D0004540

The Samaritan's Secret

ALSO BY THE AUTHOR

FICTION
The Collaborator of Bethlehem
A Grave in Gaza

NONFICTION
Cain's Field: Faith, Fratricide, and Fear in the Middle East

The Samaritan's Secret

An Omar Yussef Mystery

Matt Beynon Rees

Published by
Soho Press, Inc.
853 Broadway
New York, NY 10003

Library of Congress Cataloging-in-Publication Data

Rees, Matt, 1967-
  The samaritan's secret : an Omar Yussef mystery / Matt Beynon
Rees.
        p. cm.
  ISBN 978-1-56947-545-4
1. Samaritans--Fiction. 2. Nablus--Fiction. 3. Yussef, Omar
(Fictitious character) -- Fiction. I. Title.
PS3618.E438S26 2008
813' .6--dc22

                              2008028448

        10 9 8 7 6 5 4 3 2 1

*To my father David
and my son Cai*

Your eyes took me back to the days that are gone.
They taught me to regret the past and its wounds.
                                        —Ahmad Shafik, *Inte Umri*

Chapter 1

L ime green paint on the domes of the neighborhood mosques punctuated the khaki limestone in the Nablus casbah. Like tarnished copper tacks, they seemed to pin the Ottoman *souk* and the Mamluk caravanserai to the floor of the valley. *Otherwise even the stones might get up and run away from this dirty town*, Omar Yussef thought.

The distant siren of an ambulance rumbled in the stomach of the city and Omar Yussef felt the last crispness of dawn burn away in the sun. With his habitually shaky hand, he stroked the meager white hairs covering his baldness and clicked his tongue. These few strands wouldn't save his scalp from sunburn, and he could see that the day would be hot. Sweat itched behind his tidy gray mustache. He scratched his upper lip petulantly.

He turned from the valley and contemplated the sparse spring grass stippling the rocky flank of Mount Jerizim. *Let's see who gets burned worse—you or me*, he thought. The mountain arced, sullen and taut, to the row of mansions on its ridge, as though tensing its shoulders to endure the heat of the day.

A turquoise police car pulled up. The driver's window lowered and a smoldering cigarette butt spun onto the sidewalk. "Greetings, *ustaz*," Sami Jaffari said. "Get in."

Omar Yussef left the paltry shade of the lacquered pinewood canopy outside his hotel, opened the door of the patrol car and stretched a stiff leg into the passenger's side.

"Grandpa, morning of joy."

Bracing himself against the car door, Omar Yussef looked up. From the balcony of a second floor room, his granddaughter waved. In her other hand, she clutched a book. He wiggled his fingers to her in greeting. "Morning of light, Nadia, my darling," he said.

"Don't forget, you're taking me to eat *qanafi* today."

Omar Yussef's mustache curled downward. Sweet things were not to his taste. But Nablus was famous for this dessert of goat cheese and syrupy shredded wheat, and this was Nadia's first time in the town. He anticipated that the inquisitive, methodical thirteen-year-old would want to compare the *qanafi* from a range of bakeries and he would have to gulp it all down and grin indulgently. Even his considerable prejudice in culinary matters couldn't outweigh his love for this girl. He waved to her again. "If Allah wills it, we'll eat *qanafi* soon," he said.

"Sami, make sure you bring my grandpa back in time for a midmorning snack in the casbah," Nadia called.

"He's on official police business now," Sami shouted. "We have to investigate the theft of a valuable historical relic."

"I'm warning you. I'll tell Meisoun to call off the wedding, if you don't bring him back in time. She won't marry you if I tell her you're not nice to little girls."

Sami stuck out his tongue and put a thumb to his nose. Nadia giggled as the car pulled away from the curb. "You're going to get fat in Nablus, Abu Ramiz," Sami said, slapping Omar Yussef on the knee.

"It's you who'll start to gain weight, because by the end of this week you'll have a wife to cook for you."

Sami swerved to avoid a long, yellow taxi that drifted languidly out of a side street. He rummaged for a pack of Dunhills in the glove compartment. "Police work in Palestine keeps me thin," he said, shaking a cigarette loose and lighting it. "It's four parts nervous tension and one part genuine danger. I burn more calories thinking about my day than most people would by running a marathon."

Sami had become leaner since Omar Yussef last saw him in Gaza almost a year earlier. In the police car, Omar's initial impression was of a healthy, contented young man, but as he looked harder he sensed this was a mask for something apprehensive and angry. It was as though the police officer had been forced to swallow the criminal outrages of Nablus and had found that they ate away his muscle and left his flesh tight on his bones.

Sami picked his teeth, discolored almost to the shade of his tan by the thick coffee he drank to stay awake on long shifts. "I'm looking forward to seeing my old childhood friends at my wedding," he said. "I'm very lucky that you and your sons were able to get permits to pass through the checkpoints. It's been years since I spent time with Ramiz and even longer since I saw Zuheir."

Omar Yussef forced a smile.

Sami lifted his palm, questioningly. "What's wrong?"

"Zuheir is much changed." Omar Yussef looked at his feet. "He's become very religious."

"Then he'll be at home in Nablus. This place is one big mosque."

"He's very different from the boy who went off to study in

Britain a few years ago." He thought of the square-cut beard and the loose white cotton his son had taken to wearing, the regular prayers and the stern disapproving face. He didn't know how far his son had ventured into the unbending world of indignant imams, but the question disturbed him.

"It's lucky you gave up alcohol, or Zuheir would be trying to force some major lifestyle changes on you," Sami said with a smile.

"If I hadn't given up alcohol, it would've killed me and I might not have lived long enough to see my son become an adherent of a crazy, hard-line version of our religion."

"May Allah forbid it." Sami slapped Omar Yussef's thigh. "Enough of such thoughts. This is a day of pleasures. I have to go down to the casbah later to finalize arrangements for the wedding with the sheikh. Then we'll have a reunion with your sons at the hotel."

"After we've checked on the theft at the Samaritan synagogue and talked to their priest."

Sami shrugged. "Crime is also one of the pleasures of Nablus."

"I'm a connoisseur. Thank you for bringing me."

"I knew you'd be intrigued, as a history teacher who's knowledgeable about all elements of Palestinian culture." Sami sucked in some smoke. "They *are* part of Palestinian culture, aren't they?"

"The Samaritans? They've been here longer than we have, Sami. They claim to be descended from some biblical Israelites who remained in this area when their brethren were exiled to Babylon. In a way, they're Palestinians *and* Jews *and* neither, all at the same time."

Sami pulled over and peered out of the window. "I think it's in here," he said.

Omar Yussef raised himself out of the passenger seat with a grunt. His back ached after the long ride from Bethlehem the previous day, squashed into a taxi with his wife, his granddaughter and two of his sons. To bypass the security checks around Jerusalem, they had taken the desert backroads. He was fifty-seven and unfit, so the bumpy ride and the heat had exhausted him.

On the sidewalk, Omar Yussef straightened his spine. He pushed his remaining hair into place with his palm and nudged his gold-framed glasses to the bridge of his nose with the tip of his index finger.

He looked up a walkway of cracked steps between two apartment buildings, bright green weeds cutting through the polished stone paving, creeping over the railings at each side of the path. The door of the Samaritan synagogue, set forty yards back from the road, was a tasteless metal panel painted brown to look like wood. Seven bulbous lights on long, upright stems surmounted the stone canopy at the entrance. The building was a low square faced in the same limestone as the apartment blocks around it. Its basement level was painted pink.

"I thought it would be older than this," Sami said. He stamped out his cigarette and set off up the steps.

"They had a much older synagogue down in the casbah," Omar Yussef said, "but they left the old town fifty years ago, because their Muslim neighbors wouldn't sell them land to expand their homes as their community grew. So they moved up here."

Sami waited at the top of the first flight of steps. "But they don't even live here anymore." He pointed above the roof of the synagogue to a cluster of buildings on the ridge of Mount Jerizim. "They went up there, out of the way of everyone."

"Out of the way of the first intifada, Sami. Those were violent times in Nablus. You can't blame people for trying to get away."

They reached the final set of steps. To their left, grilles of curling black metal guarded the six arched windows of the synagogue.

"The bars on that first window are new," Omar Yussef said. "They're the only ones that aren't rusty."

Sami leaned over the railing at the side of the entrance and examined the bars. "You're right, Abu Ramiz. The window has been scorched by something, too."

Omar Yussef glanced at the ledge. Jagged black smudges slashed the polished stone. In the yard below, a square frame of rusty metal leaned against the pink wall, its bottom edge ripped away. "The original bars." He turned to Sami and smiled with one side of his mouth. "As the representative of the police, I think perhaps you might draw some conclusions from this."

Sami tapped the new black grille. "The thieves got in through this window."

Omar Yussef rubbed his chin. "Thieves who had enough explosives to blow away those bars."

"Nablus isn't short of explosives experts."

"But it *is* short of Samaritans, and even shorter of their priceless historical documents."

Sami lit another cigarette and took in some smoke with a sharp breath. "Let's go and see this priest."

Chapter 2

A long each jaundice-yellow wall inside the synagogue, ragged prayer books were wedged tight or stacked haphazardly on their sides behind the glass of their bookcases. A curtain of blue velvet embroidered with Hebrew characters in gold thread hung behind a dais at the head of the hall. The thick walls preserved the chill of night in the air. Omar Yussef shivered and pulled his French collar higher, pressing it to the slack skin of his jaw.

"It's as cold as a cellar in here," Sami said.

"Or a grave." Omar Yussef caught Sami's frown. "Don't worry. I may not be certain that this truly is a day of pleasures, as you put it, but by the time of your wedding, I'll be cheeriness personified."

Sami walked down the aisle toward the blue curtain. Between the Hebrew characters, the outline of two stone tablets had been stitched into the material. "Can you read this, Abu Ramiz?" Sami asked.

"No, but the tablets are a representation of the commandments given to the Prophet Moussa, I think. The ones that contained the Jewish law."

"The Samaritan law."

A man of about seventy years approached from a stairwell

at the back of the room. He was tall and slender, like an evening shadow. He wore a white ankle-length cotton robe, a long vest of coarse gray wool, unfastened at the front, and a fez wrapped with a red cloth so that it resembled a turban.

"The Jewish law is very similar to ours, gentlemen," the old man said, "but their holy texts include seven thousand mistakes. The books of the Samaritans are without error."

"Then you are without excuses for your mistakes." Omar Yussef smiled. "That's a terrible fate."

"No one is ever short of justification for their sins in this part of the world." The man's mild eyes appeared unfocused and bemused, like café habitués Omar Yussef had met in Morocco who smoked too much kif. He shook hands with Omar Yussef. "I'm Jibril Ben-Tabia, a priest of the Samaritan people. Welcome to our synagogue."

Sami stepped forward. "Lieutenant Sami Jaffari of the National Police. This is my colleague Abu Ramiz."

"From Bethlehem," Omar Yussef said. He glanced at Sami. His granddaughter had been trying to make a detective of him since he had been forced to investigate accusations of murder against a favorite former pupil over a year ago. Despite his insistence that he was happy as a history teacher in the Dehaisha refugee camp, Sami seemed now to have made his change of career official.

The priest tilted his head as though wondering why an investigating officer should have been brought from Bethlehem. He kept Omar Yussef's hand in his.

"The lieutenant asked me to join him because I have a special interest in Palestinian history," Omar Yussef said. He raised an eyebrow at the young officer. "I understand the crime relates to one of your historical documents."

8

"It did." Ben-Tabia let go of Omar Yussef's hand and raised his arms in a shrug. "But I must apologize, honored gentlemen, particularly to you, Abu Ramiz, for bringing you all the way from Bethlehem for nothing. The crime is solved."

Sami dropped his cigarette and ground it out with his heel. "Solved?"

The priest glanced sharply at the cigarette butt on the floor and rolled his lower lip over the edge of his mustache. "Yes, there was a theft, but the stolen object has been returned. So, you see, your intervention is unnecessary."

"Has the criminal been apprehended?"

"Everything has been sorted out to my satisfaction."

"I'm here now, so my satisfaction enters into this, too, your honor," Sami said. He held the priest's gaze.

"Very well," Ben-Tabia said. "Please, let's sit. I'm not so strong these days."

Omar Yussef and Sami sat on the front bench. The priest took a seat in the second row.

"I must apologize," he said. "I would offer you coffee in greeting, but this synagogue is only used for the first prayers of every month and no one but me is here to prepare a drink for you today."

Omar Yussef waved his hand. "Coffee is unnecessary. Your regular place of prayer is on top of the mountain?"

"As you surely know, Brother Abu Ramiz, the Samaritans have a long history in Palestine." The priest's face became grave and proud. "We have lived here in the shadow of our holy mountain, Jerizim, since the Israelites entered the land of Canaan. Our community has dwindled to little more than six hundred, but we remain, protected by Allah and our adherence to the ways of our people."

9

"It's one of the greatest traditions of Palestine," Omar Yussef said.

The priest bowed his head. "During the violence of the eighties, we moved out of this neighborhood and created a new village on top of Jerizim, including, of course, a synagogue." He lifted a long finger and pointed out of the window toward the ridge. "We wanted to be close to our holiest place."

"I'm new to Nablus," Sami said. "I've never been up there."

"Welcome to our city." Ben-Tabia lowered his head, closed his eyes and placed his palm over his heart. "The site of our ancient temple is just beyond the crest of the ridge, the smooth flat stone where Abraham prepared to sacrifice his son Isaac. It's where Adam and Eve lived when they were expelled from Eden. It's the home of Allah."

"Quite an address." Sami smiled. "I'd like to come up and see it."

Omar Yussef thought the priest hesitated before he said, "You will be most welcome, Lieutenant."

"What exactly was stolen from you, sir?" Omar Yussef asked. "It was an old religious document of some kind, I understand."

"Though we moved our community to the mountain, we maintained this synagogue and we continued to keep our most precious documents here. It was one of these that was stolen."

"From where?" Sami said.

"From a safe in the basement."

"The safe was blown?"

"Blown? Ah, yes, with some kind of explosive. But the safe has been replaced. There's nothing for you to examine."

"When was the theft?"

"A week ago. Yes, or perhaps a little more."

"You didn't report it immediately?"

The priest fidgeted with the ends of the gray vest. "I was ordered not to do so. By the thieves. They told me that if I involved the authorities, they would destroy the scroll."

"The scroll?" Omar Yussef twisted toward the priest.

"Our greatest treasure was stolen, Abu Ramiz," Ben-Tabia said. He lifted the tips of his fingers to his beard, as though he might pull it out in despair at the thought of such a calamity. "I felt terrible shame that it should be during my tenure as a priest here in our synagogue that the Abisha Scroll might be lost."

"The Abisha?" Omar Yussef's voice was low and reverent.

"What's that?" Sami said.

"A famous Torah scroll," Omar Yussef said. "The oldest book in the world, they say."

The priest raised his eyes to the ceiling. "The five books of Moses, written on sheepskin three thousand six hundred and forty-five years ago. It was written by Abisha, son of Pinchas, son of Eleazar, son of Aaron who was the brother of Moses, in the thirteenth year after the Israelites entered the land of Canaan. Every year, we bring it out of the safe only once, for our Passover ceremony on Mount Jerizim."

"It must be very valuable," Sami said.

"It's beyond all value. Without this scroll, our Messiah can never return to us. Without this scroll, we cannot carry out the annual Passover sacrifice, and if we fail to sacrifice on Passover we cease to be Samaritans and the entire tradition of our religion comes to a terrible close." The priest's eyes were moist.

11

"You said the thieves told you to keep quiet?" Omar Yussef spoke softly.

"I was blindfolded and taken to a place where I was shown the stolen scroll. They took me because they knew I would be able to recognize it and tell the rest of the community that it was safe. Then they demanded a million dollars for its return."

"Did you pay?" Sami asked.

"We don't have a million dollars."

"But the Abisha Scroll has been returned?"

"We asked for help from all our friends in Nablus." The priest lifted his hand in front of him, fingers pointing upward. "Perhaps one of them was able to influence the thieves."

"What friends?"

"We're part of the local community. My accent is like everyone else's in Nablus—I say *Oi*, when I mean to say *I*, just like the people in the casbah. We have friends among the business community, wealthy, powerful friends."

"Did one of them pay the ransom for the Abisha?"

"No one told me they did so. I finally reported the scroll stolen during the weekend, because our Passover takes place in three days and, as I told you, the entire ceremony would have to be abandoned if I couldn't carry this scroll in our procession. But the scroll was returned overnight. I came here this morning to meet you, as your office instructed me to do when I called in the theft. But then I found the scroll on the steps, safe in its box. My prayers had been answered."

"Just like that?" Sami spoke calmly, but Omar Yussef heard the suspicion in his voice. "The thieves didn't tell you they'd returned it?"

"No one comes here unless they're accompanied by me. I have the only key to the building. They must have known I'd find it."

"Who knew that the scroll was kept in the safe?"

"Many people in Nablus."

"Who knew where the safe was?"

"We often welcome guests such as you in this synagogue. Then, there are international scholars who come to study our community. Any one of them might know where the safe is kept."

"Was the scroll damaged when the safe was blown?"

"No, it's in good condition, thanks to Allah."

"Let's take a look." Sami stood.

The priest rose with some reluctance and led them to the back of the synagogue.

At the foot of a whitewashed stone staircase, he opened a heavy metal door and entered a small office. A tall green safe the size of a refrigerator stood in one corner. "A moment, please. The combination," he said, working his fingers to mime the twisting of a dial. He shut the door behind him.

When the priest allowed them to enter, he beckoned to Omar Yussef. On the desk, beside a pile of ragged prayer books, was a box with three curved sides covered in dull, blotchy hide and less than two feet in length. Omar Yussef bent close and saw that the case was overlaid with silver panels, oxidized to a dark gray tone. He lifted his hand toward it and glanced at the priest. Ben-Tabia nodded and Omar Yussef touched the box. He felt a thrill of electricity pass through his hand. He smiled at the priest. "It's one of the most beautiful objects I've ever seen," he said.

"The box was made several hundred years ago on the

orders of one of my predecessors in the priestly caste," Ben-Tabia said. "Inside is the ancient scroll, but I cannot show you that today. Only on Passover may it be seen."

"The workmanship is wonderful." Omar Yussef ran his hand over the raised silver. Under its grimy coating, it was decorated with scenes from biblical stories. At the center of one of the plates was an image of a building that looked like a castle with high walls surrounding a courtyard and a central turret. Omar Yussef stroked a fingertip around the outline of the building.

"That's our temple, which once stood on top of Mount Jerizim." The priest inclined his head toward the place where Omar Yussef's hand rested. "The Jews say the temple was in Jerusalem, where your famous Dome of the Rock now stands. But we know it was on Jerizim." He swallowed hard. "May I return the Abisha Scroll to the safe? It makes me nervous even to have it here on the table."

Sami left the room with Omar Yussef, while the priest again worked the combination on the safe.

In the stairwell, Sami pursed his lips. "He's lying," he whispered.

"You're right," Omar Yussef said. "Why would someone steal the scroll and simply give it back?"

The priest came out of the office and shut the metal door. He straightened his fez, gave a brittle, polite smile and gestured for them to lead the way up the stairs.

"Forgive me if I seem to be overprotective of the scroll, *pasha*," he said.

Omar Yussef blanched at the unearned senior rank mistakenly accorded him by the priest. *Thanks be to Allah that he doesn't expect me to arrest anyone*, he thought.

"It truly is important to the redemption of the entire world," the priest continued. "You see, our holy texts tell us that the Messiah will be born to the tribe of Levi or Joseph. We Samaritans are all that's left of those two tribes. But what makes us Samaritans? Only that we celebrate Passover and also the Feast of Tabernacles in the way taught by our tradition."

"With the Abisha Scroll at the head of your procession."

The priest opened a hand to acknowledge that Omar Yussef's understanding was correct. "If we were to miss both these festivals for a single year, we would no longer be Samaritans. The lines of Levi and Joseph would come to an end, and there would be no possibility of a Messiah being born to redeem mankind."

Omar Yussef stroked his chin with his knuckles. "Were there other ancient documents in the safe?"

"A few, but nothing else was taken." The priest looked out of the window at Mount Jerizim. "Most of our ancient documents are kept in my house on top of the mountain. Some are almost a thousand years old. But none are nearly as old as the Abisha Scroll. Only the most valuable are stored here in the safe."

"Do you preserve all your people's old texts?"

"The Torah scrolls and original manuscripts used in religious services." Ben-Tabia pointed toward the blue curtain above the dais. "When they can no longer be used, these documents are packed away there inside the holy ark."

"Why don't you throw them away?" Sami asked.

"For the same reason you Muslims don't use pages from the Koran to wrap falafel." The priest smiled, but Omar Yussef saw a glint of hostility behind the old man's outmoded spectacles. "Each page from a prayer book must be preserved, even if it's beyond repair."

He lifted a corner of the velvet curtain to reveal a low box built into the wall. At first it looked like a bench, but Omar Yussef saw that it was hinged at the back. "In here we safeguard many fragments of documents, all unusable, but still filled with the holy word. We call them 'Allah's secrets.'"

The priest dropped the curtain. "If you would like to see the Abisha Scroll itself, not just its box, please come to our Passover celebration on Jerizim later this week. I am happy to invite you."

"Do we have to convert to Samaritanism to attend?" Omar Yussef laughed with a short, coughing exhalation. "Neither Sami nor I are particularly committed to Islam."

"Conversion to our religion is only possible for women who wish to marry our men, *pasha*," the priest said. "But we should be honored to have men like you share our celebration." He laid his hand over his heart. "People come from all around the world—foreign journalists and international academics—to watch our ancient rites."

"It'll be a great pleasure, Your Honor," Omar Yussef said.

The priest went out onto the wide top step at the entrance to the synagogue. As Omar Yussef and Sami followed him to the door, they heard footsteps hurrying outside. Ben-Tabia froze, his eyes wide.

A breathless voice called to the priest from the steps: "Long life to you." Ben-Tabia looked quickly at Sami, then dropped his eyes to the floor. Omar Yussef took a short breath and felt the muscles in his back tighten. The traditional greeting meant someone else's life had ended. The voice came again: "Your Honor, we have to call the police."

Sami stepped through the door. Omar Yussef followed. A tall young man with a thick mustache stood at the foot of the last flight of steps. His thin chest heaved with the effort of running from the street. He flinched when he saw Sami's uniform.

"Who's dead?" Sami spoke sharply.

The young man glanced at the priest, but Sami descended a few steps and leaned toward him.

"Come on, what's happened?"

The breathless man looked over Sami's shoulder and called to the priest. "It's Ishaq, Your Honor. Ishaq is up on top of Mount Jerizim, at the temple."

"Why shouldn't he be?" The priest spoke slowly, as though his tongue were prodding through a minefield.

The young man coughed hard. "Your Honor, Ishaq has been murdered."

Chapter 3

A shepherd in baggy Turkish pants and an old blue seer-sucker jacket drove his herd toward the scanty pasture on Mount Jerizim. He maneuvered the goats to the side of the road, making way for Sami's patrol car. A small black kid sprang stiff-legged from a rock and landed on the shaggy brown backs of the others. Omar Yussef smiled at the little goat's exuberance. He caught the mustiness of the herd on the cool air of the mountain, an inviting scent after the exhaust fumes and trash-can stink of Nablus. But there had been a murder on this mountain and Omar Yussef narrowed his eyes to look beyond the lively animals toward the ridge where someone lay dead.

Sami called police headquarters to report that he was en route to a murder scene. He held his walkie-talkie with his left hand, steering and changing gear with his right. The car veered toward the drop at the edge of the road whenever he reached for the gearshift.

The old Samaritan watched Sami cautiously from the back seat with his dazed, faded eyes. *Maybe he lied to us simply because he doesn't trust the police*, Omar Yussef thought. *By Allah, the law around here doesn't usually inspire confidence.*

The priest couldn't know that Sami's an honest officer. The odds, after all, would be against it.

Sami slipped the walkie-talkie into its dashboard mounting and looked at the priest in the rearview mirror. "You're all related up here, aren't you? All you Samaritans?" he said. "Does this Ishaq have a big family?"

The priest flinched and put his hand over his mouth.

"Well?" Sami turned in his seat. "His family?"

Ben-Tabia leaned forward. "Are you the Sami Jaffari who was one of the Bethlehem deportees exiled to Gaza by the Israelis?" he said.

Omar Yussef saw Sami's jaw tighten.

"How did you manage to get a job back here in the West Bank?" the priest asked.

"I got a permit," Sami said. He took a last drag on his cigarette and flicked it out of the window.

"From the Israelis?"

"Obviously."

"But they deported you to Gaza because they said you were a dangerous gunman."

Sami ground the gears down into first as the road ribboned around a steep curve.

The priest persisted. "How did you change their minds?"

Omar Yussef knew how. His friend Khamis Zeydan, Bethlehem's police chief, had convinced the Israelis of the truth about Sami—the young officer had been working undercover among the town's gunmen when the Israelis arrested him. Khamis Zeydan had even obtained a permit for Sami's Gazan fiancée Meisoun to join him in the West Bank.

"Don't you think a job on the Nablus police force is a

continuation of Sami's punishment?" Omar Yussef said to Ben-Tabia.

Sami clicked his tongue. "Abu Ramiz, please, let it rest."

The priest's voice became surly. "He must have connections," he said. "That's all I mean."

And connections are suspect, Omar Yussef thought. *Tainted links to the crooks at the top, even to the Israelis.* "Sami's like you," he said. "You have a Torah like the Jews. But you're defined by the seven thousand differences between your holy text and theirs. It's the same with Sami and his connections. It's the differences that're important."

The priest folded his arms across his chest, sat back in his seat and stared out of the window.

They reached the Samaritan houses on the ridge. The well-maintained streets were neater than a Palestinian village and empty, except for a few teenagers playing basketball in a small concrete lot. They stopped their game to watch the police car pass. Blinking into the sun, the children bore the unmistakable signs of inbreeding. Their bullet-shaped heads sat askew on their necks and their big ears stuck out.

"Which way from here?" Sami said, quietly.

The priest directed Sami straight through the village. They came around a knoll at the shoulder of the ridge and up to a gravel parking lot. Signs in Hebrew and English welcomed tourists to the Samaritan holy place. Sami cut the engine and a deep silence enveloped them.

A group of five men loitered, peering down a steep slope into a glade of trees. One of them waved when he saw the priest emerge from the police car. Behind the men, the low walls of an old fortress and its domed inner buildings were silvery in the sunshine.

Beyond the Samaritan village, the ridge extended toward the mansions that had been visible from Nablus and, further away, the red and white communication towers of the Israeli army base at Tel Haras.

Omar Yussef shuffled along behind Sami and the priest. Though he was younger than Ben-Tabia, he was conscious that his movements were stiffer, his pace slower. In the silence of this remote peak, without the background racket of the town, his panting sounded prodigious. Sweat formed in his mustache, as he tried to keep up with the others. He promised himself he would take a walk every day to improve his fitness, when he returned to Bethlehem.

The men gathered around the priest as he reached them. Each shook Ben-Tabia's hand without looking at his face and kissed his cheeks three times, mumbling something to him. A slight hum rolled out of the valley. Omar Yussef heard the regular, echoing beat of a distant pile driver and the call of a single muezzin.

Among the pines on the slope, a lumpy blue and white object was wrapped around the foot of a tree. Omar Yussef pushed his glasses up to the bridge of his nose and squinted at the lifeless body of a man. "Sami, let's go and look," he murmured.

Sami put his hand on Omar Yussef's shoulder and whispered. "Abu Ramiz, I took you to the synagogue because I thought you'd be interested in the scroll. I brought you up here because I was in too much of a hurry to drop you at your hotel. But—"

"The scroll was left on the priest's doorstep and at the same time a body turned up on the edge of his village." Omar Yussef lifted his finger at the young policeman. "Come on, Sami. You promised me an investigation into the theft of a historic document, but that particular intrigue has been resolved. You owe me a mystery and that body is it."

Sami shook his head with a gloomy smile and stepped down the rocky slope toward the trees. Omar Yussef followed awkwardly. He bent to support himself with his arm and descended sideways. Slipping in the loose dirt, he struck his knee on a rock. His elbow shook, taking his weight. He sensed the group of Samaritans watching him, but he didn't look up. He was sweating with embarrassment at his frail condition. When he reached Sami, he wiped his forehead and neck with his handkerchief.

The dead man was of medium height and wore a white shirt and blue slacks. His feet were bare. His midriff folded around the tree trunk, his legs falling down the hill on one side of the pine and his torso curved around the other. His hands and knees were bound with electrical wire. Omar Yussef breathed heavily. He caught Sami's eye. The young man whispered: "He's been tortured, Abu Ramiz."

Sami pointed out the contusions around the corpse's neck and head. The thin chest was purpled with bruising where the bloodied shirt had been pulled open. The fingertips had been scorched.

The dead man was probably in his midtwenties. His sky blue eyes were open and stared at Omar Yussef with something that looked like recognition. Omar Yussef had the feeling that he had seen them before, but that didn't seem possible. He blinked and averted his face, unnerved by the familiarity in those eyes. He cleared his throat and examined the bruises. "Was he beaten to death?"

"I don't see any other wounds, at least not the kind that would be fatal. There could have been internal bleeding.

Perhaps the beating damaged his organs." Sami leaned closer to the man's head. "I suppose the neck could be broken. It's at an awkward angle."

Omar Yussef pointed to where the Samaritans stood. "He either fell or was thrown from up there. This tree blocked his fall."

"There's no blood around," Sami said. "I expect he was killed before he dropped down here."

They made their way back to the ridge, Sami following behind. Omar Yussef was grateful to him for waiting. By the time they reached the group of Samaritans, his shirt was heavy with sweat and the wind across the mountain chilled it against his shoulders and belly.

"Who found the body?" Sami said.

A short, thick man in a dirty blue shirt and a baseball cap that bore the logo of a cheap Israeli cigarette brand raised his hand. "I came up here to open the site for the tourists and I saw it," he mumbled.

"What time?"

"A little before eight. It wasn't there last night, I'm sure of that. An American arrived just before I left—someone who works with one of the international organizations—and she was surprised that there are pine trees up here." The caretaker smiled. "You know these foreigners; they only expect to see olive groves, real Middle Eastern stuff. I told her the pines were planted not long ago to reduce the wind on the mountaintop and we both looked very closely at them. I would've seen the body."

"When were you and the foreigner looking at the trees?"

"Just before sunset. About six o'clock."

"So you came along the ridge this morning and looked over the edge of the path and saw the body?"

The short man shook his head. "I saw blood on the Eternal Hill first. I thought a jackal had brought its prey here, so I looked around because I didn't want the tourists to stumble onto a half-eaten goat. Then I found Ishaq dead in the trees."

"Where's the Eternal Hill?"

The caretaker pointed across the path to a sloping rock ten yards square. Sami and Omar Yussef stepped toward it. Blood puddled black at its center. A gory trickle ran to the bottom of the gentle, rippling slope of granite. Thicker daubs led up to the top.

"He was tortured there in the middle of the rock," Sami said quietly. "These other marks must be where the body was dragged over the rock, before he was thrown into the trees. Some time during the night."

Omar Yussef turned to the priest. "The Eternal Hill is where the ancient Samaritan temple stood?"

"This rock is the peak of the mountain," the priest stammered, "the home of Allah."

"It looks just like the stone inside the Dome of the Rock," Omar Yussef said.

"The Jews say that Abraham bound Isaac there on the peak of Mount Moriah in Jerusalem. You Muslims just took over their tradition. But Mount Jerizim is where it really took place and that's why we built our temple here and made it the center of our faith."

Omar Yussef stared at the priest. "And now it's covered in blood."

The priest made a sound that was both a gasp and a sob.

A police jeep pulled into the parking lot and six officers got out. One of the officers pulled a rucksack from the jeep and walked purposefully toward Sami.

"Who was this Ishaq?" Omar Yussef said. "He was one of you? A Samaritan?"

"He's one of us," the priest said.

"What did he do?"

"He works—worked for the Palestinian Authority. He lived in the village with his wife."

The policeman with the rucksack went down the slope toward the body. He slipped in the dirt and landed heavily on his backside. The other officers laughed as they followed him over the lip of the incline. The embarrassed policeman grabbed at one of his colleagues and tried to trip him. Sami called to him sharply.

Omar Yussef rubbed his chin. "Who would want Ishaq dead?"

The priest lifted his arms and let them drop to his sides. "No one, no one."

"That can't quite be true, can it?" Omar Yussef sucked one end of his mustache. "What does the Samaritan religion say about evil things such as murder, Your Honor?"

The priest looked at the blood on the broad rock. "One of our holy books says, 'The sinner goes to the flames and I have no compassion for him.'"

Omar Yussef raised an eyebrow. "You mean the dead man was a sinner?"

"What?" Jibril Ben-Tabia blinked. "No, I mean the murderer. The murderer goes to the flames."

"He'll have to die first. The only one in danger of the flames right now is Ishaq. Do you have compassion for him?"

The priest's head dropped forward. In the quiet of the mountaintop, he whispered: "Compassion? Yes. He was my son."

Chapter 4

The priest fretted his white beard with shaking fingers. He ran his toe along the edge of the broad rock where the ancient temple once stood and stared at the blood of his son.

"Allah will be merciful upon him," Omar Yussef said.

The priest removed his glasses and rubbed his eyes hard. "Do you have a son, *pasha*?"

"I have three," Omar Yussef said. He glanced at the Samaritan men. Hands in pockets, they had the uneasy listlessness of teenagers at their first family funeral. But their eyes were alert and trained on the priest's back.

"What a blessing, *pasha*." Ben-Tabia returned his thick glasses to his nose and his eyes seemed to shrink away behind them.

Omar Yussef recalled his awkward reunion with Zuheir and his son's new religious dedication. "Thanks to Allah," he said.

He moved to the priest's side. His back ached and he would have rested his foot on the rock, but some sense of propriety prevented him. *Perhaps it's the rock's holiness*, he thought. *No, it's the blood.*

The priest's eyebrows twitched. "I don't know what friction usually passes between a father and his son, *pasha*. I know only that there was tension between me and Ishaq. I have nothing to compare it to, but I must judge myself harshly, even so." He hesitated. "It was difficult sometimes, Abu Ramiz. He was not content."

"Not content with what?"

"The village, Nablus, his wife." The priest groaned. "Certainly not with me."

"Why not?"

"I was rigid with him. What else could I do? I have two daughters, but my attention and my hopes focused on my son. You understand that, *pasha*. It's the way things are in our society. Women count for less."

Omar Yussef, who loved Nadia best of all his grandchildren, grimaced.

"When Ishaq was a boy, I was only a priest. By the time he was a man, I was a leader of our people." Ben-Tabia shook his head. "The standards that I demand of all the Samaritans applied to him even more forcefully."

"He failed to live up to them?"

"Perhaps he only failed because he wanted me to know that I had failed him as a father."

Omar Yussef realized that he had, after all, rested his foot on the holy rock. He withdrew it to the grass at the edge of the footpath. "Now is not the time for such judgments, Your Honor. A father's high expectations are natural, and a son's rebellion yet more so. You must forgive yourself, at least while you mourn."

Jibril Ben-Tabia drew a hand across his forehead. "He was a good boy, in spite of everything," he murmured. "He helped everybody. It was as though he couldn't deny anything to anyone."

"What do you mean?"

"There are some boys in the village who are, you know, not right."

"They're handicapped, you mean?"

"Ishaq always played basketball with them and talked to them. No one else bothers with them, except their immediate families. They're outsiders." The priest dropped his mournful eyes to the rock. "He was a good boy, but as his father I was forced to be critical of him."

Ben-Tabia turned to Omar Yussef and drew himself up straight. He was six feet tall, five inches greater than Omar Yussef, and his fez made him appear even taller. He took a long breath that was loud in the stillness of the hilltop. "I was Ishaq's father, but I was also his priest. That means I have certain duties now, *pasha*. His body must be washed and dressed in white. We must carry out the funeral before sunset. Our tradition is for the priest to read from Deuteronomy, chapter thirty-two, as the body is lowered into the grave. Probably you don't know it, *pasha*, as a Muslim."

Omar Yussef glanced down at the blood on the rock. "'They have corrupted themselves,'" he said. "'They are a perverse and crooked generation.'"

The priest stared at Omar Yussef, curious and wary.

"I'm Muslim, as you point out," Omar Yussef said, "but I grew up in Bethlehem back when it was still a town with a Christian majority, and I taught for many years in a Christian school. I know all sorts of things you might expect to be a mystery to a Muslim."

Sami climbed from where Ishaq's dead body lay onto the path along the ridge. "Your Honor, was Ishaq married?"

28

The priest's eyes were distant. He made a murmur of assent through his pursed lips.

Sami turned toward the Samaritan men. "Has his wife been told of his death?"

The caretaker raised his hand and pointed toward the village. "I called my wife earlier and told her to go and tell Roween. She'll have done that by now."

"Roween is Ishaq's wife?"

The short man lifted his chin to indicate that Sami was correct and turned his attention to the policemen on the slope below.

"I'd better go and see her," Sami said.

In the village, the boys were gone from the concrete lot. Sami went into a small grocery to buy cigarettes and ask directions to Ishaq's house.

Omar Yussef looked up toward the hilltop where the corpse lay. He remembered Sami's question about the Samaritans. *Part of Palestinian culture, yes. They're murdered just like we are*, he thought.

The bright morning sun made him squint, but he felt gloomy. He recalled the Samaritan priest's regrets over his son. He vowed to be as forgiving as he could about Zuheir's decision to quit his job at a British university for a position at an Islamic school in Beirut.

Sami jogged back from the shop. He lit a cigarette as he ran the car slowly along the street to a small park. The thin grass was studded with deep, rectangular pits, arranged in ranks and lined with concrete.

"This must be where they cook the sheep they slaughter for their Passover," Omar Yussef said.

Sami took a sharp drag. "Ishaq had a front row seat for the big kill, then. That's his house, right next door."

They went to the front entrance and were greeted by a short woman in her late twenties with dry auburn hair cut like a man's and parted on the left. Her thick eyebrows had been plucked, but as they grew back they met above her upturned nose. Acne mottled red and purple triangles between the corners of her mouth and her jaw.

The woman glanced past Omar Yussef to the police car at the curb and he saw that her eyelashes were wet with tears. "Please come in," she mumbled. "Feel as if this were your home and you were with your own family."

The door opened onto a living room furnished with sofas upholstered in velour swirls and an elegant cherry-wood dining set.

"Greetings. We'd like to talk to Ishaq's wife," Omar Yussef said.

The woman bowed. "Double greetings. I'm Roween al-Teef, Ishaq's wife," she said. "Please wait, *ustaz*, while I prepare coffee for you."

On the wall, there was an enlarged photo of a man bowing to receive a kiss on the forehead from the old president. Sami froze in front of the photo. Omar Yussef adjusted his spectacles and squinted: the president, wearing the checkered keffiyeh that was his trademark, puckered his lips before the smiling face of Ishaq, the son of Jibril the priest.

Sami and Omar Yussef sat on one of the stiff sofas in silence. Sami stubbed out his cigarette in a ceramic ashtray painted with a blue symmetrical design in the Armenian style and stared at the photo.

"This may have been a mistake," he said.

Omar Yussef wished he had told Roween not to bother about the coffee. It couldn't have been an hour since she had learned of her husband's death. *She ought to be looking after herself, not attending to me*, he thought.

A basketball bounced in the backyard of the house, a deep repetitive impact, as though someone were venting his anger on the concrete.

"A mistake?" Omar Yussef said.

Sami cracked his knuckles. "I don't want anything to do with that guy." He pointed at the photo of the president. "Really, a big fucking mistake."

Omar Yussef squinted at Ishaq's face on the wall. *Sami may be scared of the old president, but that young man wasn't*, he thought. The eyes once again struck Omar Yussef as familiar, just as they had when he had seen the corpse. They were knowing and conspiratorial. Ishaq seemed to be signaling to the famously duplicitous old guerrilla that he was nobody's fool, even as he accepted the benediction of those moist lips. "This isn't a condolence call." Omar Yussef turned to Sami. "You have to question her."

"You ask whatever you want, Abu Ramiz." Sami scratched his head. "I can't think straight. I really don't want to be here."

Omar Yussef was about to argue, when Roween came out of the kitchen and set the coffee on carved side tables the color of caramel.

"May Allah bless your hands," Omar Yussef said, raising his coffee cup.

"Blessings, *ustaz*," Roween said. Her voice was hoarse and restrained, as though with every word she forced herself to strangle some emotion. Omar Yussef noticed that her neck was thicker than he would have expected, taut and muscular, beneath her blue robe.

"Allah will be merciful upon him, the departed one," Omar Yussef said.

Roween sat with her hands clasped on her thighs.

"The Brother Sami is investigating the death of your husband," Omar Yussef said, ignoring the impatient drumming of Sami's fingers on the arm of the sofa. "We have been to the place where he died and Sami has examined his body."

Roween's thumb pulsed up and down where she folded it over her wrist.

"So far, all we know about him is that he worked for the Palestinian Authority and that he was the son of a priest," Omar Yussef said.

Roween's thumb pressed so hard into her wrist that Omar Yussef could see its tip grow red.

"Can you tell us more about him, my daughter?" Omar Yussef spoke quietly. "Perhaps it will help Sami identify suspects in the murder."

That word brought Roween's eyes up to Omar Yussef's face. "He was a good man, *ustaz*. Who would murder him? Couldn't it have been an accident of some kind?"

"That seems unlikely."

"He was a sweet man."

"His father says he was discontented."

"His father." Roween's lip twitched. "His Honor Jibril was his adoptive father, *ustaz*. Ishaq's parents died in a car crash when he was a few months old. The priest took him into his house, because he had no other sons."

"A car crash? Where?"

"Ishaq's parents lived in a town inside Israel, where

there's a small Samaritan community. They were on their way to Nablus, to visit this village, when their car went off the road and they died."

"What sort of work did Ishaq do for the Authority?"

Roween's mouth fell into a desolate pout as she looked at the photo of her husband on the wall. "Ishaq worked for the Old Man," she said.

"For the old president?"

"He was his private financial adviser. Perhaps because Ishaq never knew his real father, he always looked for strong relationships with older men—men who could have been his father. He and the Chief were very close."

Omar Yussef sipped his coffee. The murder of an ordinary Samaritan was a very different matter from the killing of a man who was close to the former president. He noticed Sami grip the arm of his chair tightly. He put down the coffee cup. "How long did Ishaq work for the president?"

"Three years. Ishaq studied at Bir Zeit University and got to know the Chief while he was there in Ramallah. His degree was in finance. He was extremely clever. He was always with the president, even after we married a couple of years ago. He tried to come home once a week and for our holy days, but most of the time he lived at the president's headquarters in Ramallah. The Old Man wanted to keep him close all the time."

"What does that mean—the president's private financial adviser?"

"He managed the president's money, *ustaz*." Roween opened her hands with her palms up. "The president had personal control of all Palestinian finances, so Ishaq controlled the entire budget. Unofficially, of course."

Omar Yussef thought of the bloody, beaten body on the slope of Mount Jerizim. Had his connection to the former president's money put Ishaq there?

"When the Old Man became sick, Ishaq accompanied him to Paris for his final days," Roween said. "He missed several of our important Samaritan festivals and he came back only a few months ago."

Omar Yussef recalled what the priest had said about Passover and the Feast of Tabernacles—if the Samaritans didn't celebrate these holy days on Mount Jerizim, they'd cease to be Samaritans. *This was how Ishaq failed to live up to his adoptive father's expectations*, he thought. *The expectations of his entire people*. "Was there a penalty from the community for his absence during those festivals?" he asked.

"He had to pay a fine, before he could return to live here. He had to go to the elders and beg them to let him back into the community."

"Why did he stay in Paris after the president died?"

Roween shook her head. "His business dealings kept him away," she said. "He wouldn't tell me what they were, but when he came back he went to work for Amin Kanaan."

"The famous businessman?" Sami rubbed his eyes with the heel of his hand.

"He owns one of the big mansions further along the ridge. If you have eyes in your head and your head is in Nablus, you can't miss those houses."

Omar Yussef recalled the stately pillars, the domed roofs and the plate glass of the mansions visible from all over Nablus. In a few minutes, this simple village murder victim had been elevated into the company of the former president and one of the wealthiest Palestinians.

"To my husband, Kanaan may have been another father figure. Kanaan often made deals with the president, so Ishaq handled the details." Roween knitted her fingers together once more. "Before he died, Ishaq said some strange things about one of his deals."

"What did he say?" Omar Yussef said.

"He didn't tell me much. At least, not much that made sense. He wasn't himself for the last few weeks. He was tense and often became angry, even with me. This wasn't his usual behavior. He could become very agitated and aggressive, it's true, but with me he was always gentle. Almost too gentle."

"His latest deal was on behalf of the new president?"

"No, the new president appointed different financial advisers. But Ishaq continued to work with Kanaan." Roween stroked the acne on one side of her mouth. "A few days ago, he seemed almost crazy with tension. I was worried about him."

Omar Yussef leaned forward. "Why was he so tense?"

"He told me he was dealing with something very dangerous. He said it was so dangerous he wanted to bury it all behind the temple and forget about it."

"Bury it behind the temple?"

Doubt flickered across the woman's face and her lips became tight. *She's decided to keep something from me*, Omar Yussef thought.

Roween took a sharp breath. "That's what he said. I asked him what he meant. He looked at me with pity and, I think, with love, then he put his finger to his lips as if to say that I should keep quiet. Then he said: 'It's a secret between me and the Old Man and Allah. The Old Man's dead, and when I'm dead too, it'll be a secret known only to Allah.'"

"If no one but Ishaq knew his secret, how could it be dangerous?"

Roween sobbed. "*Ustaz*, do you think Ishaq had done something wrong? People always say that the Old Man had secret bank accounts. They say he used them to pay people off. Do you think Ishaq was involved with some of these bad types?"

Bury it behind the temple. Omar Yussef thought that sounded more like a deal involving Samaritan antiquities than offshore bank accounts. But surely the killing must have something to do with Ishaq's work. When the old president died, the newspapers printed stories about secret funds hidden around the world. Perhaps someone wanted a piece of that wealth and tried to force Ishaq to lead him to it. "Did Ishaq have business dealings with anyone else? Anyone he might have talked to about his work with the president?"

"Only yesterday, I heard him tell Jibril the priest that he had an appointment here with an American financial expert from the World Bank. It was something to do with his old job. They were arguing, so Ishaq sent me upstairs where I couldn't overhear them. Even so, as I brought them coffee, I heard Ishaq refer to 'her,' which means the American is a woman. But I don't know her name."

"When she arrives, would you ask her to contact my colleague Sami? She may be able to help us piece things together."

Roween nodded.

Omar Yussef put his hands on his knees and pushed himself to his feet. "I'm sure Sami will find those responsible for your husband's death, my daughter," he said. "But now perhaps we should leave you to care for your family."

Roween flushed. "We have no children, *ustaz*. Ishaq was so often away—" She sniffled and wiped her nose with the back of her hand.

Omar Yussef and Sami drove out of the village in silence and took the winding descent back to Nablus, spread carelessly across the valley below.

"Don't drop me at the hotel yet. I'll come with you to the casbah," Omar Yussef said. "It'll help me clear my mind. I can't eat *qanafi* with Nadia while the image of that poor man's dead body is still before my eyes."

As they rounded a sharp curve, a white Chevrolet Suburban roared past them. The driver was a local, mustachioed and wearing wraparound sunglasses. In the passenger seat, a foreign woman with reddish hair tied in a ponytail was talking on a cell phone.

"What do those license plates mean?" Sami asked, as the noise of the four-wheel drive receded up the mountain.

"I didn't see them."

"They said I-B-R-D and then there was a number."

"The International Bank for Reconstruction and Development," Omar Yussef said.

"What's that?"

"The World Bank. That must have been the woman our friend Ishaq expected to meet this morning."

"It's a wasted trip for her all the way up here now," Sami said.

That depends what she's looking for, Omar Yussef thought.

Chapter 5

They left the patrol car above the casbah and Omar Yussef descended with Sami into the darkness of the old quarter. In the alleys, vaulted ceilings trapped the moldy scent of murky corners, the drifting clouds of spices from the big grinders in the shops, the gamy sharpness of donkey droppings. He wheezed on the thick air.

When they came into the *souk*, a shopkeeper, loitering with a cigarette at the entrance of his tiny store, watched Omar Yussef with insolent, blank eyes. The stare made Omar Yussef duck his head guiltily, as though he had fled from some misdeed through the grimy Turkish passageways. *Can he smell the Samaritan's blood on me?* he wondered. Glancing down at the spangly slippers and imitation Tommy Hilfiger sweat shirts laid out on low trestles outside the store, he hurried away.

At the end of the *souk*, the street opened to the sky. The high, late-morning sun dazzled off the smooth limestone. Omar Yussef caught the heavy scent of hot goat cheese from a sides treet and noticed the sign outside one of the town's best-known *qanafi* vendors. His throat tightened with remorse. Sami dodged through the crowd, eager to reach the mosque as soon as midday prayers finished. Omar

Yussef whispered an apology to Nadia for delaying her culinary expedition and followed.

The Nasser Mosque stood at the corner of a modest, rectangular plaza presently filled with junky German cars and trucks parked in ranks. Omar Yussef estimated the two-story mosque was a century old. Exhaust fumes had mottled its stone arches at ground level, and the winter's rain had streaked the upper floor black with thick mold. The dome of the mosque was a bright green and its surface was as uneven and pitted as a lime.

Taped to the metal shutter at the mosque's entrance, a colorful poster depicted famous faces from the Hamas leadership. The current chiefs smiled broadly and waved. The dead ones, all killed by Israeli helicopter missiles, were washed in sepia tones and looked a little wistful. *Like the Christian saints on the walls of the churches in Bethlehem*, Omar Yussef thought.

He tapped his knuckles against the poster. "This is your sheikh's mosque, Sami? Are you having some kind of a fundamentalist wedding?" he asked.

"By Allah, if I wasn't a fundamentalist, I wouldn't be getting married at all, Abu Ramiz." Sami winked.

The last midday worshippers filtered out of the mosque, slipping their shoes on at the door. Omar Yussef removed his mauve loafers, gave them a careful brushing with a tissue from his pocket, and placed them judiciously to the side of the worn sandals and scuffed moccasins at the entrance. Sami led him across a cheap green carpet, woven by machine and detailed with a symmetrical design of ornate gold and blue chevrons. The vinegary smell of foot sweat rose from the carpet. Omar Yussef sniffed the back of his hand, where he dashed cologne every morning to counter just such unpleasant odors.

Beside a mint green pillar in the corner of the mosque, a broad, bearded man with a casual toughness kissed Sami three times. Omar Yussef noted that a dozen bullets had pitted the pillar, gouging through the paint and thin plaster into the poured concrete beneath. An M-16 was propped against it.

"Abu Ramiz, this is Nouri Awwadi," Sami said. "Abu Ramiz is visiting from Bethlehem for my wedding."

Awwadi took Omar Yussef's hand between both of his, a motion which forced the muscles in his shoulders to rise massively. His bottom lip drooped out of the middle of his black beard, a luscious scarlet, and his skin glowed as though it had been oiled. Omar Yussef noted approvingly that Awwadi smelled of sandalwood.

"Welcome, Abu Ramiz," the young man said. He kept Omar Yussef's hand in one of his and, with the other, wagged a finger at Sami. "Why didn't you come to prayers, my brother?"

"I have no time to pray. The criminals of Nablus keep me too busy."

Awwadi laughed loudly and slapped a handshake into Sami's palm in celebration of the joke.

"Nouri is Hamas, but he's a good guy, even so," Sami said to Omar Yussef. He turned to Awwadi. "I have to see Sheikh Bader. I want to make sure everything's all set for my wedding, now that the most important guests have managed to get through the Israeli checkpoints."

"The sheikh is very busy with arrangements for the joint wedding tomorrow, but I'm sure he can spare you some time."

"Joint wedding?" Omar Yussef touched his fingers to his mustache, enjoying the scent of Awwadi's sandalwood oil on his hand.

"Hamas is paying for fifteen couples to marry tomorrow," Awwadi said. "It shows we're the only party that cares for ordinary people."

"What does marriage have to do with caring for people?" Omar Yussef laughed. "You should try funding some divorces, if you really want to help society."

"It's expensive to get married. A dowry is at least fifteen hundred Jordanian dinars. Since the intifada, hardly anyone in the casbah has work. Young men would have to save for years to be able to afford marriage."

"Hamas will pay the dowry," Sami said, "because otherwise the young men would be tempted into immorality."

Awwadi laughed and slapped Sami's hand again.

"Maybe they'd get wise and they wouldn't marry at all," Omar Yussef said. He rasped out a scratchy laugh and received a big hand slap, too.

Awwadi pointed Sami toward the rear of the mosque. "I'll keep your friend company while you bother our sheikh," he said.

"Abu Ramiz is an expert on our history," Sami said. "Show him around the casbah, Nouri, and I expect he'll be able to tell you things about your home that even you didn't know."

"May it be the will of Allah."

"I'm sure it'll be me who gets the history lesson," Omar Yussef said.

Sami entered an office behind another bullet-scarred pillar. Awwadi picked up the M-16, slung it across his chest, and led Omar Yussef by the hand to the mosque's entrance.

Omar Yussef dug his finger into a bullet hole in one of the pillars. A fine dust of stone and plaster sifted to the green carpet. "This isn't only a place of prayer," he said.

Awwadi shook his head and grinned. "Although prayer, too, is a form of jihad," he said. He took a string of green worry beads from his pocket and fiddled them through his thick fingers.

"'Paradise is in the shadow of the swords,'" Omar Yussef said.

"Abu Ramiz, you're in the right place to quote that hadith of the Prophet, may the peace and blessings of Allah be upon him. Some of my friends, may Allah be merciful upon them, were martyred in this very mosque when the Israelis came to the casbah recently."

"May Allah grant that the lost years of those who are departed should lengthen your life." Omar Yussef grunted as he bent to slip on his shoes. "Let's get out of here before I start reciting entire verses of the Koran."

"If Allah wills it." Awwadi took Omar Yussef into the street. He headed away from the small plaza toward the center of the casbah. "It isn't only in the mosque that I've lost friends," he said.

"May you live long and in good health," Omar Yussef mumbled, reciting another formulaic blessing.

Awwadi responded in kind: "May Allah preserve you." But he worked the worry beads harder and looked sternly at the limestone slabs of pavement, worn to a shine by age. "Elsewhere in the world, Abu Ramiz, a person may go his whole life without seeing a dead body. Perhaps he will never experience grief, except to weep when his father dies. Here in Nablus we aren't normal. We've finished crying. The shock of death is dead in us."

"My shock hasn't died yet."

"You've only been in Nablus a short time, I think." Awwadi smiled. "And you're not so old. You have time to witness many more deaths. Me, I feel as old as these stones, even though I'm only twenty-four, and I shall soon be martyred, if Allah wills it." He ran his fingers along the weathered wall beside the entrance to an outmoded barbershop.

"Don't you think that what you're describing is the same for all Palestinians?" Omar Yussef said. "We all face violence and loss."

"Nablus is different." Awwadi gestured to the deep cloudless blue above the confined street. "You may say that it's the same sky over every Palestinian. But where I'm taking you, deep in the covered lanes of the casbah, there *is* no sky. There's no sign that anything exists outside Nablus. It's only faith in Allah that allows you to believe that your soul might escape this town, even when you die."

Awwadi led Omar Yussef north into the heart of the casbah, under vaulted ceilings. Where side alleys made sharp turns, the corners were black as pitch. Omar Yussef caught the toe of his loafer on a drain and reached out to halt his fall, snatching at the wall. It was as clammy as the palm of a virgin on his wedding night and left a damp fur of moss on his fingers.

They came to an uncovered section of the alley. The sun angled into it with the fierce brightness of a beach at midday. The younger man smiled at Omar Yussef, squinting into the sudden sunlight. "It's a special thing, this casbah of ours," he said. "There's nothing like this in Bethlehem, is there, *ustaz?*"

"Not quite. The old part of my city is smaller and fewer people live in it, so it seems a bit less complicated."

Awwadi sighed and smiled. "Complicated, yes. Do you like our town, *ustaz?*"

"It has a great history, and it's quite diverse."

Awwadi cocked his head, questioning.

"You have the community of the casbah, the new neighborhoods climbing up the hillsides, the refugees in Balata Camp, who are a world unto themselves." Omar Yussef watched as the younger man nodded his agreement. "Then there are the Samaritans."

He noticed that Awwadi swiveled away quickly.

"I went to the Samaritan village this morning with Sami," Omar Yussef said. He kept his eye on Awwadi's broad back, a few yards ahead of him. "Sami went to investigate the theft of one of their ancient scrolls. He took me with him because I'm a history teacher and he knew I'd be interested in the scroll."

"They have many scrolls," Awwadi said. "Everyone knows that."

"This one is more important."

"I hope you had an interesting visit. The Samaritans aren't so bad."

"But their religion is false?"

Awwadi looked wary. "Of course. They should submit to Islam."

"Should they be forced to do so?"

"How can you force a man to believe?"

"Threaten him with death."

"That's against Islam, unless the man is a pagan." Awwadi's slow steps echoed as they passed under a low vault.

"Did you ever hear of the Abisha Scroll?"

"No, what is it?" Awwadi's voice was flat. Omar Yussef sensed it was bursting with tension.

"The oldest book in the world," he said. "Do you know a man named Ishaq, son of the priest Jibril?"

"Why, did he write the Abisha Scroll?" Awwadi turned to Omar Yussef and smiled. "I know Ishaq. He's the black sheep of the Samaritans. But he's useful to them because of his association with the old president."

"Now that the old president is dead, Ishaq's not so useful?"

"Ishaq still has his connections, powerful connections."

"You say he's the black sheep? Because he failed to observe their holy days and had to pay a fine to be accepted back into the community?"

Nouri Awwadi's smile was distant. "That's true, but it isn't what I meant." He walked on past the arched doorway of an old halva factory.

Omar Yussef caught the man's thick arm. "Ishaq is dead. He was murdered last night. We found him this morning on top of Mount Jerizim, bound and beaten."

Awwadi's sensuous lip dropped and he put a massive hand to his short black beard.

"I see the shock of death isn't as dead in you as you claimed," Omar Yussef said. "What was it that really made him the black sheep of the Samaritans?"

"His desires. They were unacceptable to the other Samaritans."

"What desires?"

Awwadi's face was immobile. His eyelids hung drowsily. "He was homosexual. Ishaq was gay."

"How do you know that?"

Awwadi lowered his eyes and slouched along the alley. His sandalwood scent mingled with the smell of sesame paste from a bucket outside the halva factory. Omar Yussef felt lightheaded.

He thought of the sadness in the voice of Ishaq's wife when she told him that the couple had no children. *She knew her husband was gay*, he thought. *Would that woman or her family kill a man who failed to be the kind of husband they expected? One who couldn't give her children? In our tradition, children are important, but to a community that has dwindled to only six hundred, they must be even more so.* He had thought the former president's bank accounts must have been the motivation for Ishaq's murder, but could it have been the man's sexual preference instead?

He wanted to return to the mosque to tell Sami what he had learned, but Awwadi led him further into the casbah. The sesame odor faded, overcome by the raw taint of ill-maintained drains.

Awwadi grinned. "This is the Yasmina neighborhood, the oldest part of the casbah," he said. "You always know when you've reached this place, because it feels like you've stepped into a sewer."

They passed a small spice shop. Burlap sacks circled the storefront, standing on end in the street, brims rolled back to display their contents—sandy cumin, garish yellow turmeric, cardamom ground to the color of cement. Above the entrance a dangling hand-painted sign indicated that this was the Mareh family's establishment. A framed photo of the old president, leering like a lounge lizard beneath his checkered keffiyeh, hung askew on the wall above the sacks. A tall young man in dusty blue overalls came to the door, leaned against a stack of sumac, and sneered at Awwadi.

"Peace be upon you," Awwadi said.

The man snorted disdainfully. "Upon you, peace," he hissed.

Not everyone in the casbah will be dancing at the Hamas wedding, it seems, Omar Yussef thought.

Awwadi rolled his shoulders beneath the strap of his M-16 and held the young man's glare as he led Omar Yussef into a sloping passage, open to the sky. Ornate lattices of olive wood enclosed the balconies above them, so the women of the house could watch the street in seclusion. Awwadi reached for Omar Yussef's hand and took him through an imposing, carved gateway that extended elegantly to the height of two stories.

Thick tufts of weeds grew through uneven stone slabs in the courtyard. A fountain at the center of the yard had been converted into the base for a wire chicken coop. A few goats were penned into a corner by rotting planks. Above them, cut into the wall in slashy *naskh* characters, an inscription memorialized the building's construction. Omar Yussef read that it was two centuries old. On the terrace at the top of a worn flight of steps, gray sweats and baby clothing swung on a washing line. He recognized the trademark design of the American company from the knockoff designer T-shirts he had seen piled outside the store in the *souk* when he passed through with Sami.

"The Touqan Palace," Awwadi said. "It used to be home to one of the greatest families in Nablus. But like all the other rich people they moved up the hill."

Omar Yussef glanced above the laundry to the grand mansions on the ridge of Mount Jerizim.

"Now this is the home of the poorest people, a dozen

families living in the space once occupied by a single rich man, his wife and children and servants." Awwadi shook his head. "The palace has become a slum."

"That's the story of our people, my son."

Awwadi shook his head and rubbed his beard. He looked at Omar Yussef as though he had expected better of him. "This isn't a sentimental line from the work of our national poet, *ustaz*. This is where I live."

The imitation American clothing flapped in a gust of warm air. To Omar Yussef, it seemed as if the casbah wished to blow away this cheap, foreign fashion, so the red, white and blue logo would no longer blight its exquisite architecture. The big families which once dwelled in these palaces had fled to modern homes on the mountain. They neglected their heritage, leaving it to crumble in the penniless, desperate hands of the poor. *Probably they also wear American clothes,* he thought. *But expensive, genuine ones, not the Chinese-made fakes on that washing line.*

A barefoot child stumbled across the courtyard in a grubby white T-shirt. Awwadi lifted her high, laughing with her. "My eyes," he called in a playful falsetto, nuzzling the two-year-old's cheek and rubbing her toes.

Omar Yussef smiled. "Your girl?"

"I wish, *ustaz*. She's my brother's child. My favorite niece." Awwadi placed the girl on the steps and sent her tottering up them with a gentle tap on the backside and more falsetto, urging her to find her mother. "I'm not married. Not until tomorrow."

"You're taking part in the big Hamas event, the joint wedding?"

Awwadi clapped his hands. "I'm marrying a girl who's also from here in the casbah."

"A thousand congratulations." Omar Yussef knew better than to ask for details of Awwadi's bride. The name and habits of a religious man's wife were a secret to all but himself and his close family. To anyone else, she would be known only as the wife of Nouri Awwadi and prying questions would be treated with the same hostility as if someone had reached out to stroke her skin.

A cockerel strutted past the chickens in the old fountain. He lifted his ugly leg and screeched before stepping forward, his red comb and gold neck flashing bright across the stone. Omar Yussef felt the rooster's black, cruel eyes follow him to a delicately carved doorway barred by a gate of old planks. Awwadi cooed to the darkness within. Omar Yussef flinched as a massive white head emerged from the shadows.

"He's beautiful, isn't he, *ustaz?*" Awwadi said. "The only pure Arabian stallion in the casbah. His name is *Sharik*. Partner. A good name for the horse I'll ride in the wedding procession to meet my wife."

"Yes, a good name." Omar Yussef stroked the horse's muscular neck. Its hair was rough like the stubble on a man's cheek. The horse twitched and glared down its long face at Omar Yussef. "He doesn't seem to like me. That's all right. He's your partner, not mine." He ran his hand down the horse's neck again, this time with the grain of the hair, and it was as smooth and firm as polished wood.

"The other grooms will ride horses provided by Hamas. Arabians, like Sharik. But from villages outside Nablus. I'll be the only one on a true Nablus mount." Awwadi bent to pull a handful of grass from between the floor slabs and fed it to the horse from his open hand.

The horse stamped and shifted to the side. Omar Yussef glanced beyond him to the back of the stable. A low doorway appeared to lead to a cellar, the dull light of a single bulb glimmering up through its old stone arch. As Omar Yussef peered toward the light, Awwadi stepped in front of him, yanking the bridle so that his movement might seem to have been dictated by a toss of the horse's head. *What does he have down there that's so secret that he doesn't want me to see?* Omar Yussef thought.

Awwadi gave Sharik a slap on the back, made his assault rifle comfortable across his shoulders, and guided Omar Yussef toward the entrance of the Touqan Palace. "We should go back to the mosque," he said. "Sami will think you've been kidnapped by Hamas."

Chapter 6

O mar Yussef found Sami in a corner of the mosque, leaning close to a sheikh who stood stiff and straight in his camel-colored robe and tarboosh. As Omar Yussef crossed the green carpet in his stockinged feet, the sheikh turned an imperiously immobile face toward him. He had a frown like a thousand fatal fatwas.

"Let me introduce you to Sheikh Bader," Sami said. "Abu Ramiz is a schoolteacher in Dehaisha Camp and a neighbor of my family. He's in Nablus for my wedding."

Omar Yussef greeted the sheikh, who briefly dipped the point of his gray beard in acknowledgement. His black eyebrows pulled toward each other like baleful rainclouds. *When this man frowns and those two clouds meet*, Omar Yussef thought, *there'll be thunder.*

Nouri Awwadi bowed his head and whispered respectfully to the sheikh. He stuffed his worry beads into the pocket of his jeans and smiled at Sami. "Did you finalize all the arrangements for your wedding?"

"Our Honored Sheikh has been very accommodating," Sami said, "despite the much bigger wedding he's organizing for tomorrow."

Awwadi lifted a finger. "In two days, Sami, I invite you to

join me at the baths. I'll relax after my wedding and you can get a massage to prepare yourself for your own happy day." He turned to Omar Yussef. "You, too, *ustaz*. After all, you're a history teacher. What better way to relax than to enjoy the steam in a historic bathhouse."

"Where is it?" Omar Yussef asked. "It's been years since I went to a good Turkish bath."

"Just along the street. The *Hammam as-Sumara*."

"The Samaritan bathhouse? Do they run it?"

"No, but it's in what used to be their ancient quarter of the casbah. The neighborhood still bears the old name, even though everyone who lives there today is Muslim." Awwadi smiled. "I'm going to the baths now to relax before my wedding tomorrow. But I'll meet you there in the morning two days from now."

"Thank you, Nouri. I have a lot of work and the preoccupation of my own wedding, so I won't have time," Sami said. He raised one eyebrow at Omar Yussef. "But I'm sure Abu Ramiz would be delighted to meet you at the baths. He seems to be very interested in the Samaritans, and he's not busy."

Omar Yussef held Sami's gaze a moment before he put his hand over his heart and smiled his assent. "If Allah wills it," he said.

Awwadi headed for the door, shaking hands with two brawny men as they removed their muddy boots. They wore black and carried M-16s at the ready across their chests. Once inside the mosque, they slumped in a corner with their heads against the wall and closed their eyes. *Tired from a nighttime operation*, Omar Yussef thought. *The house of prayer is the safest place for them to rest.*

After Awwadi left, Omar Yussef smiled at the sheikh. "Nouri showed me the horse he'll ride in the wedding procession tomorrow," he said. "A beautiful Arabian stallion."

The sheikh inclined his head with deliberate graciousness. "All the grooms will ride like this."

"The event must be expensive," Omar Yussef said.

"The Chastity Committee takes care of it all." Sheikh Bader snapped his fingers.

"That's a Hamas institution?"

"It's an important occasion for the whole city. The money isn't significant and neither is the group that organizes it. Marriage is the most important thing in life, *ustaz*." The sheikh's speech was slow and grave. "It keeps men away from illegal sex and bad influences and perversions."

"Illegal sex?" Omar Yussef jerked his head as though contemplating something inconceivable. "You don't mean that there are prostitutes in Nablus?"

"Of course not."

"Then you must mean homosexuality?" *Ishaq could have told you that marriage doesn't put an end to forbidden desires,* Omar Yussef thought. *Only death can stop those urges, and Ishaq would know about that, too.*

The sheikh frowned. "The cost of a dowry is very high. Men have been putting off their weddings for lack of funds, due to the economic problems of our town during the intifada." He hesitated. "Their physical needs were satisfied in desperate moments, instead of being fulfilled by their family life. Many of them made mistakes."

"Our Honored Sheikh, wouldn't it be better if we allowed young men to be intimate with women, instead of forcing them to seek release with other youths?"

"Woman is seduction itself and must be hidden. You know our saying, 'Women are the devil,' " the sheikh said. "Yet keeping them hidden is a delicate balance. Men must have women to protect them from immoral acts with each other. Still, failure to keep women separate leads to other transgressions of our religious commandments. There have been weddings in Nablus where men and women danced together and drank alcohol."

"So the Chastity Committee isn't just there to make marriage affordable," Omar Yussef said. "It's to prevent people celebrating."

"If the style of the celebration is against Islam." The sheikh lifted his chin. Omar Yussef saw the hairs in his broad nostrils quiver.

Omar Yussef gestured around the mosque. "From the poster on the door, it's clear this is a Hamas mosque. The joint wedding is a big Hamas rally, isn't it?"

Sheikh Bader smiled, but his eyes maintained their superior, fierce cast. "My charitable work is in the cause of Islam. If it's funded by Hamas, it's still for Islam."

"The wedding will bring political gain, though."

"I will make a speech at the wedding about morality. But the morality I speak of won't rest solely on the responsibility of young men to follow a healthy, family path with their wives." The sheikh's brows squeezed down above his dark eyes. *Here comes the thunder,* Omar Yussef thought. "I shall make an important disclosure during my address— hitherto secret information about a failure of morality that will have tremendous political significance for Nablus and for the future of all the Palestinian people."

I was waiting for thunder and he gives me lightning, Omar

Yussef thought. "If that speech makes people support Hamas, then it's all in the cause of Islam?"

Sami cleared his throat. "Abu Ramiz—"

Sheikh Bader raised his hand. "It's all right, Sami. Your friend is a modern teacher. He demands logical reasoning."

"But I also don't condemn some of the illogical things people do when their bodies demand it of them," Omar Yussef said. "For them to do otherwise is to court depression and suicide, and that's certainly against Islamic law."

"You can't mean you see nothing wrong in homosexuality? The holy Koran condemns homosexuals as *Loutis*, the people of Lot from Sodom."

"Homosexuals suffer enough in our society without me hating them, too."

"What if you learned that one of your sons was such a pervert?"

Omar Yussef gave a rasping laugh. "I'd blame his mother. But he'd still be my son."

The sheikh looked him up and down with disdain. His eyes left Omar Yussef self-conscious about his physical frailty. *I'm paying the price now for what my body demanded of me over the years, for all the drinking and smoking,* Omar Yussef thought. *He's older than me, but he's dignified and strong. He wants society to look like him, not like me.* "A society is an accumulation of experience, Our Honored Sheikh," he said. "Life can't be parroted the way you teach children to memorize the Koran. When the experience of a society is broad, everyone's happiness can be taken into account in a spirit of tolerance."

"That's a dangerous path, *ustaz*." The contempt in Sheikh Bader's black eyes reminded Omar Yussef of the arrogant cockerel in the Touqan Palace.

"Danger lies in denial. As a teacher I can tell you that when you order children to learn by rote, it's soon forgotten, because they don't understand *why* it should be remembered. They grow up not knowing how to think for themselves and then they're easy to manipulate."

"In the sura of The Poets, the holy Koran says, 'Will you fornicate with males and eschew the wives whom Allah has created for you? Surely you are great transgressors.' My pupils are obedient to Allah and to the holy Koran."

"Obedient to you, above all." Omar Yussef's finger shot out, pointing shakily at Bader.

One of the armed men in black came out of his snooze and rose slowly in the corner of the mosque. The shoulder strap of his assault rifle clicked against the darkened metal barrel. Sheikh Bader lifted his hand and the man sat down, but his eyes remained open, watching Omar Yussef. "Evidently obedience was not part of *your* education," the sheikh said.

"My dear father taught me to think for myself." Omar Yussef had a sudden remembrance of the stern sheikhs who used to come to his father's house when he was a boy, urging the old man to join the new political groups campaigning for Palestinian rights. They always entered the room purposefully, hurrying as though their political cause might spoil in the sun. At the time, Omar had thought his father weak for refusing them. Now he saw how wise he had been.

He withdrew his finger and looked at Sami. The policeman raised an eyebrow, glanced at the two gunmen in the corner and dipped his head toward the door of the mosque. *Time to go*, Omar Yussef thought. "My dear father also taught me to show respect. I hope you don't mistake my bluntness for disrespect, Our Honored Sheikh."

"May Allah forbid it," Sheikh Bader said. "If you'll excuse me, I have to finish the arrangements for tomorrow's wedding. We must be sure that Nouri Awwadi isn't the only one riding a horse. I have to get fourteen more such mounts into the casbah by the end of the day. May Allah grant you grace."

In the small plaza outside the mosque, Sami gave Omar Yussef a smile. "Are you so opposed to marriage, Abu Ramiz, that you want to insult the sheikh until he refuses to carry out the ceremony for me?"

"As a matter of fact, I think you and Meisoun are a perfect pair. But men like him make me angry." He jerked his thumb in the direction of the mosque. "Many years ago, when I was still a drinker, I once told a particularly self-important sheikh to go screw himself. Evidently he took my advice, because he has given birth to many others like him and now we're inundated with arrogant, self-righteous religious leaders."

Sami grinned. They turned toward the shops along the casbah's main street.

Chapter 7

At the entrance to the *souk*, Omar Yussef detected something savory in the air. He twitched his nostrils, searching beyond the aroma of walnuts and dates from the *ma'amoul* shortbread pyramided on wide trays outside a sweetshop. Sami pointed into the half-light of the market. "You've picked up the scent of Abu Alam's restaurant," he said. "Now I'll prove to you that I'm not marrying Meisoun just so that I'll have someone to fry my eggs in the morning."

They weaved between the women in the *souk*. The presence of the crowd calmed Omar Yussef. In the empty casbah, there always seemed to be some man, menacing and solitary, sloping along close to the wall on the shadowed side of the alley. As the women milled past the small stores, the brush of their shoulders against Omar Yussef felt like a soothing caress. *I could almost forget that I saw a dead man today*, he thought.

Just past a toy shop selling bright plastic machine guns and tricycles, Sami dodged into a storefront, its door and window the width of a man's arm span and open to the street. The sizzling of oil in a frying pan drew Omar Yussef inside. He could rarely stomach food that wasn't prepared by his wife, but his exertions at the summit of Mount Jerizim and his walk around the casbah had made him hungry. He noticed that he was salivating.

Sami reached over the counter to slap hands with the owner, who was making hummus in a bucket-sized mixer. Abu Alam squeezed two large lemons over the chickpeas, tehina and garlic. He wiped the juice from his fingers on his soiled shirt, before reaching out a thick forearm to grasp Sami's hand. His fat face glistened with perspiration.

"So you're a pal of Sami's from Bethlehem?" Abu Alam's voice was hoarse from shouting orders to his cook over the din of the busy *souk*. "Welcome, *ustaz*. Things down there aren't violent enough for you, so you decided to come and see what life is like in a real war zone?"

"Thanks for your welcome." Omar Yussef raised a finger and smiled. "How do you know I'm not on the run from the Israelis? Maybe I decided to take refuge here where they can't get at me."

"You may see gunmen walking freely around our casbah in the afternoon, it's true, *ustaz*. But believe me they're not out of reach of the Israelis, even here. Only last night, the Israelis came right to the door of my restaurant." Abu Alam pointed toward a metal concertina shutter folded back from the entrance. The light green paint was smeared a cloudy black. "That's from a grenade or some other explosive, and it wasn't like that when I locked up yesterday."

Omar Yussef touched a finger to the blackness. It came away dirty, with a smell of burnt plastic. "What happened?"

"The Israeli special forces come in every night to arrest some gunmen. We're not very deep in the casbah here, so the Israelis can enter this far and still know where they stand." Abu Alam waved a big hand at the door. "But they don't like to go further. They're at a disadvantage in the alleys and the old tunnels. The streets are too twisty for their tanks, and our gunmen know their way around much better than they do."

"In Bethlehem the army comes at night once or twice a week," Omar Yussef said.

"Nablus isn't like Bethlehem or the rest of the West Bank. It's more like Gaza, *ustaz*," Abu Alam said. "We used to run the most prosperous businesses in Palestine and produce its greatest poets. Now our casbah is a factory for gunmen and the only literature is written on posters advertising the latest martyr."

"Most of the gunmen in Bethlehem have been arrested by now."

"No matter how many the Israelis kill or capture, Nablus still has a good supply."

"Maybe if you gave the gunmen free eggs and hummus, they'd be too fat to run away from the Israelis and then your town could get some peace."

"I'm doing my best. The men of the resistance eat free here, *ustaz*, and you know that hummus makes you sleepy." Abu Alam wiped the sweat from his forehead with the back of his wrist.

"What about the police?" Omar Yussef squeezed Sami's shoulder. "Do they eat free of charge?"

"The brother Sami will never get fat, and my prices are affordable, even for a man on a police salary." Abu Alam smiled. "The usual, Sami?"

"Yes, and the same for Abu Ramiz."

Sami took Omar Yussef's elbow, led him down the single

row of tables, and sat facing the door. Against the opposite wall, a thin youth in baggy jeans took a few eggs from a cardboard pannier and cracked them one-handed into a charred frying pan. He turned up the heat on a row of gas burners, wiping a smear of egg yolk onto his white apron. Behind Sami, another youngster was wedged between a deep stainless steel sink and a waist-high cooking-gas canister in the violet glow of an electric fly trap. He split a baked eggplant, scraped out its pulpy innards, and tossed the skin onto a pile of trash, where it lay, bruise-black and limp, like a gutted crow. Abu Alam shouted to the boy, who went quickly to the counter and ferried a few small plates to Sami and Omar Yussef.

Sami curled a wedge of flatbread around his forefinger and scooped some *khilta* into his mouth. He wiped a dribble of the yoghurt from his chin. "Try it. It's good," he said. "Even your dear wife wouldn't object to this place."

"I think she might take issue with their cleanliness," Omar Yussef said, glancing at the charred gobbets of egg on the gas burners.

The yoghurt was appealing, though, dotted with the brightness of finely chopped tomatoes and red peppers. He ate, enjoying the freshness of the dish. When he tried the soft slices of avocado soaked in olive oil, he sensed himself relaxing. He was supposed to be on vacation and he hadn't planned for dead bodies in his itinerary, so it was comforting to taste hearty, traditional food prepared simply and to forget about the corpse on the mountain. *It's Sami who has to worry about the dead Samaritan*, Omar Yussef thought, *and his killer.*

The young man who had been working the burners laid

an omelette, glistening with oil, on the table and grinned at
Omar Yussef with betel-stained teeth. In the kitchen, a
jagged crackle and a stutter of violet light marked the
sudden demise of a fly.

Omar Yussef took some hummus, but as he brought it to
his mouth, a dollop slipped off the bread onto his shirt. He
cursed quietly and held up his hands, while Sami wiped at the
stain with a wet paper napkin. The men at the other tables
smoked and drank tea and talked, bending low over their
plates when they ate. Omar Yussef leaned close to Sami.

"Ishaq was homosexual," he whispered. "Awwadi told me."

"You've been interrogating Awwadi?" Sami mumbled
through a mouthful of hummus. He scrubbed once more at
Omar Yussef's stained shirt, looking sharply at his friend.
"You're supposed to be in Nablus for my wedding, not to
play detective."

"Weddings depress me. I need to focus on a murder to
cheer myself up."

Sami dropped the damp napkin in the ashtray and examined the hummus stain on Omar Yussef's shirt with suspicion.

"Will the stain come out?" Omar Yussef said.

Sami shrugged. "You think Ishaq's death is connected to
his homosexuality?"

"Ishaq may have had access to money hidden by the old
president in the foreign accounts people always talk about.
He also had a personal secret that could shame him before
his community. Sounds like a good basis for blackmail."

"But he was murdered. Why kill someone you want to
blackmail?" Sami swirled the hummus with his bread.

"Blackmailers are like anyone else—they make
mistakes." Omar Yussef rooted for a sesame seed trapped

between his teeth. "Even your great Sheikh Bader isn't right all the time. Eventually someone will refuse to follow his sacred rules."

Sami cut a piece of omelette with the edge of his fork. He held it with a small piece of bread and rolled it in a hot dish of fava bean *foule*. "Mistake or not, it's a mystery, and that's that." He shoved the omelette into his mouth and wiped his fingers on his combat pants.

"It's not just a mystery. It's a murder case." Omar Yussef's eyes widened.

Sami chewed his food. "You're a good friend, Abu Ramiz, so I'm going to be straight with you. Nablus has many murders, but it has very few murder trials."

"What do you mean?"

The young policeman sucked the last remnants of bread from his back teeth. "You know that I don't follow the sheikh's sacred rules, as you call them. I have my own guidelines in life, and accordingly there's only so far I can go with this case."

Omar Yussef straightened in surprise. "I smell corruption on your breath."

"Don't be dramatic. Abu Alam's hummus just has too much garlic," Sami grinned. "Corruption makes me choke just as hard as you."

"Then what's the problem?"

Sami picked at his thumbnail. "The sheikh warned me not to pursue this case."

"Then start your investigation with him. Why would he want the case of a dead Samaritan to be dropped? He must be involved."

"Abu Ramiz, I was just transferred back to the West

Bank after five years in Gaza, in exile," said Sami. "I'm about to be married to the woman I love and I want to have a family. My deportation already delayed these things and I can't afford to take risks."

"Risks?" Omar Yussef's hands shook. He gripped the edge of the table to steady them.

"This isn't just a case of the murder of some anonymous Samaritan."

"Are you saying you don't care about his death because he was homosexual?"

"I'm saying I care very much about his death and I certainly don't intend to drop the case completely. But there may be limits to how far I can take my inquiries." Sami picked up a strip of cheese and pretended to roll it in the dish of *khilta*. He spoke quietly, urgently. "The case isn't simple. It's obvious to me that it reaches far into the politics of Nablus. It'll surely concern influential people."

"I agree," Omar Yussef said. "After all, Ishaq managed the Old Man's money."

"The money suggests this wasn't just a crime of passion, even perverted passion. Someone powerful was after all that cash. If they have the money now, they won't be happy with anyone who investigates it, and if not, they may kill again to find it." Sami squashed the spongy finger of cheese onto his plate as though it were a cigarette. "The political leaders of Nablus are violent, ruthless men. I can't go up against them."

"You fear the sheikh will kill you, if you ignore his warning?"

"Someone might have Meisoun's permit revoked, sending her back to Gaza. They could even harm her, or have me posted to Gaza again."

"Who are *they?*" Omar Yussef brought his hand down on the table. The plates rattled. He looked about him, but the noise of cooking and conversation went on as before.

Sami lit a cigarette and called to Abu Alam for two glasses of tea. He expelled twin streams of smoke from his nostrils. "You know me well enough to understand that I uphold my principles as much as possible, Abu Ramiz. But in this society, where does it get me?"

"Am I wrong to stand up for *my* principles?"

"With respect, Abu Ramiz, lecturing the little girls at the UN school isn't as tough as confronting the corrupt political establishment of Nablus."

"How do you know you'd have to go up against the entire political system? What did the Sheikh tell you?"

"You saw the photograph on Ishaq's wall. The Old Man was kissing him."

The tension in Sami's jaw betrayed his shame to Omar Yussef. *He's a fine boy and a good policeman,* he thought. *He has sacrificed so much for a rotten system. He only wants to do something for himself now.*

Omar Yussef wondered whose side his friend, Bethlehem's police chief, would take, when he arrived for the wedding. *Probably he'd defer to Sami,* he thought. *He'd tell me that Sami has an instinct for danger, knowing when to charge the guns and when to take cover. My instincts, on the other hand, are less practical.*

"If I help you identify the killer, will you arrest him?" he said.

Sami puffed out his cheeks. "If Allah wills it, of course. I'll even pay for your tombstone."

"My sons can cover that."

Omar Yussef knew that Ramiz, his eldest, would agree with Sami. He always avoided trouble. Zuheir, however, was principled and combative, like Omar Yussef. He would want his father to seek justice, even when the law failed. Omar Yussef noticed that Zuheir's approval was important to him.

"A good tombstone is expensive," Sami said.

"I'll tell my boys to start saving."

"For some things, you never finish paying."

Sami's mobile phone vibrated on the tabletop. Abu Alam set their tea beside it. Sami put his finger on the phone to stop it wandering across the Formica. His tired, yellowy eyes stared hard at Omar Yussef and his lips were tight with irritation. He picked up the phone.

Chapter 8

Sami whispered into his cellular and the muscles of his face relaxed. With the tiny silver phone pressed to his ear, he rose, dropped some coins on the counter and gave Abu Alam a light handshake. He crooked a finger for Omar Yussef to follow and moved into the flow of people through the *souk*.

Omar Yussef sipped at his tea, but the glass was too hot for him to hold and the mint stuck to his teeth. He put it down before it burned his fingers and picked a flaccid leaf from his lip. The hummus felt heavy in his stomach.

"Did you enjoy the food, ustaz?" Abu Alam shouted above the sizzling of falafel in a blackened frier. He flattened a green ball of mashed fava beans between his palms and slid it into the hot oil.

"Your plan to bring peace to the town by making the gunmen sleepy with hummus may work. It has succeeded with me," Omar Yussef said. "Leave a big plate outside your door at night and in the morning you'll find a group of contented Israeli soldiers snoozing in the street."

"I could poison the hummus, but I doubt the soldiers would notice the difference. Have you ever tasted Israeli hummus, *ustaz?* You can tell it's made industrially. There's not enough lemon and the chickpeas are ground too fine, as though it was meant to be eaten by little babies."

"Whereas your hummus merely makes me want to sleep like a baby." Omar Yussef turned to the street. Sami was edging away through the crowd, waving to someone over the heads of the shoppers. "Thank you for your food. The avocado was very good."

"To your double health, *ustaz*. Thank you." Abu Alam smiled. "May Allah grant you good health."

Omar Yussef peered along the passage, looking for Sami. Dusty pillars of sunlight from ventilation grates in the ceiling illuminated the crowd, but all the men had identical short, black hair and every woman covered her head in a cream scarf.

A stocky tradesman with gray stubble and a dark mustache leaned over his handcart and lifted a quartered watermelon. "Come on, watermelon, watermelon, it's almost free," he bellowed. Omar Yussef flinched at the volume of the man's sudden call and glared at him. The vendor caught Omar Yussef's indignant eye, but only raised his chin and his volume: "O Allah, it's free."

A hand reached up out of the crowd, and another next to it. Someone was waving to him. Then he saw Sami's face below the raised hands, and he started through the throng.

His wife emerged from the crowd of Nablus women in their long gowns and headscarfs. Maryam's head was uncovered and she wore black slacks and a thin black sweater. On her shoulder, she carried a dark blue handbag with gold clasps that Omar Yussef had bought for her in Morocco. She lifted her arms and hugged Omar Yussef, her plastic shopping bags slapping his back.

Sami guided him out of the flow of the crowd and into the entrance of a shop selling gaudy housecoats for women. He opened his palm to present a slight young woman. "Abu Ramiz, you remember Meisoun?"

Though her head was draped with the scarf of a religious woman, Meisoun dropped her chin to one side coquettishly and fluttered her long, delicate lashes at Omar Yussef. When they had first met, Meisoun had been working at a hotel in Gaza and was kind enough to respond with good humor to Omar Yussef's innocent flirting. *I'm sure she considered me just a harmless old man,* Omar Yussef thought, *and she probably still does.* He felt more regret than he would have expected for the passing of the days when women might have described him as charming, handsome and even dangerous. *Now I'm only charming—provided I'm in a good mood.*

"Miss Meisoun, I came to Nablus solely to see you," Omar Yussef said. "The West Bank needs Gazan beauties like you to make life more bearable here. But you betrayed me and agreed to marry another man."

"I have several unmarried sisters in Gaza, *ustaz.*" Meisoun smiled at Sami to show that she enjoyed teasing Omar Yussef. "They would be glad to meet an accomplished man of intelligence like you."

"He's not so smart." Maryam slapped Omar Yussef's wrist and wagged a finger at her husband. "Omar, it's only peasant men in the villages who take more than one wife these days. Anyway, why would you want a second wife? You always complain that one is too many."

"The political power of the Islamists is growing, Maryam," Omar Yussef said. "It's important to stay in their good books. If I take a second wife, they'll assume that I'm religious, and I won't even have to pray to prove it."

"Would you agree to let Sheikh Bader officiate at the wedding?" Sami smiled, but Omar Yussef detected a hardness in his friend's eyes.

"All the grooms at the big Hamas wedding will be mounted on white stallions." Omar Yussef laughed. "Given the condition of my health, if I tried to ride such a horse, Sheikh Bader might have to arrange a white ambulance to bring me to my new bride."

"And they'd take you away in a coffin," Maryam said.

Meisoun laughed. "I certainly wouldn't want my wedding to be like the big one Hamas is planning," she said. "You know I'm religious, *ustaz*, but Sheikh Bader has planned more of a political event than a wedding, from what Sami tells me. Men and women should be separated for the sake of decency, but they shouldn't be celebrating on different planets, like they will at the Hamas event. The women will be at one end of the casbah and the men at the other."

"My wedding to Meisoun and our married life together—these are the most important things to me." Sami spoke to Maryam, but Omar Yussef knew this was aimed at him. "I suffered a long time in Gaza away from my family, but perhaps it was Allah's will that I be sent there to meet this perfect wife and mother."

Maryam laid a hand on Meisoun's arm and smiled. "I don't think we'll have to wait long," she said.

Omar Yussef sighed. After the marriage, people would refer to the couple as Abu Hassan and Umm Hassan—the father of Hassan and the mother of Hassan—because most

Palestinians considered Sami obliged to name his first child after his father, Hassan. *Of course, it had better be a son,* Omar Yussef thought, *or there'll be commiserations all around.*

At times like this, Omar Yussef found Maryam utterly conventional, but he was never able to maintain his discontent with her for long. *That either means I'm also rather conventional,* he thought, *or I must love her.* He recalled the taxi ride from Bethlehem to Nablus. Maryam had chattered all the way about the lace on the bridal gown, how tall the wedding cake might be, and how many children she expected Sami to sire. As the hot breeze had buffeted Omar Yussef through the taxi window, his irritation at her babble had grown and he had wondered what had ever made him marry her. When the taxi finally approached the Hawara checkpoint at the edge of Nablus, she had tidied the few strands of white hair crossing his bald head and touched his cheek with her palm. With that gesture, his resentment had ceased and he had remembered that there was little enough in her life to bring her joy. His eyes tearing, he had taken her hand and kissed it. Sometimes she seemed like the most average woman alive, but it was too late to wonder why he loved her.

"No, we're not going to have to wait very long at all for a little one to arrive." Maryam leaned close to Sami and spoke with an excited quaver. "Are we, Abu Hassan?"

Omar Yussef threw his arms wide and let them slap down against his thighs. "Maryam, allow them to enjoy their marriage. Don't pressure them."

"Who's pressuring them? You don't think children are the greatest pleasure of marriage?"

"Marriage has many benefits, not only children."

"If you had your way, I'd have given birth to a shelf full of books, instead of three sons." Maryam examined Omar Yussef's shirt. She brushed her hand across his chest. "Omar, is that hummus?"

Omar Yussef glanced hopelessly at Sami.

"It's my fault, Umm Ramiz," Sami said. "Abu Ramiz didn't want to eat, but I was very hungry and I forced him to taste the hummus at my favorite restaurant."

Omar Yussef touched the tips of his mustache, nervously. "It wasn't as good as yours, my darling," he said.

Maryam jerked her head back and opened her dark eyes wide. "Of course it wasn't. Perhaps you want a second wife so that she can make your hummus. She can wash your underwear, too."

Omar Yussef smiled and put his hand to his wife's cheek. "Very well, she can wash my underwear. No one but you will make hummus for me, though." He looked down at Maryam's bags. "What have you bought?"

"A nice new shirt for Nadia to wear to the wedding." Maryam opened one of the plastic bags and Omar Yussef looked inside. The shirt was pink and lacy. Maryam held up the other bag. "I also picked up some American T-shirts for Miral and Dahoud."

"Nadia will love it." He smiled approvingly and kissed his wife's cheek. "So will our newest little pair." He had adopted Miral and Dahoud after the death of their parents, friends of his, little more than a year ago, and found in them a delight that made him feel young once more. He thought of the Samaritan priest, robbed of his adopted son by a murderer, and shivered at the thought of losing either of his new charges.

"Can I take you both back to the hotel?" Sami asked. He tilted his head and stared hard at Omar Yussef as he spoke. "You must be tired, Umm Ramiz. You too, Abu Ramiz. You've done enough for one day."

He doesn't want me arguing with him about the investigation into Ishaq's murder, Omar Yussef thought. *I can't force him to face down the powerful people he says are involved in this case, but I know Sami's a good policeman. He'll come around, if I don't push him too hard.*

"Why should Omar be tired? He's only been loafing around, eating other people's food." Maryam wiped at her husband's stained shirt with the corner of her handkerchief. As they moved into the stream of shoppers, she turned to Omar Yussef. "How was your visit to the Samaritan synagogue? Did they show you their historic scrolls?"

Omar Yussef suddenly felt light-headed and panicky. He thought of Ishaq's corpse. The busy street around him dissolved into darkness and he slipped on the puddle from the ice melting in the watermelon vendor's cart. Sami caught him under the arm and maneuvered him into a side alley.

"The car is just here, at the top of the casbah, Umm Ramiz," he said. "We'd better take your husband to the hotel."

"I'm fine," Omar Yussef murmured.

"Sami, I don't know how you find your way around these alleys," Maryam said. She looked suspiciously at Omar Yussef.

They rounded a dark corner and pushed into a dim, vaulted stretch, aiming for a bright spot where the tunnel emerged twenty yards away.

"Meisoun, there's nothing like this in Gaza," Maryam said. "Are you getting used to it?"

Meisoun wiggled her head. "It's true, the surviving older buildings of Gaza aren't as impressive as the casbah here in Nablus. This is one of the most important places in Palestine, historically."

"Have you been taking lessons from the schoolteacher here?" Maryam jabbed a finger at Omar Yussef.

"I would be honored," Meisoun said. "But actually I studied the ancient commerce of Palestine for my business degree. Nablus was always much more important as a center of trade than Jerusalem."

They came into the light. Vivid green weeds fell in thick clusters over the wall.

Sami smiled. "My fiancée is much smarter than me," he said. "I want her to start a business here in Nablus."

"With her knowledge of history, she could be a tour guide," Maryam said.

"That's not exactly a growing business. You may be the first tourists to reach Nablus in five years. But if you like, I can be your tour guide." Meisoun smiled, lifted her arm, and marched forward. "Follow my finger, come on, my group."

Sami fell into step behind her, dropping his shoulders like the indolent tourists who shuffled about Bethlehem on organized tours. Omar and Maryam joined, too.

Meisoun halted at the end of the overgrown wall and cupped her hand beside her mouth like a guide with a bull-horn. "Listen, my group, most of the casbah dates from the last eight centuries. But beneath our feet are remains of the Roman town built for veterans of the legions and called

Flavia Neapolis. Nablus is a corruption of the name 'Neapolis.' "

Omar Yussef held up his hand. "Miss, miss, what was the town on this site called before it was rebuilt as Neapolis?"

"Quiet, you troublemaker." Meisoun put her finger to her lips. "The Jews say they lived here two thousand years ago in a town called Shekhem, but I'm not allowed to say any more about that or I'll lose my official tour guide license."

"Perhaps you should choose another business that's less politically sensitive," Omar Yussef suggested.

"I'm encouraging her to get into cell phones, in partnership with Ramiz," Sami said. Omar Yussef's son ran a cell phone business in Bethlehem. "You're right that it's best to avoid politically sensitive issues." He angled his neck toward Omar Yussef to emphasize his warning.

Meisoun put her finger on her lips again. "My interest in cell phones, too, is a secret no less explosive than the ancient Israelite history of Nablus." She smiled. "Someone else might steal our idea."

"I'm very discreet, Miss Meisoun," Omar Yussef said. "Unfortunately, my wife is a chatterbox. If you want to prevent Maryam from exposing your secret, you'd better bury her at least as far down as the Roman remains."

Maryam slapped Omar Yussef's shoulder. "Then who would make your hummus?"

They laughed, but Meisoun grew quiet. She stepped closer to the wall and peered into the shadows cast by the falling weeds. She ran her hand across the smooth, tan stone and circled three bullet holes with her forefinger. Powdered limestone came away on her nail when she probed one of them. A flattened slug of lead dropped to the floor. "You see, Umm Ramiz. I'm right at home in Nablus. It's just like Gaza."

They walked on in silence. Meisoun rubbed the dust from her finger and reached for Sami's hand. The young man looked into her eyes with a strained smile.

Omar Yussef reached out and pinched Maryam's earlobe affectionately. She was stroking his hand, when they heard quick footsteps around the corner.

Four men came into the alley. They wore green fatigues and their faces were disguised by black stocking caps. Two of them held thick lengths of wood. A short, bulky man slapped a tire iron into his palm. They barred the alley, poised on their toes, ready to spring.

Sami pulled Meisoun behind him. Omar Yussef looked back along the passage. It was empty and dark.

The short man chuckled, jeering and mirthless. "You're Sami Jaffari, aren't you, you son of a whore?" He stepped toward Sami, the men with the timbers at his elbow.

Sami pushed Meisoun away, ducked his head and charged at the short man, hitting him in the chest with his shoulder. The man went down, but Sami took a two by four across his shoulders and dropped to his knees. Another blow flattened him.

Omar Yussef let go of Maryam's hand. "Stop this, by Allah, stop it," he shouted. "Shame on you."

The fourth masked man was tall and trim. He shoved Omar Yussef on the collar bone with the flat of his hand, but the schoolteacher kept his balance and moved forward.

"Calm down, Little Grandpa." The tall man leaned close. Omar Yussef smelled cardamom on his breath, as though he had been chewing seed pods.

"*Your* grandpa would be ashamed of you," he said, "and I hope he'll curse you for this."

The tall man raised his hand and slapped Omar Yussef hard. His glasses fell and he spun toward the wall. He struck it with his shoulder and doubled over.

Maryam spread her arms in front of him. "Don't touch my husband, you filthy dog," she said.

Omar Yussef's myopic eyes were tearful from the blow and his nose was running into his mustache. He saw a blur of green, hooded shapes lifting something from the floor and heard the tall man's voice: "Consider this a warning, Jaffari, you worthless shit." An arm swung. Omar Yussef heard a light crunch like cutlery rattling in a drawer, and Sami bellowed.

"Peace be upon you, Lieutenant." The tall man's voice was mocking. Omar Yussef heard someone expectorate and saw Sami flinch when the spittle hit him.

The men went back around the corner. Omar Yussef listened to their footsteps recede. Maryam handed him his glasses and stroked his stinging cheek.

Sami was hunched over his knees on the flagstones of the alley. Meisoun hugged his shaking body.

Omar Yussef kneeled beside him. He gave his handkerchief to Meisoun, who wiped the gob of sputum from Sami's cheek. The young policeman's face was pale and sweating. He cradled his right arm with his left.

"They've broken my arm," he gasped.

This time Omar Yussef didn't ask who *they* were.

Chapter 9

The sun slipped behind the mansions on Mount Jerizim, as though their prodigiously wealthy residents had bought it and stashed it in their gardens. *Why not?* Omar Yussef thought. *Everything's for sale in Palestine, if you bribe the right people.* He gathered his breath for the steps outside his hotel, coughing on the exhaust fumes as his taxi pulled away, and followed Maryam toward the entrance.

Few of the rooms in the Grand Hotel were lit. In the dark, its seventies façade of rippled concrete looked like the exhausted face of a man moments from death. Meisoun, playing the ironic tour guide, had said the violence of Nablus discouraged tourists, and her wedding guests accounted for almost every illuminated window in the hotel. Omar Yussef hoped not to have to be the one to tell them that the groom was in the sick bay at police headquarters with his broken forearm in a sling.

As Omar Yussef tracked Maryam across the empty lobby, the hotel manager wrenched a jammed sheet of paper from the fax machine on the reception desk. "Peace be upon you, *ustaz*," he said, a little breathlessly.

"And upon you, peace."

"This might be a reservation." The manager beamed

desperately at Omar Yussef. He had eyes the pale brown tone of cigarette filters and gray skin, so that his face looked like a heavily used ashtray with two new butts stubbed into it. He wore an expression of hopeless fragility that made him look as though he would, indeed, blow away about as easily as a pile of cinders. With the shredded fax close to his face, he struggled to read the text. His mouth tightened and he crushed the sheet into a ball, tossing it hard into a wastepaper basket.

Maryam caressed Omar Yussef's face as they waited for the elevator. While they had watched the doctor set Sami's arm, Omar Yussef had felt the sting in his cheek and wished the masked man in the alley had punched him instead. The slap had been contemptuous, as though he were a woman or an infant. He couldn't help but resent Maryam's sympathy.

"Darling, I'll wait down here while you change for dinner," he said.

He kissed her and entered the lounge. Lit a ghostly blue by glimmering fluorescent tubes, the room was noisy with the sententious voice of a presenter on the Abu Dhabi cable news channel resonating from a big-screen television on the far wall. At a breakfast bar of the same pale pine as the reception desk, a waiter in a white shirt and flashy striped vest leaned over a newspaper. As Omar Yussef approached, he shoved himself off his elbows and straightened the bottom of his vest over his paunch.

"Evening of joy," Omar Yussef said.

"Evening of light, *ustaz*," the waiter mumbled. He looked nervous and defeated, as though he already knew he wouldn't be able to fulfill any order to Omar Yussef's satisfaction.

"A coffee, please. Prepare it *sa'ada*." Omar Yussef always took his coffee without sugar.

The waiter ducked below the counter.

"Please turn the volume down on the television, too," Omar Yussef said. "The news is always bad enough without it having to be loud, as well."

The waiter remained on his haunches, reaching up to a shelf behind him for the remote control.

The room had been recently whitewashed, but its furniture was a decade old. The couches were low squares of foam covered in nylon and corduroy with no armrests or support. Omar Yussef winced, wondering how he'd ever be able to get up, once he had sunk into one of them.

With the hotel almost empty, there was only one group in the lounge. In the far corner, Nadia balanced on the edge of a couch of spongy cushions upholstered with a russet fabric in an angular pattern. She was in conversation with her uncle Zuheir and a red-haired foreigner in her late thirties. Omar Yussef would have preferred to sit alone, letting the adrenaline that still thundered through him after the attack by the masked men dissipate. But if he didn't join them, Nadia would want to know why and he preferred not to talk to her about Sami's beating.

By the way Zuheir's lips puckered and his thick beard twitched, Omar Yussef sensed that he was suppressing a powerful anger. The schoolteacher's second son was twenty-eight years old. He wore a white dress shirt buttoned to the neck, its tails falling outside white cotton pants. It was the clothing of a religious zealot and Omar Yussef searched beneath it for the excitable, curly-haired boy he had secretly favored over his other sons, when they were children. Zuheir's dark eyes flitted between the foreigner and Nadia. *If his niece weren't here*, Omar Yussef thought, *I suspect he'd give that red-haired woman a mouthful.* He smiled. He was suspicious of Zuheir's newly devout demeanor, but he was happy that the boy's habitual truculence hadn't deserted him.

Nadia noticed Omar Yussef picking his way between the empty couches and waved. His favorite grandchild was skinny and tall and so pale that her grandmother's main mission in life was to force food upon her in the hope of adding color and size. Her mischievious intelligence impressed Omar Yussef more every month. As he came close, she suppressed a smile. *I know that look*, he thought. *She has a surprise for me.* He bent to kiss her smooth forehead. Her hair had a clean bubble-gum scent and Omar Yussef felt embarrassed by the sweat on his shirt and socks from the scuffle in the casbah.

"Grandpa, this is Miss Jamie King," Nadia said, in English. She gestured to the foreigner with the spine of a paperback, keeping her place in the book with her forefinger. "Miss King, this is Omar Yussef Sirhan from Bethlehem. He's a schoolteacher—with a secret life." She opened her black eyes wide.

The red-haired woman stood and shook Omar Yussef's hand with a strong yank that started at her hips. She wore a blue chalk-striped suit and a thin gold chain over the freckled, sunburned skin at her collar bone. "What secret life is that?" she asked.

"He's a detective," Nadia said.

"In my granddaughter's imagination." Omar Yussef raised his eyebrows and lifted a finger to caution Nadia. "I work for the United Nations, as a school principal."

"That's an excellent cover for a detective." The American moved closer to Omar Yussef. "Actually I've come across your name before, *ustaz*. I'm based in Jerusalem and I'm a good friend of your boss, Magnus Wallender. He told me how helpful you've been to him in his job running the UN Relief and Works Agency schools."

Omar Yussef smiled. "Magnus is a good man."

"Miss King is from Los Angeles," Nadia said. "We're planning a crime together."

Zuheir grunted testily and tugged on his beard. Nadia grinned at him and he averted his eyes.

Omar Yussef lowered himself onto a short sofa. The foam was even softer than he expected and he felt himself falling backward. He needed both arms to right himself, and the muscles in his back and abdomen twinged. "My granddaughter is corrupting you, Miss King," he said, breathing heavily.

"I'm impressed that she's already reading in English," King said.

Nadia flashed the cover of her book at Omar Yussef. He only had time to notice that it was by a man named Chandler. "Miss King is going to help me to write a novel in the style of my favorite American detective writer," she said. "I started it today, because I was bored waiting for my grandfather to come and take me to eat *qanafi*."

Omar Yussef gave a thin smile. The waiter brought a small coffee cup and set it on the low table. "May Allah bless your hands," Omar Yussef said.

"Blessings," the waiter said, putting a plastic ashtray and a glass of water beside the coffee cup.

"Nablus is famous for *qanafi*, Miss King," Nadia said.

"It's a very sweet dessert made with wheat and cheese and—Grandpa, what do you call *fustoq halabi* in English?"

Omar Yussef scratched his chin. "I don't know. Aleppo peanuts?"

From behind his hand, Zuheir murmured: "Pistachios."

"Ah, pistachios. Nablus is famous for this dessert and for making soap in old factories in the casbah. They make the soap out of olive oil." Nadia giggled. "If my grandfather ever takes me out of this hotel, I expect to find the people of Nablus are very fat and very clean."

"What's the title of the book you're writing, Nadia, my darling?" Omar Yussef asked.

"*The Curse of the Casbah.*" Nadia shared a smile with Jamie King.

Omar Yussef noticed that the American tapped her finger impatiently against her chair, despite her grin. "That sounds exciting," he said.

"The murder victim in my book is going to be killed with poisoned *qanafi.*"

Omar Yussef tasted his coffee. Its bitterness pleased him, but it was too weak, so the grounds floated in it, instead of sinking to the bottom. He turned to frown at the waiter, but the man was leaning on his elbows, staring at his newspaper.

He twisted toward the American. "Miss King, I believe I saw you on the road today," he said. "Do you work for the World Bank?"

"Do I stick out that much?" King said. "With this security situation, I guess there aren't a lot of foreigners around Nablus."

"Not driving in big cars with IBRD plates." He put down his coffee cup and sucked the grounds off his teeth.

"You looked like you were on your way to the Samaritan village on Mount Jerizim, when I saw you in your car. I was on my way back from there."

King looked grave. "For me, it didn't quite work out as planned," she said.

"I was returning from a visit to a Samaritan woman named Roween."

King grimaced.

Omar Yussef smiled at Nadia. "My darling, will you go upstairs and ask Grandma what time she wants to eat dinner?"

Nadia bit her lower lip. *She knows I'm getting her out of the way and that she's about to miss something interesting*, he thought. Reluctantly the girl left the lounge.

"She's very bright," King said.

Omar Yussef watched through the glass wall of the lounge as Nadia blew him a kiss from the lobby and entered the elevator.

Zuheir sat forward and spoke quietly in Arabic. "Don't you think it's a waste for Nadia to spend so much time reading these American detective stories?"

Omar Yussef smiled awkwardly at Jamie King and reached out to grasp his son's knee. "Whatever excites us when we are young eventually turns to ice, Zuheir," he said. "Later we look back with contempt on our early enthusiasms."

Zuheir pulled his knee away.

"Many of us in Palestine pour that youthful idealism into an uncompromising hatred." Omar Yussef looked intently at Zuheir, but the young man averted his eyes toward the television. "So let Nadia enjoy this harmless pleasure of hers. Perhaps it will stay with her and not freeze inside her, as politics does."

"And religion, too?"

"I'm not talking about you, my son. Only about Nadia."

Zuheir scowled and was silent.

Omar Yussef turned to the American. "Miss King, you know that Ishaq the Samaritan was murdered."

King nodded slowly.

"I examined the murder scene with a friend from the local police force. His wife told me Ishaq had been scheduled to meet you, but he was killed first. What was the meeting supposed to be about?"

King sucked on her lip and cast her eyes down.

"I think Miss King is attempting to say, 'It's none of your business,'" Zuheir said.

"Well, I'm dealing with some very significant issues that have a major influence on international policy," King said. "I'm not at liberty to discuss details."

"I think my translation was accurate." Zuheir smiled, bitterly.

Omar Yussef linked his fingers. "Miss King, if you don't discuss it with me, I'm sorry to say that you will be forced to endure a very lonely silence."

King frowned. "Our friend Magnus told me that you're something of an amateur detective, but really I think I'd better share information only with the official police investigators. You said you were at Ishaq's house with the police. Aren't *they* investigating?"

Zuheir snorted contemptuously.

"This time my son's translation is only partially accurate," Omar Yussef said. "There is an investigation underway, but the police will not exactly be devoting their full resources to resolving Ishaq's murder."

"But why not? A man was killed."

"That man is dead and he'll stay dead. The police are concerned that, if they probe any further, they might end up in the same condition." Omar Yussef looked around to be sure he wouldn't be overheard. The waiter was engrossed in his newspaper, his forefinger rooting in his ear. "Already someone—we don't know who—has attacked the investigating officer and given him a nasty beating. The fact that Ishaq was responsible for the old president's secret finances also disturbs the police. When there's big money involved, the case is sure to involve powerful, ruthless people."

"So the police are going to ignore the murder?" King's features sagged. "That's a disaster."

"Many people are killed in Palestine all the time." Omar Yussef's voice sounded frail and he was ashamed of what he said. He realized that the men in the alley had scared him badly.

"Of course, but in this case it's a bigger issue than a single murder, and it's quite urgent," King said. "My job is to trace the funds cached around the world by the late president. My team has tracked down about eight hundred million dollars, so far. Each time we find something, it's incorporated into the official Palestinian Authority budget, so that the international donors know their money is being utilized as they intended."

"I see. For education, or services. Not for funding the gunmen."

"That's right. Under the former president, the money was all handled off the books. Politicians in Washington and Brussels felt they were dumping aid into a black hole. After all, when you look around Nablus, you wonder what all that money bought. Where are the modern hospitals? The schools and infrastructure?"

Zuheir jerked forward. "Where do you think our leaders learned such corruption? In exile, in the West."

Omar Yussef coughed and raised his eyebrows. His son sat back in indignant silence, his arms folded.

"I won't argue with you," Jamie said, extending her palm toward Zuheir. "But that's not an explanation that will appease the international donors."

"You haven't finished locating all the money?" Omar Yussef said. "That's why you're here?"

King pointed a finger at him. "Right. We think there's another three hundred million dollars out there."

"And Ishaq knew where it was?"

"He told me he could lay his hands on the documents within an hour of meeting me."

"Did he want anything in return?"

"I don't know. Maybe the usual sort of stuff I've come across in my investigations. Some folks want green cards or American passports. Some want cash. I had only one brief phone conversation with Ishaq. I couldn't say which category he fell into." King stroked the amber hairs that grew lightly down her cheeks beside her ears. "To tell the truth, I was surprised to learn that such a people as the Samaritans even existed. I know the biblical parable about the Good Samaritan, but I didn't know they were still around."

"Only a bit more than six hundred of them."

"On the phone, Ishaq told me they're descended from some of the original tribes of Israel."

"That's their claim. Other research suggests they're the

descendants of captives brought to repopulate the area after the Babylonians exiled all the Israelites." Omar Yussef shrugged. "As you Americans might say, the bottom line is that they've been here a long time, and they're isolated and few in number."

"Since you mention the bottom line," King set her hands flat on her thighs and sat very straight, "I have to send a report to the World Bank board in Washington on Friday. If I can't find that three hundred million dollars by then, the board will block financing to international organizations working here, cut off all funding to the Palestinians."

"Why?"

"Before they send any more money, they want to recover some of the cash the president salted away and see that it's spent correctly. The Bank gave the new president some time to track that money, but we're about out of patience."

"That's why you needed Ishaq."

King nodded. "If he had given me the details of that last three hundred million dollars, I could've prevented this boycott."

"These Western governments train our leaders in corruption and deceit," Zuheir said, "then they punish the people."

"Unless we find that money by Friday, all our aid will be cut off. It'll be an economic disaster." Omar Yussef slapped his fist into his palm.

"We?" Zuheir scoffed.

"You can stay here on this couch, if you wish, but I'm going to help Miss King track down this money." Omar Yussef shifted in his seat, angry and excited.

Zuheir sat upright and opened his eyes wide in outrage.

I've seen that same face when I look in the mirror, Omar Yussef thought, *despite the thick beard and the cropped hair.*

"Don't imagine you'll be the only one on the trail of that money," Zuheir said. "Whoever else is after it won't hesitate to kill, Dad."

Omar Yussef recalled the splintering sound when Sami's arm broke. He shivered and glanced at Jamie King. Zuheir had switched to Arabic, but King, staring into her teacup, hadn't seemed to notice. *She's preoccupied with her investigation,* Omar Yussef thought.

He spoke to his son in his native language. "I don't say I'm not nervous about the dangers of tracking such a large amount of money. But even so I'm surprised at you. Are you content to accept the terrible way things are in our society?"

"Content?" Zuheir lifted his arms and slapped them onto his chair. "O Allah, do I seem content to you? Did I turn to Islam because I'm *content* with the state of Palestine? The Prophet, blessings be upon him, said that Islam and government are brothers—'Islam is the foundation and government the guardian.' I've accepted Islam because I want to help meet half of that requirement, but there's no government here to make the society complete."

"I'm surprised at your cynicism. One would almost think you prefer our people not to receive this aid money."

"If your generation had returned to the way of Islam, perhaps you could have liberated Palestine years ago." Zuheir struck his thigh in frustration. "At least, you could have set up a responsible government in Palestine, instead of the corrupt mess we have now."

Omar Yussef gave a faint, apologetic smile to Jamie

King. *So my son thinks I'm a failure*, he thought, *me and my whole generation. That's why he wears the sheikh's costume. Perhaps I did fail by allowing society to deteriorate around me, as long as I was able to live a comfortable life. But maybe if I take the risks I avoided long ago and succeed, I can win his respect.*

"Zuheir, have you ever wondered why we keep herds of goats in the Middle East, rather than sheep?"

Zuheir's cheek twitched in annoyance.

"It's because Middle Easterners are extremists," Omar Yussef said. "Sheep crop the grass when they eat. It grows back, and they eat some more. But goats rip out the grass at the roots to get a little more food right away. In the end, it's disastrous, because the grass that is ripped out doesn't grow back and the soil on the bare hillsides is blown away. The next year, the goats find nothing but rocks to eat."

"I'm a goat? Is that what you're saying?"

"Don't be childish. I mean that we Arabs dismiss gradual change. We're only interested in all or nothing. But if I wait until I can rip corruption out by the root, or until the government announces that justice will henceforth be upheld, I'll wait forever. If I nibble at the problem, it's a start." He turned to the American and spoke in English. "Miss King, I'll see to it that the police help you find that money by Friday."

King nodded—with more politeness than hope, Omar Yussef thought. Then her eyes darted away from him as quick footsteps entered the lounge. Omar Yussef followed her glance and saw Khamis Zeydan advancing with a grim face.

"I need you to come with me," the policeman said brusquely.

"And a good evening to you, too," Omar Yussef replied. He gestured toward Jamie King. "I'm in the middle of something."

Khamis Zeydan leaned forward and extinguished his Rothmans in the empty ashtray by Omar Yussef's coffee cup. He exhaled the smoke over Omar Yussef and looked briefly at King. "Sorry, dear lady, I have to interrupt," he said, in English. "It's really very important. Don't worry, I'm not arresting him."

Khamis Zeydan folded his arms so that the navy blue sleeve of his police uniform hid his prosthetic left hand from the American. Omar Yussef knew this chariness about his false limb for a sign of extreme agitation in his friend.

"What's wrong?" he asked.

"I'll tell you on the way. This is urgent," Khamis Zeydan said. His sharp blue eyes were pleading and his nicotine-stained mustache twitched.

"If you'll excuse me a moment, Jamie." Omar Yussef took Khamis Zeydan a few paces away and put his arm around his friend's back. "What's going on?"

"Who's the sheikh?"

"That's Zuheir."

Khamis Zeydan looked confused.

"My son," Omar Yussef said. "He flew in from Britain a few days ago."

The police chief raised his eyebrows and glanced toward the young man, who was now leaning close to Jamie King and speaking quickly. "By Allah, I'd never have recognized him. He's changed." He turned to Omar Yussef. "I have to go up to Amin Kanaan's place."

"The businessman?"

"I see you read the financial page. He lives in one of the mansions on Mount Jerizim."

"Did something happen there? Something related to Ishaq's death?"

"Whose death?"

"Ishaq, the son of the Samaritan priest. The Old Man's financial adviser."

Khamis Zeydan let his head roll back as though he'd just put together the pieces of a puzzle. "Sami, you silly boy," he muttered.

"What?" Omar Yussef stepped back toward the couch. "Jamie, will you be staying in Nablus?"

"Until the end of the week. Unless I get any leads some-place else on—" she glanced at Khamis Zeydan and lowered her voice "—you know."

"We'll talk some more, I hope."

King took a business card from her handbag. "My cell phone number is on there," she said.

Omar Yussef slipped the card into his pocket. Its very touch felt incriminating and dangerous, as though the men who had beaten Sami would find it on him and punish him for intruding where a schoolteacher had no business. *I should pass the American's details on to Sami and be done with it*, he thought. "Zuheir, I'll see you at dinner, my son." He waved and followed Khamis Zeydan to the lobby.

The police chief took his elbow and moved toward the door. "I arrived in Nablus an hour ago, but before I checked in here I went to police headquarters to see Sami."

"So you saw, some thugs broke his arm."

"Lucky for those bastards they didn't try to break his head.

They'd have wasted a lot of energy, because it's hard as hell. He wouldn't tell me what it was all about, but now I see."

"You do?"

"You just told me."

Omar Yussef first felt callow and unsophisticated, but then he was sad for his friend. Khamis Zeydan was so accustomed to the corruption of the Palestinian militias that he had immediately made the connection between Sami's beating, his murder investigation, and Ishaq's job managing the president's money.

"After I left Sami," Khamis Zeydan said, "I ran into Kanaan."

"How do you know him?"

"From Beirut. Years ago, during the Lebanese Civil War."

"He was a fighter like you?" Omar Yussef glanced at the prosthesis, encased in a black leather glove. It was a substitute for the hand Khamis Zeydan had lost to a grenade in Lebanon.

"That bastard never fought for anything but dirty contracts." Khamis Zeydan looked about him as though he wanted a place to spit. "Unfortunately he saw me at the police headquarters."

"So what?"

"He'll tell his wife. She'll know that I'm in town. I can't come to Nablus and not visit her. She'd be offended."

"Is she such a good friend?" Even as he said it, Omar Yussef knew how naive he sounded.

"Back in Beirut, she and I—" Khamis Zeydan coughed.

"But not any more?"

"It was before she married Kanaan. We were rivals for her."

"Does he know?"

"Certainly he does, and he's just the kind of bastard to tell her he saw me. I can hear him now: 'Your loverboy is in Nablus and he hasn't even come to visit you. Maybe he never cared about you at all.' That'd be just what he'd say."

"Do you want to go up there to prevent her from feeling hurt, or to prove your rival wrong?"

"It doesn't make a difference. The point is I can't go up there alone."

"From the standpoint of morality, you mean? A man and woman alone, particularly with such a romantic history? But surely she has servants who could be present, for propriety's sake."

Khamis Zeydan rocked his head from side to side indecisively. "I don't trust myself," he said, faintly. "She's still very beautiful."

Omar Yussef took a backward step and his mouth dropped open. "Are you serious?"

"Don't look at me like that, you moralizing bastard," Khamis Zeydan said.

"You have a wife and children in Jordan."

"I have nothing to hide. My marriage is crappy. My wife preferred to stay in Amman, when I accepted this job in Bethlehem. And my children always take their mother's side."

"Your son was good enough to come from Jordan to visit you last month."

"My blood's still boiling from all the arguments I had with him."

Omar Yussef glanced back into the lounge where Zuheir talked animatedly to the American woman. *If my son is as religious as I think he is, why is he sitting alone with a woman?*

Maybe he can't stop himself from setting her straight, even though he would consider it more appropriate to ignore her presence.

He put his arm on Khamis Zeydan's shoulder. "Your son takes after you," he said. "Argumentative."

"No, he's just like his damned mother. He's stupid and self-righteous and he never says what he really means." Khamis Zeydan took Omar Yussef's hand. "Please, let's go."

Omar Yussef felt like a sordid accomplice to adultery. But Ishaq's wife had said that the dead man was working with Kanaan. This visit might be a good pretext to enter Kanaan's home and see what he could uncover there to help Sami's investigation.

The electronic bell of the elevator sounded and Nadia stepped into the lobby. "Uncle Khamis," she called, running to the policeman. Khamis Zeydan gave her a hug. "I'm writing a detective story about Nablus and there's a character based on you, Uncle Khamis."

"Is he a good guy or a bad guy?" Khamis Zeydan grinned.

"That depends on whether you take me to the casbah to taste the *qanafi*," she said.

"That's my job." Omar Yussef reached for his grand-daughter's hand. "Nadia, Abu Adel is a diabetic. If he eats sweet desserts like *qanafi*, his feet will go numb and he won't be able to walk. Besides, he's probably too busy to take you to the casbah."

"How can he be busy? He's a *Palestinian* policeman." Nadia giggled and Khamis Zeydan raised his arms in mock outrage. "Grandma wants to eat dinner in an hour."

"Tell her I'll be back in two hours and apologize on my behalf," Omar Yussef said. "I'm going on a mission of the heart."

Chapter 10

The last scattered houses on the outskirts of Nablus receded, pale in the first glimmering of the moon. Khamis Zeydan sped up the twisting road across the steep flank of the mountain. His fingers tight on the gearshift, he wiped sweat from his forehead with the sleeve of his uniform and swerved to avoid an old rockslide. He swore under his breath.

"The Hill of Cursing is on the other side of the valley," Omar Yussef said. "The Jewish Torah gives that name to Mount Ebal over there. Jerizim was called the Hill of Blessing."

"Then it's lucky I'm not a Jew, because I curse every stone on this mountain."

Omar Yussef put his hand on Khamis Zeydan's shoulder. "I've seen you face terrible dangers without flinching," he said. "But here you are, sweating with fear over a woman."

Khamis Zeydan leaned across to the glove compartment and took out a half-pint of Johnnie Walker. "In battle, I know how to handle myself," he said, wedging the bottle between his legs while he unscrewed the cap.

"In love, you're all at sea?"

The policeman tossed back a hard swig and put the

bottle between his legs again. He sucked at the ends of his white mustache. "They say, 'A man with a plan carries it out. A man with two plans gets confused.' I know how to fight. I never learned anything else."

"Am I supposed to stand at the door, like a bodyguard, and drag you away if things get out of control?" Omar Yussef said. He averted his eyes from his friend's bottle. The smell of the forbidden alcohol made him resentful and irritable. "Or do you want me to recite love poetry to her on your behalf, if the man of action gets tongue-tied?"

"Do you want to walk all the way back down to the hotel?"

"You demanded that I come with you, remember? Why can't you be a bit more likeable?"

Khamis Zeydan took another drink, rattled some phlegm in his throat, and spat out of the window. "I try to be likeable, but it's just not me," he said. "The more likeable I am, the more I hate myself. I feel dishonest. Smiling makes my face hurt."

"So tell me your history with this woman."

The red and white communication towers of the Israeli base on the ridge took shape in the darkness up the slope. Omar Yussef and Khamis Zeydan fell silent. When they reached the next curve, the mountain hid the Israeli camp and they saw the mansions again, like short men puffing out their chests on the lip of the mountain.

Khamis Zeydan spoke in a whisper no louder than the sound of his exhalation. "It was in Beirut in 1981. I was one of the Old Man's special operations people, when I met Liana. She was beautiful, but most important she was free."

"What do you mean?"

The policeman snorted and shook his head. "My dear old friend, you're a wonderful, educated man with an open mind about the world. Your only problem is that you've only seen that world in books. By Allah, you've lived your whole life in Bethlehem, a town which has remained provincial and conservative despite all the changes around it."

Omar Yussef stiffened his jaw and glared ahead at the mansions. "You forget our student days in Damascus. That was enough action for an entire lifetime."

"Okay, we were hard-living students. But I graduated to Beirut, which was an entirely different class of wildness. I was at the heart of our people's liberation movement. I traveled to Rome, Brussels, Amsterdam, on operations for the Old Man."

"Call them what they were—cold-blooded murders." Omar Yussef slapped the dashboard hard.

"Calm down. Not always murders, no. But if you insist, you can call some of them murders." Khamis Zeydan bit his thumbnail. "I was young, just thirty-three, and she was the same age. My wife was much younger than me and very traditional. My dear father chose her for me and I'd never have gone against his wishes, may Allah have mercy upon him. But he picked me a simple girl from a refugee camp with whom I had nothing to talk about. Liana was so worldly in comparison."

"You don't need to make excuses. Just tell me what happened."

"We slept together; that's what happened. But it isn't the whole story." Khamis Zeydan turned his pleading eyes toward his friend.

Omar Yussef breathed deeply. He was pressing him too hard. "This road winds a lot on the way to the top of the hill. I took it this morning to get to the Samaritan village, so I know we still have some distance to go. Carry on with your tale."

Khamis Zeydan stared hard at Omar Yussef.

"Just try to keep your eyes on the road, while you're talking to me, will you?" Omar Yussef said. "Your driving is making me nervous on this mountain."

"Liana is from Ramallah, but she grew up in Europe. Her father worked there for King Hussein. She had experienced some of the freedoms of life in the West." Khamis Zeydan wiggled his hand at Omar Yussef. "You know what I mean?"

"I'm unworldly, as you note, but I can guess what you mean."

"I had never met that kind of woman, at least not among Palestinians. Suddenly I could experience all the intelligence and progressiveness of a Western woman, while also sharing the bond of Palestinian culture, of our struggle against the Israelis."

"So you had an affair?"

"Her job with the party newspaper brought her to the Old Man's bunker all the time. We often saw each other there. I was close to him in those days."

"What attracted her to you? Your pretty blue eyes? Or your gun?"

Khamis Zeydan bared his teeth as though he had bitten down on the pit of an olive. "If you were forced into proximity and comradeship with such a woman, you'd have done the same thing. I was in love, and so was she," he said. "I even considered divorcing my wife."

The police chief was quiet. The engine bawled as the Jeep climbed a steep section of road. Omar Yussef stared ahead, waiting for him to continue.

"When the Israelis invaded in 1982, I went to fight them from the refugee camps in southern Lebanon. Liana stayed in Beirut. I lost my hand in the fighting and was in a hospital for a while with some other injuries. I don't remember much about that time. I was very depressed."

Omar Yussef touched his friend's arm lightly. He knew Khamis Zeydan's destructive boozing had started after his injuries in Lebanon.

"By the time I returned to Beirut," Khamis Zeydan said, "Liana was no longer around."

"Where did she go?"

Khamis Zeydan's pale eyes darted toward the mansions on the ridge.

"Kanaan?" Omar Yussef asked.

"That bastard used to come to Beirut to do dirty financial deals with the Old Man. He'd waft into the bunker in a Saville Row suit, trailing eau de cologne and primping his long hair. While I was in the hospital, he married her and sent her back here to his hometown."

"She didn't visit you in the hospital?"

"She wrote to me later that she had come once and I hadn't recognized her. I suppose it's possible. I was badly wounded, drugged up and depressed. Maybe I even told her to fuck off. You know my temper." Khamis Zeydan raised his good hand, palm upward.

Omar Yussef laughed. "It's an old acquaintance of mine."

"I've seen her at official functions from time to time," Khamis Zeydan said. "Only ever really across a room."

"But you've never been to see her at her home?"

They passed the first of the mansions and fell silent once more. Omar Yussef was accustomed to the poverty of his people and it shocked him that there were Palestinians with the resources to build such palaces. Their designs reminded him of the Taj Mahal, the Topkapi in Istanbul, and Thomas Jefferson's Monticello. In the electric light shining from their tall windows, the grass threw off a hectic green like the Saudi flag. Elsewhere in Palestine, water had to be saved for the olive trees and the cabbages; here thin cypresses lined the lawns, a ravishing, wasteful opulence that was in contrast to the jagged rocks and garbage strewn over every open area in Nablus.

They came to Kanaan's mansion, a rectangular three-story building with massive pillars topped by a Greek pediment. The house stood in a formal garden built into the slope of the ridge, its terraces supported by tall buttressing walls. A peacock fanned its tail on the floodlit lawn and strutted into the trees.

Khamis Zeydan pulled up and beckoned to a man in a leather jacket leaning against the gilded gate. The guard slouched toward them, spitting the shells of sunflower seeds into his palm. When Khamis Zeydan broke the wondering silence in the car, it was to answer the question Omar Yussef had asked him before they reached the row of mansions. "Here?" he said, looking along the avenue of cypresses that led to the house. "No, I haven't been to see her here. I've never been anywhere like this."

Chapter 11

A servant in a collarless blue tunic with gold buttons and a brocaded hem showed them into a spacious salon and tiptoed out as though he were getting away with something. His dainty steps made a subdued patter on the pink marble.

Inlaid mother-of-pearl shone coral and white from the Syrian chairs, like teeth snarling through bared lips of teak. The wrought-iron coffee tables were patterned with Armenian ceramic tiles, figured with fruit and fish in yellow and brown. In the corner, a gaudy palm tree had been painted onto a thick board and cut out, so that it stood up like a six-foot exercise from a children's book. The artist had signed the tree across the roots.

Omar Yussef gestured toward the painting of the palm tree. "Surely there's room in here for a real one."

"A real one wouldn't cost a hundred grand." Khamis Zeydan lit a cigarette. His good hand shook and he glanced at Omar Yussef to see if he had noticed.

To save his friend embarrassment, Omar Yussef turned to the door, his eyes tracing its arabesque relief. The little servant in the blue tunic opened the door and stood aside to allow a short woman in a pink suit to enter.

Liana reached out to stroke the polished surface of an art nouveau table as she came toward her guests. *That gesture is like a gambler's tell. She's as nervous as my friend Abu Adel,* Omar Yussef thought. She held Khamis Zeydan by the upper arms and brought him down for three kisses on the cheek, advanced a step toward Omar Yussef and offered him her hand.

Her eyes were deep, black and cool, like the eyes in an ancient Pharaoh's portrait, and they were painted with the dramatic shades of green and blue the Egyptians used for the hieroglyphs of their tombs. *That great beauty Cleopatra might have looked like Liana,* Omar Yussef thought, *had she lived longer, but no more wisely.* Her hair was dyed black and rolled back in high lacquered waves, so that it resembled the shell of a snail. She kept her chin high. Omar Yussef wondered if that was out of a sense of superiority or to give the parallel wrinkles across her neck room to breathe.

Liana invited them to the ornate Syrian sofas before the picture window. Khamis Zeydan seemed so loath to sit that Omar Yussef pushed his jumpy friend gently into a chair. Another servant in an identical blue tunic brought coffee on a silver tray. He held out his hand and, with an encouraging smile, caught an inch of ash from Khamis Zeydan's cigarette. He lifted a gold ashtray from one of the Armenian tables and set it next to the policeman's coffee cup.

"I'm happy that you brought your friend to see my home, Abu Adel," Liana said.

Khamis Zeydan grunted.

"You're most welcome here, *ustaz*," she said to Omar Yussef. "Consider it as your home and as if you were among your family."

Omar Yussef was about to give the formal reply, when Khamis Zeydan spoke, louder than was necessary, as though he had to force the words out. "Are you glad I brought myself?"

"Abu Adel, I always want to see you. I wish you'd come often."

"Really?" Khamis Zeydan sounded bitter.

Liana sucked in her cheeks, patiently. "Agreeable company is always a pleasure on this lonely hilltop."

Khamis Zeydan stubbed out his cigarette and looked up at her. His blue eyes were sad and lost.

"My life here is like a dream," Liana said. She fixed her eyes on Khamis Zeydan. "People always describe a pleasant experience as being like a dream. But how many of your good dreams do you remember? I seem to recall my nightmares much more clearly."

Liana and the policeman stared at each other in silence.

Omar Yussef cleared his throat. "Perhaps people mean only that it's a feeling they know is destined to pass quickly," he said. "Like our memories of dreams, which are so vivid while we sleep, only to seem vague once we awake."

"Are you a friend of Abu Adel's from here in Nablus, *ustaz?*" Liana asked.

"From Bethlehem," Omar Yussef said. "I've known Abu Adel since we were students together in Damascus. We renewed our friendship when he returned to Palestine to become police chief in Bethlehem after the peace agreement with Israel. We had lost touch during his period in Beirut."

Khamis Zeydan and Liana locked eyes once more at the mention of the Lebanese capital. Omar Yussef bit the end of his tongue at his indelicacy.

"Abu Adel and I are in Nablus for the wedding of our young friend Sami Jaffari. He's a policeman, but he's also involved with the Fatah Party, so you may have heard of him."

"I also will be attending that wedding," Liana said. "I attend all the Fatah functions."

"Your husband is an important figure in Fatah," Khamis Zeydan said.

The woman looked at him with pity. "Have I become such a minor character that I wouldn't receive any invitations if it weren't for my husband?" She waited, but Khamis Zeydan kept his eyes on his ashtray. Liana turned to Omar Yussef. "We used to live closer to the town, but we built this house ten years ago. The views are wonderful, although it's a little isolated. Few people come up here to the peak of Mount Jerizim."

"I was up here only this morning," Omar Yussef said.

Liana inclined her head to the side. One of her large silver earrings rattled into her leathery neck and she stroked the lapis scarab embedded in it with her index finger.

"I was with a Samaritan priest when he heard there had been a murder in his community," Omar Yussef said. "We found the body of a dead Samaritan man at the site of their ancient temple just along the ridge from here."

"Allah will be merciful upon the deceased one," Liana murmured.

"May Allah preserve you," Omar Yussef said.

Ishaq had worked for Liana's husband. Omar Yussef wondered if Liana would betray anything that might be useful to Sami's investigation. "The dead man was an associate of your husband, I believe."

Liana sat up and flattened her pink skirt against her thighs.

A trace of fear crept across her eyes. She blinked, and the eyes came back as dead and dull as the surface of the water in a neglected well. "Who?" Her voice was cautious and throaty, as though she feared Omar Yussef might reach out to catch the word and slap her face with it.

"Ishaq, the son of Jibril the priest."

Liana turned her face away from Omar Yussef and examined the diamond rings on her hands.

"Did you know him?" Omar Yussef said.

"Ishaq?" She spat the word down toward her rings and her jaw shivered. "I was acquainted with him."

"Your husband's acquaintance with Ishaq was quite a close one, I believe."

"My husband makes friends easily. Most multimillionaires do." Liana threw back her head and her face contorted as though she wanted to prevent a tear from escaping her eye. She sighed and thrust an arm out straight to Khamis Zeydan. "Give me a cigarette, Abu Adel."

Khamis Zeydan pulled a cigarette from his pack. She took it and leaned forward for him to light it. Her hand shook and the cigarette missed the flame. Khamis Zeydan gently steadied her wrist with his prosthesis, while he lit the tip.

Liana sucked on the Rothmans and blew out a stream of gray smoke. Khamis Zeydan glanced with confusion at the leather glove covering his prosthetic hand.

Omar Yussef watched Liana take another long drag and shiver as she exhaled. *Is it merely the mention of her husband and his money that made her suddenly so edgy?* he thought. "Your husband attracts friends only because he's rich?" he said.

She swallowed hard and looked at Omar Yussef. "My husband is charming and charismatic. But there's no way to make hundreds of millions of dollars and remain a nice guy, *ustaz*. The more money a man makes, the greater his egomania and childish brutality, and the more so-called friends he requires to allow him to indulge such traits."

"Doesn't that depend on whether the money is made legally, or through crime?"

"I was a student radical in the late 1960s and a campaigning journalist in the 1970s, *ustaz*. I believed then that for one man even to possess a million dollars would be a crime. No matter how much the Prophet Muhammad is said to have praised the life of the merchant, I always believed there would have to have been some sort of crime involved in the acquisition of such a sum. That opinion hasn't changed." She looked at Khamis Zeydan. "Being with my husband hasn't changed many of my opinions since those days."

Ishaq's name seems to make her furious and nervy, Omar Yussef thought. He wondered if Amin Kanaan and Ishaq, the homosexual, had shared more than just a business partnership. "Was your husband especially close to Ishaq?"

Liana looked sharply at Omar Yussef. Her eyes were wide and fierce. "It was undoubtedly one of my husband's closest relationships," she said, her bright lips quivering. "Brother Abu . . . ?"

"Abu Ramiz," Omar Yussef said.

"Brother Abu Ramiz, I would like to discuss something privately for a few moments with my old friend Abu Adel," Liana said. "If Allah wills it, we shall meet again soon, at your friend's wedding perhaps."

"If Allah wills it," Omar Yussef said.

Dismissed, he raised himself from the couch. Khamis

Zeydan lifted his hand hesitantly, as though he might pull Omar Yussef back onto the sofa for protection. *Protection from himself*, Omar Yussef thought. He gave a peremptory grin to his nervous friend and made for the door.

Omar Yussef crossed the hall to a pair of high glass-paneled doors at the back of the house. He touched a smooth pillar of green Indian marble and looked down at the scattered lights of Nablus in the valley. Dull and orange, they nestled between the mountains like the final glowing coals of a dying campfire. *In five days, even those few lights will be turned off, if the World Bank flips the switch*, he thought. *Face it, Omar, there's nothing you can do about it. It isn't that you don't care, but you're just a schoolteacher. If you try to keep the lights on, it could easily be you who's snuffed out.*

Something moved in the darkness outside the window, flickering in front of the distant city lights. Omar Yussef put his face close to the glass and cupped his hands around his eyes to block out the lights of the hall. Among the cypresses bordering the lawn, a group of men was gathered. Omar Yussef watched for a minute, but could make out very little in the dim radiance cast from the mansion. Within a minute, most of the men moved away from the house into the dark and went over the buttresses at the edge of the garden. As they jumped, one of them lifted his arm for balance and Omar Yussef saw that he was holding an assault rifle.

The last man turned and strode across the grass to the house. He was tall and his thick white hair fluttered back from a wide forehead, swept by the wind that came over the hilltop. He padded quickly up the steps. Omar Yussef hid behind the pillar, but the man turned along the terrace toward the mansion's northern wing without looking around.

Omar Yussef had seen him clearly enough to recognize a face familiar from the newspaper's business page.

It was Amin Kanaan.

The door opened behind Omar Yussef and Khamis Zeydan came into the hall. Omar Yussef folded his arms and leaned against the pillar, as though he had been waiting casually for his friend to emerge.

Khamis Zeydan waved his arm impatiently and headed for the door.

"What was the secret chat about?" Omar Yussef asked.

"She wanted to sing me a few lines from our favorite old love song. She's sentimental like that," Khamis Zeydan said. "Let's go. I need a drink."

They drove in silence along the avenue of cypresses to the gate. Khamis Zeydan unscrewed the cap of his Johnnie Walker but he didn't drink until they were on the road. *Does he wish to present a dignified front while still on Kanaan's property?* Omar Yussef wondered. Khamis Zeydan turned downhill, sped up and slugged hard from the bottle, his gulping throat working rhythmically, like a part of the engine.

He wiped his hand across his mustache. "What do you think you're doing, grilling Liana about some dead Samaritan?"

"He wasn't just any Samaritan. You seemed to know exactly who he was when I told you about him earlier." Omar Yussef grabbed for the whisky, wrested it with both hands from Khamis Zeydan's grip and tossed it in the glove compartment. "You must have met Ishaq on your visits to the Old Man's office in Ramallah."

"I'm not finished with that bottle," the policeman said.

"You can drink after you've negotiated this dangerous

road." Omar Yussef swept his hand toward the boulders at the roadside, menacing in the stark beams of the headlights. "I asked her about the Samaritan, because I wanted to help Sami with his investigation."

Khamis Zeydan sighed, impatiently. "Help Sami? If you want to help Sami, keep your mouth shut."

"What do you mean?"

"Sami's not investigating. He's in danger."

"He's a policeman. Even Palestinian policemen are supposed to trace criminals."

"Not if it means ending up dead."

"If those men wanted to kill him, they could have done it in the alley."

"You think it's a small step to kill? Even for thugs like that? If you exhumed all the murdered police investigators in the world, I bet you'd find that none of them had a broken arm. No one's stupid enough to push on after that kind of warning."

Omar Yussef tapped Khamis Zeydan on the shoulder. "That's what Liana wanted to talk to you about alone, isn't it?" he said. "She's big in Fatah, so she wants the Party to have the money, not the World Bank. Her husband was close to the dead Samaritan. Was he involved in the murder? She told you to make sure Sami hushes up the murder, didn't she? Well, he won't."

"What money?" Khamis Zeydan looked thirstily at the glove compartment and bit his lip.

Omar Yussef hesitated.

"Shall I beat it out of you?" Khamis Zeydan said. "Come on, let's hear it."

"The American woman at the hotel works for the World

Bank. She reckons Ishaq hid three hundred million dollars in secret accounts around the world for the Old Man, and she's trying to track these funds. Ishaq was about to talk to her, when he was killed."

"Obviously she's not the only one who was looking for that money."

"Then we have to find it first. If the World Bank can't trace the money by Friday, all Palestinian aid money is going to be cut off."

"What? Now I'm going to beat you just for being a stupid bastard." Khamis Zeydan punched his fist against the steering wheel. "Whoever is trying to get hold of that three hundred million dollars isn't going to share it with you. They're going to kill anyone who attempts to beat them to it."

"But the aid—"

"It's the World Bank's job to find the money, not yours. It's better for the aid to be terminated than your life. Didn't you think of that?"

Omar Yussef considered lying that he hadn't, but instead he turned away.

Khamis Zeydan whistled. "My dear brother, I despair of you sometimes."

Omar Yussef stared at the road dropping toward Nablus. Lurking among the dim lights on the valley floor, there were men who would kill him for three hundred dollars, let alone three hundred million. *He's right. I have to leave this to the American woman*, he thought.

"I took the business card of the World Bank lady," he said. "You're right that I shouldn't be involved in this. I'll give her card to Sami. He doesn't know about the money. But maybe he'll have an idea of how to trace it."

"Sami's already dropped the case," Khamis Zeydan said. "When I saw him in the sick bay at police headquarters, he told me the broken arm wasn't the only threat he'd received."

"I know. The sheikh warned him off."

"Which sheikh? The Hamas guy? Sheikh Bader?" Khamis Zeydan shook his head. "This was something else. He got a phone call. A threat to kidnap Meisoun."

"So put her under the protection of the police."

"What good would that do? The kidnappers might also be policemen. This is Palestine. The men with the guns don't carry them out of civic duty." The police chief reached out, gave a gentle slap to Omar Yussef's face, and rested his hand on the back of his friend's neck. "You remember the old story about the Arab conquest of Egypt? The caliph decided to name one of his generals as military governor and planned to put someone else in charge of the treasury."

Omar Yussef knew where this was going.

"The general refused, saying that it would be as though he held the horns of a cow, while the other guy milked it. That's how it is here. The men who beat Sami were holding the horns of the cow, but they were sent by the guy who's milking it."

The jeep jolted through a pothole. Omar Yussef spread his hands against the dashboard to brace himself.

"I can't let this case be dropped," he said.

Khamis Zeydan looked at him with fierce eyes. Omar Yussef knew the police chief had heard the desperate strain in his voice. He had to explain himself, though the more he talked, the shriller and more wretched he sounded. "The stakes are very high. All our people's aid money, cut off, and you don't seem to care."

"Are you surprised that the Palestinians should get screwed again?"

"If Sami won't do it, you must."

"Not me." Khamis Zeydan waved his prosthesis. "I've only got one hand. If they break my other arm, I'm out to pasture."

"Well, I can't do it. I can't." Omar Yussef's cheek throbbed where the masked man had slapped him. His stomach convulsed with shame and fear. A trickle of sweat ran from his palm down the dirty black dashboard.

"You're right about that, my brother," Khamis Zeydan said. Quickly, he opened the glove compartment and pulled out the bottle before Omar Yussef could react. He grinned. "Even someone as stubborn as you can't save the Palestinians. Everyone has to figure out a way to save themselves. This is my way." He brandished the whisky.

"You talk as though you and I weren't Palestinian."

"Palestine? It's up there on that ridge, inside all those mansions. It's nothing but a corrupt business deal. Sometimes the P.R. is good and the world shovels in the cash. Sometimes it's bad and the peasants suffer. But people like Liana still visit conferences in Europe on the rights of refugees and stay in the most expensive hotels. Save Palestine? Let it go to hell." He swigged from the bottle.

Down the slope in Nablus, a meager fluorescence glimmered from the narrow, arched windows of the old quarter. Omar Yussef shuddered. Khamis Zeydan might find the reality of his people's struggle in the mansions above them, but Omar Yussef knew that it was below him, in the hidden alleys of the casbah.

Chapter 12

A hundred years ago, on the periphery of the casbah, the Turks had built a tapering clock tower rising sixty feet to a cinquefoil window. Omar Yussef admired the simplicity of the design, as much as he regretted the undignified atmosphere around the structure's base. The bleached stones were draped with green Hamas flags and a pair of loudspeakers on the roof of an old, olive drab Volkswagen van blasted Islamic songs at a volume so thunderous that he feared the tower might collapse.

He wrinkled his nose at the ripeness of the men packed into the square and hunched his shoulders against their jostling. The men at the back of the crowd strained over the heads of those in front to see the dais at the foot of the clock tower. Omar Yussef felt dizzy. He stuck a finger in his ear, worried that the loud music might have damaged it.

Sami slipped his left hand beneath Omar Yussef's upper arm and guided him to the edge of the square, where they could observe without being pummelled by the shoving newcomers. Sami wore a brown leather flying jacket, its right side loose over his shoulder, his broken arm slung tight against his body in a bulky cast. Khamis Zeydan pushed level with them. He was also out of uniform, wearing a checked sport jacket and blue tie. His eyes were watery and his skin was almost as pale as his white mustache.

"This is no place for a man with a fucking hangover," he said.

"Perhaps instead of drowning your problems in drunken silence all night, you ought to confide more in your friends," Omar Yussef said.

"You have problems enough of your own. Don't try to take on other people's woes, my brother. Whoever pats scorpions with the hand of compassion gets stung."

"Are you going to sting me if I suggest you should have had a bigger breakfast to settle your stomach?"

Khamis Zeydan pinched the slack, liver-spotted skin on the back of Omar Yussef's wrist. "I'm not ready to sting yet, but I'm warning you."

Omar Yussef smiled and rubbed his hand.

Sami laid his good arm across Omar Yussef's shoulder. "Over there, Abu Ramiz, is where they'll celebrate the big wedding. On that dais by the tower. Then everyone will go to a big party in the social club at this end of the square."

"Where's the women's celebration?"

"Somewhere down that way, farther into the casbah. The brides will be there already."

"As Meisoun said, on another planet."

A cheer went up among the men at the entrance to the mosque. Bearded youngsters leaned out of the upstairs windows, hammering the air with their fists and chanting. Their words competed indistinctly with the song from the loudspeakers, but soon Omar Yussef picked out the rhyming declaration that there was no god but Allah and that Muhammad was his prophet.

Sheikh Bader made his way from the mosque to the dais. He stepped up to the platform and took his place at its center, drawing his robe together in front of his abdomen and lowering his bearded chin to his chest. He appeared unaware of the crowd, but commanded it merely by the mastery he had over himself.

The attention of the crowd turned to the alley behind the clock tower. The loudspeakers' volume crept higher. A deep bass and a susurrating tambourine pulsed around the voices of the singers. Nouri Awwadi appeared at the head of the line of grooms, riding on Sharik. The white stallion tossed its head and glared down its long muzzle at the bearded faces around it. The file of young grooms moved through the crowd. Some riders looked around with wide smiles, waving at friends. A few held tight to the reins, as nervous as their shying mounts.

The horsemen formed a rank before the dais and the music was shut off in midchorus. Nouri Awwadi sat very straight on Sharik and stared over the crowd with a proud, stern expression, as though transformed into a statue of some victorious ancient warrior. *A statue he'd destroy, because it'd violate the Islamic prohibition against the making of idols*, Omar Yussef thought.

Sheikh Bader's rhythmic speech came through the loudspeakers, beginning the marriage sermon. He read the brief details of the fifteen marriage contracts, the names of the brides and grooms, and exhorted them to a life of piety and mutual love. He recited verses from the Koran and recounted a hadith, one of the sayings of the Prophet, which urged believers to fear Allah, to pray, to fast and to marry a woman.

Omar Yussef recalled his own marriage, more than thirty years before. He remembered that, at this moment in the ceremony, the sheikh had prayed for Omar and Maryam, for their families, their town and the broader Muslim community. He smiled. *Omar and Maryam came out just about all right*, he thought. *On the other hand, their town and their community have had it pretty rough.*

Sheikh Bader prayed for the grooms and their families. When he came to the prayer for the Muslims, he halted and raised a finger above his head. "Brothers, the community we pray for here, the community of all the Palestinians, is sinking into a time of ignorance."

Omar Yussef glanced at Khamis Zeydan. His friend raised an eyebrow. The *time of ignorance* was the term Muslims used to refer to the days before Islam.

"There's a rot among the leaders of our people," the sheikh continued. "Brothers, you know the complaints—the corruption and violence and the collaboration with the Occupation Forces. None of this is new to you. And you know who the men behind it all are. Hamas fights them on your behalf. I call on you all to redouble your own commitment to this fight in the name of Allah, the Master of the Universe."

Though the loudspeakers were at full volume, the sheikh barked himself hoarse, his voice cracking and his fist punctuating the swinging cadence of his speech. "What more urging does a man need than the commandments of the Prophet, blessings be upon him? You should require nothing more to impel you to oppose the present leaders of our people. Yet men say to me, does not the holy Koran also command us to obey the government? It's true. But what kind of shameful government do we have, and must it still be obeyed in its shamefulness?"

The crowd murmured angry agreement.

"O Muslims, how far have our rulers deviated from the path of the rightly guided caliphs who were the companions of the Prophet, may Allah bless him with peace and still more peace? Today I offer you new evidence that the men of a certain political party are devils and monkeys who live their lives in contravention of all the proscriptions of the Prophet, may the peace and blessings of Allah be upon him."

Khamis Zeydan gave a little whistle. "I'm glad Sami and I didn't wear our uniforms today. This speech would've made us unpopular."

The sheikh lowered his voice. "The man who led that certain political party, the man who purported to lead the Palestinian people for decades, the man who cast the founders of Hamas into his jails—that man died of a shameful disease."

"By Allah," Khamis Zeydan said.

The men in the crowd stirred.

"Brothers, you'll tell me that you have heard this rumor and that it's a lie spread by the Jews and that in fact the Israelis poisoned him. While no evil is beyond the Jews, I tell you that this is not the case. We have obtained proof, documentary proof of the cause of this man's end. This man, who was our president and who dared to call himself the symbol of our suffering—this man was autopsied in a foreign hospital and the leaders of his faction suppressed the results. But Hamas has obtained the autopsy report and we have learned that he did, indeed, die of the shameful disease whose name you all know and which is the result of immorality and forbidden acts."

The murmur in the crowd grew. Nouri Awwadi's horse

shied and bumped the next stallion with his flanks. His iron shoes rattled on the stones of the square.

"Hamas knows what to do with this information," the sheikh said. "When we pray now for our community, for the Muslims and for Palestine, think of these men whose only creed is immorality. Think of the power they wield over our honorable Palestinian people, and let us wrest that power from them. Allah is most great."

The men joined Sheikh Bader in proclaiming the greatness of Allah, swaying and stumbling in the crush. Omar Yussef was pressed against the metal shutters of a vegetable store. The horsemen maneuvered their bucking mounts through the crowd to the social club at the end of the square and dismounted. As they entered the building, they accepted the happy kisses of the men around them like the victors of a sporting event.

As men followed the grooms into the social club, the throng in the square thinned out.

Omar Yussef put his face close to Khamis Zeydan's ear. "Did you hear anything about an autopsy on the Old Man?"

"No. There never was an autopsy, as far as I heard," Khamis Zeydan said. "But if the Old Man died of AIDS as Sheikh Bader implied, it's conceivable the party chiefs would keep it even from senior officials like me."

"He has been rumored to have died that way."

"If such rumors were true, then famous people must have been immortal until that disease came along to strike them all down."

Omar Yussef shook his head. "We aren't talking about a pop star or an actor. This was our president. People expect different morals from such a figure."

"I'm surprised you aren't glad to hear this news. You hated the Chief, after all."

"I didn't hate him," Omar Yussef said. "I thought his methods were distasteful, but so are yours, and I consider you my best friend."

"Thanks be to Allah." Khamis Zeydan picked at his teeth.

Sami linked his good arm around Khamis Zeydan's elbow. "Are you coming to the party, or are you waiting for a ride on one of the horses?"

Omar Yussef looked around the square. The posters and banners and music had been irresistibly exciting to the mob that now pressed into the Hamas social club. *It's just as the sheikh told me*, he thought. *This shows that Hamas is working for the people. And the old president's purported death from AIDS is a perfect moral contrast.*

Sami and Khamis Zeydan moved toward the social club. Omar Yussef walked slowly to the dais where Sheikh Bader had stood. The horses had left neat piles of dark brown feces in a row before the platform. Omar Yussef wondered if the sheikh had seen the horses defecating, their tails lifted toward him as he gave his speech, or if he had smelled their dirt on the ground.

He crossed the square and followed his friends into the social club.

Chapter 13

S heikh Bader stood unmoving and silent at the head of
the receiving line. He acknowledged each handshake
with a slow blink and the deceptive calm of a cruel father
daring his children to call down his outrage.

Omar Yussef worked his way through the crush in the
social club. The sheikh's black eyebrows lowered when he
spotted him.

"A thousand congratulations, Our Honored Sheikh,"
Omar Yussef said.

Sheikh Bader's hand was limp in Omar Yussef's grasp. He
inclined his head and whispered his welcome.

"This was more than just the political rally I predicted."
Omar Yussef kept the sheikh's hand in his and pulled him
close. "This was very dangerous."

"Are you threatening me, *ustaz*?"

"Don't worry. I'm only a teacher in a United Nations
school, and corporal punishment has been banned."

The sheikh's nostrils twitched. "The danger is not in *my*
statements. The danger is in our people's leadership, which
ignores the corruption and impropriety in its ranks."

"I won't argue with that." Omar Yussef laid a second
hand across the sheikh's fingers. "But if you're wrong—"

"I'm not wrong."

"—there'll be a price paid in violence. A backlash."

"Allah is named in the holy Koran as the Executor of Justice. He will protect me in this struggle."

Omar Yussef inhaled sharply. He was sure Khamis Zeydan was right to warn him off the case of the dead Samaritan, but the sheikh's condescending certainty needled him and he had to strike back. "Maybe it's in the name of Allah, the Executor of Justice, that you told Sami Jaffari to back off his investigation into the murder of Ishaq, the Samaritan?"

The sheikh took back his hand with a tug and touched it to his beard.

"Did Allah tell you about the three hundred million dollars in the possession of the dead Samaritan?" Omar Yussef jerked his jaw toward the sheikh, quivering with anger. *O peace, schoolteacher, you can't keep your mouth shut, can you?* he thought.

The haughtiness went out of Sheikh Bader's face. "I don't understand."

"Your boy Nouri Awwadi knew Ishaq. Ishaq's dead. You warned Sami away from the murder. So where's the three hundred million dollars?" Omar Yussef sucked on his mustache. "See if you can figure it out, Our Honored Sheikh. Without the inspiration of Allah."

Sheikh Bader swallowed hard and reached for the extended arm of another well-wisher, who shouldered Omar Yussef gently aside.

Omar Yussef breathed deeply and tried to calm himself. At the back of the crowded social club, he found Nouri Awwadi. The young man threw his thick arms wide and kissed Omar Yussef five times on the cheeks. His loose white wedding shirt smelled of the sweat he had shed keeping his anxious mount under control in the square, but his beard still gave off the scent of sandalwood. His big hands gripped the schoolteacher's shoulders.

"Welcome, dear *ustaz* Abu Ramiz. What did you think of the wedding ceremony, dear friend?"

Omar Yussef's laugh was rasping and cynical. "I wouldn't have missed it for anything," he said. "I enjoy gossip."

Awwadi frowned. "You picked up some gossip?"

"The sheikh broadcast it."

"That wasn't gossip, *ustaz*." Awwadi leaned in close to Omar Yussef. "That was based on documents, real evidence that Hamas has obtained."

"From where? From whom?"

Awwadi smiled, but raised a warning finger. "Are you investigating the death of the Samaritan on the hilltop? Or are you investigating Hamas?"

"I'm not a policeman. By Allah, the police force doesn't seem to be in a hurry to investigate, anyway. But I'm naturally curious."

"Take my word for it, we have the proof."

"If I was going to take someone's word for it, the sheikh's would have sufficed." Omar Yussef laid a hand on Awwadi's deep chest. "Nouri, in the Arab world, you may not need proof to accuse people of certain things, but in this case it's such a scandalous accusation that you're really going to have to produce some evidence."

Awwadi waved a dismissive hand. "Everyone knows what killed the Old Man."

"No, everyone has a conspiracy theory. No one knows what actually killed him."

Awwadi took Omar Yussef's hand and led him through the crowd. He whispered to a brawny, bearded man at the door, whom Omar Yussef recognized as one of the gunmen he had seen watching over the sheikh at the mosque. The man handed an M-16 to Awwadi and stared blankly at Omar Yussef.

Outside, a few small boys kicked a soccer ball against the shutters of the vegetable store where Omar Yussef had stood during the ceremony. The sun was at its zenith, but a raw wind whirled down from the mountain and ruffled the green banners on the clock tower. The metal shutters rattled and the football bounced through the horse dung by the dais, making the boys laugh. One of them rolled the ball back into the square and gave it a strong kick. His playmates doubled over as the manure sprayed off the ball into the boy's face. Omar Yussef followed Awwadi down the steps of the social club.

"It was I who obtained this evidence for the sheikh," Awwadi said, quietly.

"How?"

"On behalf of Hamas, I acquired files containing dirt on all the top Fatah men." Awwadi glanced about him and shifted the weight of the M-16 across his chest. "You're a friend of Sami Jaffari. He's Fatah, but so far he's pretty honest. The rest of them are crooks. You shouldn't trust them. Certainly don't listen to what they say about me."

"From whom did you buy the files? How do you know they're real?"

"I got them from a Fatah guy. He gave them to me, because he was just like the rest of those people—all he cared about was getting what he wanted for himself, and even his own party could go to hell."

"It could be a plant." Omar Yussef hugged himself against the cold wind.

"Why would they plant information that'll make *them* and their former leader look bad?" Awwadi took Omar Yussef's hand and led him into the alley beside the social club, sheltering from the wind. "*Ustaz*, most of the information we obtained was from the files of the Old Man himself. He kept scandal dossiers on everyone around him, so that if they ever became too popular or tried to confront him, he could blackmail them into submission."

"But the information about the president's illness—that couldn't have come from him."

"That was a little bonus thrown in by the man I did the deal with."

The metal door of the social club swung open. The wind caught it and it struck the wall with a heavy resonance. Awwadi stepped further into the darkness of the alley, pulling Omar Yussef after him. Khamis Zeydan appeared on the steps, lighting a cigarette. He scratched his head and called back inside. Sami emerged and the two walked toward the newer part of town.

Omar Yussef watched Khamis Zeydan hurry down the street, his shoulders hunched against the wind. The police chief limped on his left foot. *His diabetes is acting up*, he thought.

"Brigadier Khamis Zeydan. He's with your friend Sami. Is Zeydan a friend of yours, too?" Awwadi murmured.

Omar Yussef turned toward the young man. "Do you have a file of dirt on him?"

Awwadi nodded. "Want to read it?"

"I want to destroy it," Omar Yussef said.

"I thought you were a historian. These are the unofficial archives of Palestinian politics."

"They stink."

"So does Palestinian politics."

"Is there a file on Ishaq?"

Awwadi clicked his tongue to signal a negative.

Whatever this man reveals about these dirt files should hardly surprise me, Omar Yussef thought. *What could they contain? Theft, rape, corruption? Murder? There's no injustice that I wouldn't believe those who rule over the Palestinian people to be capable of.*

"These aren't just historical documents," he said. "They could change the future, too. They could make it more bloody—cause a civil war between Fatah and Hamas."

"We're in a civil war now. A long one, with some breaks so everyone can pretend it's not their fault. But it's a war anyway." Awwadi came closer. "You ought to know the truth about these Fatah people who ruled us for so long. The things they've done, the shameful things. All the billions of dollars in aid our people received—wasted. Look at our town. We have no theater. We have no cinema. But the whole place is a circus. Thanks to the people whose names are in the files I obtained."

Even the board of the World Bank is about to come to that conclusion, Omar Yussef thought. *But why must everyone in the Middle East who aims to right a wrong do so with violence?* "How much did you pay for the files?"

Awwadi shook his head.

"A million dinars?" Omar Yussef stepped toward the big man. "What do you think will happen to the money you paid? You're part of Fatah's corruption now, don't you see?"

Awwadi's eyes grew angry. "I didn't pay Fatah anything. I made a trade. I gave them the Abisha Scroll."

"But the Samaritans showed me that scroll yesterday. Who gave it back to *them?*"

"I gave the scroll to the Samaritans. There are Samaritans who're in Fatah. It was one of them who gave me these dirt files."

"Ishaq," Omar Yussef said.

Awwadi exhaled. Omar Yussef smelled garlic on the man's breath.

"You stole the Abisha Scroll from the synagogue. Then you swapped the scroll for these dirt files," Omar Yussef said.

"If you say so."

"How did Ishaq come to have these files?"

"They were the Old Man's files. After he died, I figured Ishaq would be able to get them for me. If he didn't have them, they might be in the possession of his friend Kanaan, who'd do anything Ishaq asked. So I stole the Abisha and forced him to give me the files in return for his people's holy scroll. It was a good deal."

"You think so?" Omar Yussef stroked his mustache with his thumb and forefinger. "Ishaq also had the Old Man's secret account details. I imagine he feared people like you would try to track down the money. So he offered you these dirt files to throw you off the scent."

"This information is very valuable. I got a good deal."

"Is it worth three hundred million dollars?"

Awwadi grunted, as though he'd taken a light punch in the stomach.

"That's how much Ishaq had stashed away for the Old Man. He pulled the wool over your eyes and now someone else is going to get the money. Maybe someone from Fatah already has it. That sort of cash could buy enough weapons to wipe out Hamas."

The younger man scratched his head angrily.

Omar Yussef narrowed his eyes. "Is there a file on Amin Kanaan? Or his wife Liana?"

"No, there isn't."

"Why not?"

"Maybe they're clean?" Awwadi sneered.

What would my file look like, if anyone ever bothered to compile it? Omar Yussef wondered. *I did some jail time when I was young. I can explain it, of course, but on paper it would be stark and accusing and make me look like a criminal. There'd be a record of my drinking days, things that I can't even remember doing during my drunken blackouts. Files like this can't tell you the essence of a person. They can only smear someone with a surface of filth.*

"Once a man has sinned, he ought to have the chance to redeem himself," Omar Yussef said. "One of our Arab sages wrote that he who wishes to purify his soul can't do it by a single day's worship, nor can he prevent it by a single act of rebellion."

"I've read Ghazali, too, *ustaz*, and you're leaving something out. He concluded that one day's abstention from virtue leads to another and, thus, the soul degenerates little by little." Awwadi lifted his index finger. "The file on Khamis Zeydan didn't get to be as bulky as it is from only a single day's sinfulness."

"Stop it. He's my friend."

"Maybe you don't know enough about him to judge whether you ought to be his friend. The real Khamis

Zeydan is the one in his dirt file, not the man you think is your friend."

"Where are the files?"

Awwadi lifted his chin and shook his head. He stepped past Omar Yussef to return to the wedding hall. The motion reminded Omar Yussef of the way Awwadi had blocked his view of the cellar behind the horse's stable at the Touqan Palace. *It isn't weapons you've cached in that cellar,* he thought. *You've got the files in there, haven't you?*

Awwadi hesitated on the steps to the social club. "I'll still see you tomorrow morning at the Turkish baths," he called.

Omar Yussef saw that the young man regretted their confrontation. He nodded and waved. He waited for Awwadi to enter the hall, and went into the casbah.

Chapter 14

O mar Yussef retraced the route he had taken with Awwadi through the vaulted alleys, until he once more breathed the dense sewage stink of Yasmina. The people of the casbah had gravitated to the Hamas wedding and the passages seemed emptier than ever. Omar Yussef recognized the small spice shop of the Mareh family, where Awwadi had stared down the hostile young man in the blue overalls. Though its entrance was locked, the shuddering hum of the electric grinders rose from a basement window and the dim air was clouded with the gray dust of crushed cardamom pods. Omar Yussef stopped to savor the bouquet. As he inhaled, he recalled a thousand delicate coffees flavored with this spice that he had shared with his good friends. Then he remembered the same odor on the breath of the masked thug who had slapped him and he looked down the alley to the next corner, wondering if that man waited for him there.

He turned right and descended toward the Touqan Palace.

Ishaq was with the Old Man at the end, when he died in Europe, he thought. *Perhaps Ishaq knew what really killed the president. Could the young man have been murdered by someone in Fatah because he passed that knowledge on to Hamas?*

At the bottom of a sloping alley, he stopped. He was sure the Touqan Palace had been down here, but he had reached the end of the lane and hadn't seen the tall gate of the old mansion. He retraced his steps and went right, assuming Awwadi's home was on the next parallel street, but the alley led him diagonally up the hill. He cursed his sense of direction. He had to get to the Touqan Palace to examine that cellar before Awwadi left the wedding celebrations. That gave him little more than an hour. There might be many files to sort through, if he was right about Awwadi's hiding place. Omar Yussef cared little about the leaders of Fatah and he could hardly destroy the entire set of files, even if he did manage to find them, without bringing down the wrath of Hamas. But he wanted to protect Khamis Zeydan, to find his file and dispose of it.

Here you are, running around like a rat in a maze, he thought, as he checked his watch. *The clock's ticking and you're wasting time wandering these old alleys.*

He felt sure the palace had been lower on the hillside, so he cut into a smaller alley and dropped down some steps. He sniffed. The drainage scent seemed less ripe here. Had he taken a wrong turn and left Yasmina altogether?

He came to the head of a flight of steps, which descended beneath a dingy vault, and noticed the capital of a Roman column built into the base of the wall. It was worn almost beyond recognition. Omar Yussef bent to touch its rough, knotty surface.

Something whipped through the air above him and struck

the wall with a sudden hiss. His hand still on the ancient stone, he glanced behind him. *That was a bullet*, he thought. *What have I walked into?*

He stood, and another bullet cut away a chunk of the Roman capital, spraying dust onto his shoes. In the alley behind him, he heard feet approaching fast. *Only one pair of boots*, he thought. *I haven't stumbled into a gunfight. Someone's after me.*

A shot came out of the alley. Omar Yussef saw the muzzle flash orange in the shadows and threw himself to his right. He landed on the steps and rolled into the darkness, protecting his head with one hand and clasping his glasses with the other.

He held himself rigid, as he fell. He would have ugly bruises, but so long as he didn't allow his body to bend nothing would break. He slammed to a halt against a box of rotting chicken bones and a startled cat fled the impact. He lay groaning, until he heard the shooter coming along the alley toward the steps. He pushed the box to the center of the passage, groped fast along the wall and turned a corner. He saw light through an arch ahead and he hobbled toward it.

When he emerged from the dark, he was in the empty *souk*. On any other day he would've been safe in the crowd, but everyone had shuttered their shops to attend the big wedding. Behind him, he heard someone tumble over the box of chicken remains and curse.

Across the *souk*, an iron fence caged some old tombs. A building had been erected behind and above the graves, but the wall beside the fence lay in a pile of smashed bricks. The Israelis must have entered on one of their night raids, blowing a gap to search for weapons hidden behind the tombs. Omar Yussef edged through the hole.

Stumbling on a loose brick, he grabbed for the nearest

grave. The stone was smoothly dimpled like an orange. He scrambled behind it and squatted, pressing his face against a decorative rectangle of Koranic verse carved in stately *thuluth* calligraphy. He ran his fingers over the text and picked out the Touqan name engraved on the limestone. *It's the tomb of a wealthy man who once inhabited the palace where Awwadi lives,* he thought.

Omar Yussef stared at the stone until the face of the corpse within seemed to glow through it. *Please be quiet,* he told the corpse. *I'll forgive you any sins you committed centuries ago, so long as you don't give me away now.*

He heard someone running through the *souk*. With a limp. *Probably from falling over the box of trash,* he thought. He tried to emulate the dead beneath the gravestones, who obliged him with their silence.

The footsteps halted outside the iron fence. Omar Yussef heard a man breathing hard. He thought he smelled the scent of cardamom and recalled once more that same spice on the breath of the man who had slapped him. The metal fence squeaked. *He's coming inside,* he thought. But then he heard the feet move along the *souk*.

A door swung open, slamming against a wall some distance away, and cheerful voices rushed into the street. Omar Yussef heard his stalker curse in a low voice and turn back toward the casbah.

Omar Yussef dropped to the ground, his back against the Touqan tomb, and breathed desperately, like a swimmer surfacing from a long dive. He closed his eyes and shivered. *Whoever that was, he probably saw me with Nouri Awwadi. Whatever I know about the dirt files or Ishaq's murder, that man must suspect I know even more. He'll try to kill me again.*

A strong wind swept through the casbah and the evening sun dropped behind Jerizim. A deep chill emanated from the old tombs. It was too late to return to the Touqan Palace to hunt for the files. Omar Yussef climbed over the rubble, lowered himself onto the worn flagstones of the *souk* and rushed away.

Chapter 15

O mar Yussef disliked restaurant food. He suspected professional chefs of cheating, adding extra fat or too much salt, rather than taking the time to follow traditional recipes. Anticipating such second-rate fare at the hotel restaurant, he waited sullenly by the window of his hotel room, tapping his finger on a book he had been trying to read, while Maryam dressed for dinner.

Isolated blue lights were scattered across the hillside below. The people of Nablus had eaten early and gone to bed, leaving the streets to the gunmen and the Israeli patrols. *And to the man who tried to kill me.*

The stillness outside his hotel window seemed illusory to Omar Yussef, like the quiet of a corpse. *A dead body appears motionless,* he thought, *but the serenity of death is only a mask for the assiduous decaying of flesh. I would have said Ishaq's cadaver was lifeless when I inspected it on the mountaintop. In reality, it was being eaten away by countless awful microscopic organisms. This peaceful cityscape, too, is no less riddled with destructive undercurrents than a putrefying carcass.* He clasped his hands anxiously. *Perhaps if I just talked to the American woman again, I could get a better idea of why Ishaq died. I might be able to guide her toward the money, without really being involved.*

Without taking any more risks.

"I hope the hotel doesn't overcook the *shish tawouk*." Maryam stepped out of the bathroom, slipping a small gold earring into her earlobe. "These restaurants always ruin chicken, so that you have to drown the food in lemon juice to give it any life."

Omar Yussef laughed. "Next time we travel, I'll rent a hotel room with a kitchen for you," he said. "That way we'll be able to avoid restaurants entirely."

Maryam pulled on a black woolen jacket. "Omar, these restaurant people do all kinds of terrible things with food. They don't love the food or the people who eat it."

Omar Yussef noticed Maryam had left his short-sleeved shirt hanging from the shower rail in the bathroom, damp across the chest where she had scrubbed away the hummus stain. The food at Abu Alam's snack bar had been good, even if it had offended Maryam that he ate there. Perhaps he shouldn't be so quick to condemn restaurant meals. "My darling, tonight's dishes may not be so bad."

His wife raised a scolding finger. "Yes, maybe the meal will be as good as the hummus in the casbah."

Omar Yussef's mouth dried up, like the overdone chicken on which he imagined he'd soon be choking. *Can she read my thoughts*, he wondered, *or just my guilty conscience?*

"I'm going to taste the salads," Maryam said, "and if I don't think they've made them correctly, I won't even touch the main course."

She frowned, lifted his hand, and inspected a greenish bruise on his wrist. "Did that happen when you stumbled after that scum slapped you?"

Omar Yussef hoped there was a limit to his wife's ability

to see through him. "That must be when it happened," he said. He pulled back his hand. He ached all over from his tumble down the steps, but he didn't want to alarm Maryam.

"I still don't understand why they would hurt Sami."

"He's a policeman. They're criminals."

"I'm proud that you tried to stop them."

Omar Yussef set his book on the dresser. He had tried to reread some poems by a famous Nablus writer, but the book had frustrated him. The poet struck a heroic tone that seemed to Omar Yussef as false as the melodrama of a newscaster. The poems praised people who, instead, ought to have been shaken to their senses before they made useless sacrifices of themselves. *Even our artists can't tell us the truth*, he thought. *It's no wonder our politicians find it so easy to lie.* "I'm going down for a quick coffee while you finish getting ready, Maryam," he said. "It'll relax me."

"Of course, my darling." She blinked hard. "I just have to tidy my hair and then I'll join you."

Omar Yussef smiled at his wife. Beside her black clothes, her skin appeared gray, though it was really a yellowed brown like the flesh inside an eggplant. She blinked frequently when spoken to, an idiosyncrasy she had developed during the years of the intifada. Omar Yussef worried that it was the result of excessive tension, of repressed concern for her family amid the violence of Bethlehem. *Perhaps she's just surprised that she's still alive, after what our town's been through*, he thought.

Maryam went back into the small bathroom. "I worry about Zuheir," she said quietly, as Omar Yussef turned the door handle to leave the room.

He took his hand away from the knob. "Because he's become religious?"

Maryam snapped her face toward her husband. "Because he's all skin and bones. He isn't eating well."

"It's just the stupid loose clothes he wears, like some Saudi herdsman," Omar Yussef said. "Or maybe it's because he's fasting twice a week like a good Muslim."

"Omar, don't criticize the boy. He's stubborn, just like you. If you tell him he's taking the wrong path, it'll only make him more determined."

She leaned close to the bathroom mirror and, with a finger and thumb, toyed with the sagging skin at the corners of her mouth.

"Maryam, turn away from that mirror," Omar Yussef said. "When you look at yourself like that, it reminds me how much worse my own reflection appears. Do you want to be cruel to your poor husband?"

Maryam twiddled the brass buttons on Omar Yussef's blazer and brushed the lapels. "Don't worry," she said. "You look smart, as always."

It wasn't true that, confronted with a mirror, Omar Yussef examined himself critically. He saw more than a trace of the handsome young man he had been. He even imagined that he might be less bald than in fact he was and that his gray mustache gave him a manly gravity. But he was unsure of himself tonight. The mirror might catch him with haggard, drawn eyelids and new lines scored beside his mouth like scars.

He kissed his wife's forehead and opened the door. She reached for her hairbrush, as he went out.

In the elevator, the mirror challenged him. He glimpsed

a sallow face, streaked with deep gray shadows. He turned his eyes swiftly to the flickering fluorescent lights in the ceiling, keeping them there until the elevator doors opened on the lobby and allowed him to escape his reflection.

Jamie King stood in the center of the lobby with her hands resting together in front of her. Her eyes wandered around the room as though she were waiting for someone. She wore her red hair down and Omar Yussef admired its thickness. A surge of purpose overcame his melancholy. *I must talk to her before Maryam arrives*, he thought. As he approached her, the American straightened her jacket, smiled and extended a firm hand to greet him.

"I hope I'm not intruding," he said.

"No, in fact, I—"

"Jamie, I need to continue our talk about Ishaq, the Samaritan," Omar Yussef said, moving close to her. "Ishaq was very young to be in charge of the Old Man's secret finances, wasn't he?"

"There weren't many people the president trusted." King stroked the soft hairs by her ear. "The people who first told me about Ishaq all used the same phrase: 'Ishaq was like a son to the Old Man.' But I wouldn't rule out the possibility that the president simply had something on Ishaq."

"Some sort of dirt?" *His homosexuality*, Omar Yussef thought.

"Something that would give him power over Ishaq. So that if Ishaq ever tried to pilfer the cash, the president could ruin his family."

"He went to Paris with the president, when the Old Man was dying," Omar Yussef said. "Once the president died, Ishaq could've kept all the money."

The American dipped her head closer to Omar Yussef. "Unless someone else also knew his secret and was in a position to blackmail him."

"If that were the case, why would he return to Palestine? He was walking right into the arms of his blackmailers." Omar Yussef shook his head. "What do you think happened to the money?"

"I've traced no recent transactions that would suggest the money has been moved. I assume Ishaq still controlled the secret accounts when he was killed."

"Where's the money likely to be?"

"What we've found so far was in accounts in the Bahamas, Belize, Panama, those kinds of places. There were also investments in companies all over the world. Telecom businesses in Libya, food distribution companies in Saudi Arabia, all sorts of industries. But most of it was in easily accessible cash accounts, to pay for things the president needed quickly. I'll keep trying to track it all down— my investigators are in Geneva at the moment, following up a couple of leads. But I'm worried. If someone killed Ishaq for the details of the accounts, they might have cleaned them out by the time I catch up."

"Whatever you discover, perhaps you'll share it with me?" Omar Yussef whispered. "It might help you to consult someone who knows the culture."

Jamie King gave a distant smile of politeness that Omar Yussef knew well from years of working with foreigners at the United Nations. *I won't be waiting up for a phone call from her*, he thought.

The elevator sounded its electronic tone. When the doors opened, Maryam was close to the mirror, pulling at the bags under her eyes and Nadia was mimicking her grandmother and giggling. The girl hurried across the lobby, beaming at Jamie King. "Grandpa, I invited Miss Jamie to join us for dinner," she said.

Omar Yussef touched his fingers to his mustache, trying to hide his surprise. "Are you going to talk about your book with her all night, Nadia?"

The girl shook her head. "I won't give away anything else about it," she said. "You're going to have to guess who the bad guy is, first."

Jamie King shook Maryam's hand. "Nadia tells me this meal will be a very inferior experience compared with your home cooking, Umm Ramiz," she said.

Maryam kissed Nadia. Omar Yussef watched the pleasure that overcame her tired face when she held her granddaughter. He couldn't help but think of his wife as a simple woman whose pleasures were all in the domestic, familial things a woman was supposed to enjoy. Yet, he often felt sure that there were complicated elements of her character about which he knew nothing. He would have enjoyed reading all Maryam's secrets, if they had been included in the dirt files Awwadi had procured for Hamas.

In the dining room, Nadia spotted her father, Ramiz, and her uncle, Zuheir, near the window and made her way toward them. Maryam stopped to chat with a woman at the next table, where other friends of Sami's family from Bethlehem were sharing skewers of lamb and chicken.

Omar Yussef greeted the Bethlehem people with some jokes about the rarity of finding Maryam in a restaurant and sat beside his wife. Ramiz stroked his daughter's long, straight hair and whispered to her. They laughed together and the healthy chubbiness at Ramiz's jaw rolled. Zuheir cradled a glass of water and stared at the cigarette burns on the white tablecloth. The waiter came over with a wide tray of small salads and spreads. He laid them out on the table.

Ishaq thought he was free, once the president died, Omar Yussef thought. *He returned from the safety of France to the village on Mount Jerizim to be with his wife and his adoptive father. He believed the president had taken his secret with him to the grave. But someone knew Ishaq's shame and used it against him. Could it have been Nouri Awwadi?* The Hamas man had told Omar Yussef that Ishaq was gay. He had also managed to obtain the dirt files from Ishaq. Perhaps he had murdered him, after all. Had he squeezed the president's secret bank accounts out of Ishaq, too, under threat of blackmail? *Awwadi may have told me about the scandal dossiers on the Fatah men because he wanted me to believe that they were all he received from Ishaq.* Omar Yussef fretted at a small rip in the tablecloth. *But when I told Awwadi that Ishaq had the president's millions, he seemed totally surprised. Unless he's a very convincing actor, he doesn't have the money. Not yet.*

Sami and Meisoun crossed the dining room. She linked her hands demurely. They were allowed to be together in public before the wedding, but they had to behave with reserve. Sami stopped at the table next to Omar Yussef's to greet his family friends, grinning sheepishly when they joked about the cast on his arm. He caught Omar Yussef's eye and his smile wavered. The schoolteacher turned away. Meisoun kissed Maryam. As she hugged Nadia, she quickly appraised Jamie King and spoke to Omar Yussef. "So, *ustaz,* it seems I'm to be relegated to your third wife."

Omar Yussef's face grew hot.

Sami bent to kiss Ramiz and Zuheir, muttering quiet greetings. He sat beside them, hunched forward with his eyes on the tablecloth and his broken arm hidden beneath the table.

The poor boy's ashamed that he isn't working on Ishaq's case, Omar Yussef thought.

Maryam dropped a crisp chip of fried flatbread onto her plate, clicked her tongue and folded her arms. "The yoghurt in the *huwarna* is too thin," she said in English.

King leaned over the small plates spread across the table. "Which dish is that?"

Maryam pointed at a shallow bowl of plain yoghurt, dotted with tiny dark pods. "All you have to do is wash the mustard seeds and put them in the yoghurt. How difficult can that be? They didn't even add the slightest bit of mint." She wanted to be angry, but she couldn't help smiling as she explained the local food to the foreigner. "I always put fresh mint in my *huwarna* just before I serve it, to give it a little extra flavor."

Omar Yussef scooped some of the yoghurt dip onto a bread chip and crunched it in his mouth. "Ignore her, Jamie," he said. "It's really quite good."

Maryam glared.

"It's not as good as yours, of course, darling," he said, in English. Then he switched to Arabic. "Nadia, tell your Grandma that she'll starve in Nablus if she refuses to eat the rotten food in this restaurant."

Maryam lifted a small dish of greens and spooned some onto King's plate. "Jamie, try this. It's *jarjeer*. It's a very traditional part of Palestinian meals. It's a leaf that in English I think you call 'arugula.' To make the salad, you add lemon juice and this purple ground spice, which we call sumac. I don't know what it is in English."

King ate appreciatively. "It has a very zesty taste."

"The lemon highlights the fresh flavor of the arugula leaves," Maryam said.

"Jamie, they say this salad makes a man vigorous in bed," Omar Yussef said with a laugh. "Which is why Maryam hasn't given me any."

Maryam dropped the dish of *jarjeer* on the table in front of Omar Yussef. "Eat it all, and see if I care," she said.

Nadia sniggered and blew some of the cola she had been drinking out of her nose, which made her fall to the table in a fit of giggling. Omar Yussef watched her and chuckled. He stroked the back of Maryam's hand and smiled at her until she, too, laughed.

Zuheir picked at a few spoonfuls of *baqdounsiyya* on his plate. The seething intensity with which he avoided looking at King seemed to draw the American to him.

"And what kind of salad is that one?" she asked him.

Zuheir barely looked up as King pointed to his plate. "Chopped parsley and sesame paste," he mumbled.

Maryam leaned toward him. "And what else?"

Zuheir gave a reluctant smile. "Salt and olive oil and lemon juice, Mama."

Maryam bowed, proudly.

"Zuheir, when we spoke earlier over coffee, our conversation was all about politics," King said. "I forgot to ask if you also live in Bethlehem."

Zuheir sucked on his bottom lip and glanced at his father.

"I've been living in Britain for some years, studying and teaching," he said. "But I'm returning to the Middle East now. I'm going to teach in Beirut."

"I love Beirut. It's a wonderful city," King said.

"Westerners always love Beirut. That's its problem." Zuheir pushed his plate away. "In reality, it's full of all different kinds of extremists. I hope that by teaching there, I can do something to reduce their fanaticism."

"Why not do the same thing here?"

"My father is the one who'll have to deal with the Palestinian extremists."

Sami looked sharply at Zuheir.

"What are you trying to say, Zuheir?" Omar Yussef said, through a mouthful of *baqdounsiyya*.

Zuheir lifted his eyebrows. "The Palestinians have isolated themselves once again, and you're the only one who wants to lie down in the filth so they can step to safety on your back."

"If we're dependent on the strong back of our dear father to save the Palestinians, then may Allah protect us all," Ramiz said. "He's no bodybuilder." He laughed and reached for the hummus.

Zuheir and Omar Yussef watched each other silently, as the waiter removed the salads and brought the grilled meats of the main course.

"Do you have any vacancies for a business graduate at the World Bank?" Maryam touched Jamie King's arm and pointed at Meisoun.

Ramiz shook his head. "Mama, don't let the World Bank steal away my new partner."

"I'm going to open a franchise of Ramiz's cell phone business in Nablus, after my wedding," Meisoun told King.

"Great. Where did you study?"

"In Cairo. I intended to obtain a higher degree, but the border between Egypt and my family home in Gaza was closed because of the intifada. I had to find work in a hotel in Gaza City."

"That's too bad."

Meisoun smiled. "Not so bad. That's how I met my future husband. Otherwise, I might have married some puffed up little Pharaoh in Cairo."

"But at least Cairo's not a war zone." Ramiz slapped Sami on the shoulder.

"If a woman doesn't choose the right husband, she creates her own war zone." Meisoun lifted a finger to scold Ramiz. "Sami and I will have peace, no matter what troubles engulf Nablus."

"So when's the big day?" King asked.

"Friday. But it isn't a big day quite like the American weddings I've seen on the television," Meisoun said. "It's a big party."

"But no religious ceremony?"

"Some religion, but we already made our vows to each other."

"The main thing was getting her father to agree," Sami said.

"Evidently her father said yes." King raised her glass of juice as if in a toast.

"Well, he didn't actually *say* yes. He gave Sami sweetened coffee."

Nadia took Meisoun's hand to signal that she wanted to

explain. "When a man goes to ask permission to marry a woman, the host serves coffee at the end of the visit. If the coffee is sweetened with sugar, it means the family agrees to the marriage. If it's bitter, the answer is no."

"I guess that's an effective signal."

"Everyone prefers sweet coffee. Except Grandpa. He always drinks his coffee bitter." Nadia made a sour face at Omar Yussef.

King excused herself after the coffee at the end of the meal. As the American left the dining room, Omar Yussef noticed Khamis Zeydan crossing the lobby. The police chief swayed and rested his shoulder against the door of the restaurant. He took a big, rasping intake of breath through his nose, coughed up some phlegm and spat on the floor. The waiter glanced at him nervously.

Omar Yussef touched Maryam's arm. "I'll see you upstairs, after you've finished dessert," he said. He raised his eyebrows toward Khamis Zeydan. Maryam followed his sign and her lips parted in pity.

Sami stood and rounded the table. Omar Yussef rose. "Sit with your fiancée a little longer," he murmured. "This is one thing that I hope you'll allow me to take care of."

"Just this one thing," Sami said stiffly.

Meisoun beckoned for her fiancé to sit. The skin of the young man's face grew tight until it looked stony and inhuman.

Chapter 16

The waiter headed reluctantly for the drunk at the door, but Omar Yussef shook his head and gestured for him to return to his station by the kitchen. "Let's go to your room," he said, catching Khamis Zeydan by the arm.

"I haven't had a proposition like that in years, darling," Khamis Zeydan said. He slurred his words and laughed bitterly with an exhalation that smelled like a dirty ashtray doused in scotch. Omar Yussef held his breath.

At the elevator, Khamis Zeydan needed two hands to get his lighter to the end of his cigarette and, in the corridor to his room, he leaned so hard on Omar Yussef that the schoolteacher's knees almost buckled.

"Amin Kanaan's a fucking bastard," Khamis Zeydan said. He dropped his keys outside his door.

Omar Yussef held his listing friend against the doorjamb with one hand and bent to pick up the keys. He opened the door and maneuvered Khamis Zeydan inside.

The room smelled of cigarettes and urine. Khamis Zeydan pulled a pint of scotch out of a tubular olive kit bag on the bed. He propped himself against the headboard and drank. Omar Yussef flushed the stinking toilet and glanced with distaste at the cigarette butts floating in a mug by the sink.

"Kanaan stole your girlfriend twenty-five years ago," he said, sitting in an uncomfortable desk chair at the foot of the bed. He leaned back in it. *It creaks almost as much as me*, he thought. "Isn't it time you put all that behind you?"

"Everything's behind me. Everything good." Khamis Zeydan wiped his mustache with the back of his hand and stared with hate at the glove covering his prosthesis. "They're all fucking bastards."

"Who?"

"All of them, the whole fucking bunch."

When you're sober, no one is more boring than a drunk, Omar Yussef thought. He had never seen Khamis Zeydan this far gone and he wanted to get out of the room.

"My wife is a bastard," Khamis Zeydan said. "My sons, my daughters, everyone. Fucking bastards." He shook his head and drank. He considered the bottle for a moment and his eyes became teary. "Not Sami. Sami's like a son to me."

Omar Yussef stood. "I've had enough of this stupidity. Pull yourself together." He heard the words, angry and harsh, and paused. It seemed as though another man had entered the room to yell at the sot on the bed. Yet no one else was there, only the bottle and his feeling of how much he hated to want it as he did, and then he recognized the voice as his own.

Khamis Zeydan waved his scotch at the schoolteacher. "He's like a son to me. The son I should've had instead of those milquetoast little shits in Jordan. Fucking mama's boys. How dare they . . . they called me a . . . I'm not a . . ." He lost the thread of his anger, took another swig of scotch and came back at full volume: "How dare they?"

"My brother, don't blame your children for resenting

you. You were always away from home while they were growing up."

"Fighting for our people."

"And they're fighting for their mother, who was the only person who seemed to care for them."

"It's easy for you to say that. You're a good man and everyone tells you so."

Omar Yussef sighed. He sensed tears coming and he blinked hard. "You're a good man, too, Abu Adel."

"People always seem to like me better than I like myself," Khamis Zeydan said.

"Is that because they don't have as much information as you do?"

Khamis Zeydan paused with the bottle halfway to his lips, examining the schoolteacher.

Omar Yussef thought of the file of dirt about his friend that Awwadi had hidden somewhere. He looked at the police chief's pale eyes. *He knows what'd be in his file,* he thought. *He can't imagine anyone could love a man who's done such terrible things, no matter in what cause he was fighting.*

Khamis Zeydan took a slow swig of the scotch, as though he had suddenly lost his taste for it. "I've been betrayed all my life," he said. "Maybe I overreact to my family's complaints about me. Whenever I'm criticized I feel like it's the prelude to some greater betrayal. That's how it was in exile with the Old Man. People like Kanaan would scheme behind my back, smear me, create rumors to discredit me. I had to be at headquarters all the time to cut off the plots before they went too far. That's why I could never be with my family, never experience the love everyone else gets from their children."

"That's finished now. You're not in exile anymore." Omar Yussef lowered himself once more into the uncomfortable chair.

"It's not over. I saw that much in Kanaan's face when I bumped into him yesterday at the police headquarters." Khamis Zeydan put the bottle on the nightstand. "I'll never be free of it. Now it's happening to Sami, too. People suspect he must've done something for the Israelis. They think that otherwise he wouldn't have been given a permit to return to the West Bank from Gaza."

Omar Yussef remembered the Samaritan priest's questions and the angry embarrassment in the young man's response. If Sami's story had made its way to the Samaritan village on the peak of Mount Jerizim, how much more suspicion must surround him down in the casbah? "It won't be the same for Sami," he said. "He's in love with Meisoun. They'll have a good marriage. He'll be happy."

Khamis Zeydan shook his head. "He needs me to be a father to him."

"He has a father. In Bethlehem. Hassan's my neighbor, and I can tell you that he's a good man."

"Then Sami needs me to be his godfather. So that he doesn't end up like me."

"You're drunk, my brother."

"His hand." Khamis Zeydan stared at his prosthesis. "Even Sami's hand is the same as mine. Broken, useless."

"He only has a broken arm. It'll heal. And, believe me, you're an admirable man. Sami would be proud to be like you."

Khamis Zeydan dabbed away a tear with his fingertip. He tried to hide the motion by wiping his nose with the back of his hand, but Omar Yussef saw it.

"Sami shouldn't take any risks," the police chief said. "You know what I mean, don't you? This dead Samaritan. Forget about him."

Khamis Zeydan's voice was suddenly firm and intense. Omar Yussef wondered if his friend had faked his drunken self-pity to soften him up for this. He straightened in his creaking chair. "If you'd seen the Samaritan's corpse, beaten and bloodied, could you forget it?" he said.

"Sami has a chance to live a secure life here in Nablus with his new wife—to have the kind of family I never had. Don't try to make him investigate this case. It'll force him to confront powerful people. They'll finish him. At best they'll destroy his career and send him to swelter in a crappy one-room village police station chasing goat thieves for the ignorant Bedouin down south. But they might even kill him or Meisoun."

"Sami isn't involved. Don't worry about him."

"Should I worry about you?"

"I'm not involved either." Omar Yussef stood and stretched his back. "Tomorrow morning I'm going to the Turkish baths in the casbah. Does that sound like the action of someone obsessed with tracking down a murderer? Why don't you come?"

"Sweat out the hangover?"

Omar Yussef squeezed Khamis Zeydan's shoulder. "More than just the hangover. You can purge yourself of all the suspicion and loneliness."

"I might flood the entire casbah, if I start to sweat that out."

"Why not? I need to cleanse myself, too. I just hope our pores are big enough for the job."

The two men smiled as Omar Yussef left. He went along the corridor to his room and found Maryam in a pale blue nightdress, spreading cold cream over her cheeks and forehead. "Is he all right?" she asked.

Omar Yussef hung his blazer on the back of the door and went to the window. "He'll never be all right."

His wife layered a final smear of cream around her lips and raised her eyebrows, questioningly. "What is it?"

"Why did you stay with me, Maryam?"

"Omar?"

"It isn't so many years ago that I was like our dear friend Abu Adel."

"You were never quite like that."

"I was a drunk. I was easily angered. I couldn't believe that anyone really liked me and I suspected everyone of mocking me behind my back."

"But I never allowed you to be lonely, as he is." Maryam linked her hands behind Omar Yussef's neck.

He smelled the rosewater in her lotion and kissed her. When he came away from her, there was cold cream in his mustache. She smoothed it into the white hairs and twisted the ends upwards.

"I would never leave you, Omar," she giggled. "Not even if you oiled your mustache like a stuffy old Turkish *pasha*."

Chapter 17

I n the alley outside the baths, Khamis Zeydan blew loudly through pursed lips, rubbed his bloodless gray forehead and swallowed hard. "I don't know if I'm up for this," he rasped. "If I go into the steam room, I might pass out."

"What about all the sweating you need to do?" Omar Yussef followed his friend up the steps.

"If I sweat those things out, they'll leave traces of my dirty history all over the tiles in the baths for people to read."

Someone has already unearthed those secrets, my friend, Omar Yussef thought. He wondered if he ought to tell Khamis Zeydan that they were about to meet Awwadi in the bathhouse. By introducing them, he hoped to persuade Awwadi that Khamis Zeydan was a good man and to prevent him using his dossier of dirt against the police chief. With his friend irritable and hungover, though, he wasn't sure Awwadi would take to him.

"Never mind," Khamis Zeydan said. "The sooner I get some hot water on my head, the quicker we'll know if this is the hangover that's finally going to kill me." He labored toward the doorway.

The main hall of the Hammam al-Sumara centered on an old fountain of scalloped limestone. Water spouted softly from a stone column in the middle of the fountain into a pool tiled turquoise. The window at the peak of the high domed ceiling was sectioned into blue, green and orange triangles. Long vines grew around the glass and emerald mold streaked the white plaster. The room was light, but the dampness gave it the scent of an old cellar.

Nouri Awwadi lay on a divan by the entrance. When he noticed Khamis Zeydan, he raised his eyebrows and pushed his chin forward at Omar Yussef, as though complimenting a host on a finely prepared dish. He played his thumb across the keypad of his cellular phone and pointed it at a bulky man beside him, who directed his own phone at Awwadi. They laughed as the handsets sounded the refrain of a cloying Lebanese love song. Omar Yussef recognized the tune from the music video channel to which Nadia sometimes danced about the living room.

Awwadi gave his companion's heavy shoulder a slap. He turned to Omar Yussef. "We're swapping ringtones."

Omar Yussef frowned. He resented their loud laughter and the intrusion of the idiotic jingle into this traditional place. "When they built these baths five hundred years ago, cell phones were one annoyance they didn't have to suffer," he said.

Awwadi's friend smiled. His thick black hair was slicked back from a low forehead and his beard shone with oil. "This was always a place for meetings, *ustaz*. If you return later in the day, this hall will be filled with men smoking the *nargila* and playing backgammon."

"In that case, I'm glad we came early."

"Do you think in Paradise there are no people?" The dark-haired man lifted his arms wide. Under his black-and-white checked shirt, his chest expanded and he rolled his neck. "People are part of Paradise."

"If everyone made it to Paradise, you'd be correct." Omar Yussef wagged his finger and smiled. "But I hope that Allah, the King of the Day of Judgment, will weed out anybody who tries to take their cell phone into Paradise."

"If Allah wills it." The heavy man laughed, reaching out to give him a big, slapping handshake. "I apologize for some mess you may find here and there around the baths. An Israeli special forces unit came last night."

"Why?"

"Looking for something."

"For what?"

"I failed to qualify for the Israeli special forces, so I'm not privy to such information. My name is Abdel Rahim Dadoush. I'm the manager of the baths."

"And the best masseur in Nablus, too." Nouri Awwadi stood up and greeted Omar Yussef with three kisses. He took Khamis Zeydan's hand.

"Good, I need a massage," Khamis Zeydan said. "My body's as stiff as a donkey's cock in midpiss."

Awwadi clapped his hands and laughed.

"Only the pain of a rough massage can free you from this stiffness," Abdel Rahim said. "I will kill you with my massage and make you feel alive again. But first, the baths."

In the narrow changing room, Omar Yussef pulled a thin white towel around his slack waist. Khamis Zeydan took an extra towel and draped it casually over his arm to disguise his prosthetic hand.

Awwadi smiled as they entered a wide room filled with steam. "Once a man has been in the baths with another man, they have no need for secrets," he said.

Khamis Zeydan glanced at the towel over his lost limb, but Omar Yussef knew that Awwadi wasn't referring to the prosthesis. *He's telling me that Khamis Zeydan's file won't be used against him*, Omar Yussef thought.

The three men lay on the floor of the steam room. Colored light radiated out of the vaulted ceiling, passing through small circular shafts each with a pane of stained glass at the top. Omar Yussef felt the mulberry scent of the steam opening his lungs.

"When you experience the warmth of this air, it's like a drug," Awwadi said. "You feel that nothing can harm you."

"Steam can't protect you from a bullet," Khamis Zeydan murmured.

"What can make a man bulletproof?"

"Money."

"Perhaps I will soon have enough of that to deflect every bullet in the arsenals of all the Palestinian factions, and the Israelis, too." Awwadi winked at Omar Yussef.

He's close to finding the secret account documents, Omar Yussef thought. *Or perhaps he already has them. How am I going to persuade him not to use the money for Hamas operations? He has to turn it over to Jamie King.*

Awwadi rose and slapped his palms on his smooth pectoral muscles. "Excuse me for a while, please. I like to have my massage when I'm sweating like this," he said.

"Nouri, there's something you ought to know," Omar Yussef said. "On Friday, the World Bank—"

"In a few minutes, Abu Ramiz. I'll rejoin you later for the hot water."

The steam closed behind him.

Omar Yussef and Khamis Zeydan went to the next chamber. The walls were divided into cubicles as wide as a man is tall. In each cubicle, a cinder block lay on the floor on either side of a low stone basin. Khamis Zeydan sat on an upturned block and ran the hot water.

Omar Yussef stared at the black mold surrounding the basin and creeping along the grouting between the cream-colored tiles. Higher up the wall, the plaster was streaked with a lime green mold so bright that at first it looked like paint. "Why don't they clean this off? It's disgusting."

"Don't be a pansy," Khamis Zeydan said. "Sit down and pour." He lifted a red plastic beaker, scooped hot water from the basin and tipped it over his head. He shuddered and bellowed.

Omar Yussef lowered himself onto the other block. Khamis Zeydan handed him a beaker and he doused himself. The long strands of white hair he combed over his baldness washed down across his brow and his glasses fogged. The warmth sank deep into him and he scooped the hot water again and again, until he wondered if he would ever be able to stop.

Khamis Zeydan splashed his beaker back and forth in the basin to cover his words. "What did that Hamas bastard mean about secrets?" he whispered.

"Can't you relax for a while?" Omar Yussef closed his eyes and poured another beaker of water over his scalp and onto his sloping shoulders.

"He looked at you as though you'd know just what he meant."

The dirty faucet splattered water into the basin. Omar

Yussef listened, but they were alone in this part of the baths. "Awwadi procured some files for Hamas," he whispered. "Files that were compiled by the Old Man. With scandalous information."

"Dirt?"

"Dirt. I don't know who's included in the files, but it's clear from what Awwadi says that it concerns a lot of top Fatah people."

Khamis Zeydan opened his mouth. Omar Yussef held the palm of his hand in front of his friend's face. "There's a file on you," he said. "But don't worry. I'm sure that's what Awwadi meant just now. He won't use that file against you after we've shared a bath together."

"Are you fucking crazy?" Khamis Zeydan slopped the water around in the basin noisily. "He was letting me know that he has something on me. He might use it any time."

"You're being too suspicious."

"Put yourself in my position. You'd be highly suspicious."

Omar Yussef tapped his beaker on the stone edge of the basin and felt the urge to be nasty creeping toward his lips. "I'm tired of your constant negativity," he said. "Anyway, I'm not in your position. I haven't lived a dirty life. I don't have to fear that I'll be blackmailed for all the wicked secrets hidden in my past."

"You don't have skeletons in your closet?" Khamis Zeydan looked scornful. "You were fired from the Frères School, weren't you? You always told me it was over nothing. But maybe there was something to it. Don't forget Damascus, either, when we were students and you were a political hack at the university. You were into all kinds of shady things back then, don't deny it. And what about that son of yours in New York? The Israelis had him in jail a couple of years ago. What has he been up to?"

"Ala was never charged."

"You sound like his lawyer, not his father," Khamis Zeydan said. "Go into anyone's past and you'll find that we're all dirty liars who manipulate the truth."

"Lies are one thing. Running all over Europe and the Middle East committing murder is quite different."

Khamis Zeydan sneered, as though Omar Yussef had thought to knock him down with no more than a slap from a wet towel. "It's no secret that I did those things, which means it's no scandal. But for all I know, you could be a murderer."

"How dare you," Omar Yussef said. He thought of the time he had spent in jail in Bethlehem before he went to university, on a false murder charge. "And if you heard that I was a murderer, you'd believe it?"

"I never believe anything I hear," Khamis Zeydan said. "But you seem content to assume the worst about me."

They poured hot water on their shoulders, but the relaxation was gone.

"We all try to keep our past quiet," Khamis Zeydan said. "All silence is guilty. I've done so much dirty stuff that I ought to be put away forever. But instead I'm a law enforcement officer. Welcome to Palestine."

Omar Yussef put his hand on Khamis Zeydan's pale, bony knee. "We can try to get your file from Awwadi."

"Those files aren't for his personal use, by Allah. Even if Awwadi and I have bonded in our towels, Sheikh Bader hasn't hung out naked with me. I don't imagine Awwadi has the sheikh's dispensation to give up that file, even if he were prepared to do so. The sheikh will use it against me, if I ever try to arrest someone from Hamas. In Palestine, you can never allow another man to have power over you."

"'Call a man your master, and he'll sell you in the slave market,'" Omar Yussef said.

Khamis Zeydan snapped his fingers. "This is where the sheikh got the idea that the Old Man died of that disease, isn't it? From the files."

"Could be."

"But how? They were the Old Man's files. He wouldn't have the details of his own death in there."

Omar Yussef took a breath. He was about to tell Khamis Zeydan how Ishaq had been with the president at the end and had also given the files to Hamas, but there was a cry from further back in the bathhouse.

Khamis Zeydan's towel spattered water behind him on the tiles as he disappeared into the shower room. The cry could have come from someone suffering as his knotted muscles were massaged too strongly, but Khamis Zeydan must have recognized something harsher in the voice. *He's heard men in pain and he's heard men in despair*, Omar Yussef thought. *He didn't hang around to listen for a second scream.*

Another voice howled from the same direction. This time it was no cry of pain. It was a shriek of horror.

Omar Yussef slopped across the wet floor. His heel slipped in a pool of water, and he grabbed a shower curtain to break his fall. The plastic rings along the shower rail popped one by one and dropped him awkwardly to the cold, damp tiles. He cursed and rubbed his tailbone where it had hit the floor. His slip had quickened his pulse even more than the scream.

He found Khamis Zeydan kneeling before a massage

bench. The baths' manager leaned against the wall with the expression of a man who had just been punched hard. On the bench, someone lay on his belly, his feet hanging off the end.

Omar Yussef carefully crossed the puddled floor. The massage chamber seemed cold, after the steam bath and the hot water.

The bench was made of thick, clumsy chunks of olive wood, blackened with the sweat of many men despite the gray, smeared towel wrapped across it. As Omar Yussef approached, he saw that the body on the bench was muscular and hairless. When he smelled sandalwood, he gasped. He knelt by Khamis Zeydan, as his friend lifted Nouri Awwadi's hand from where it dangled to the floor and laid it beside his heavy torso.

"His neck is broken," the police chief said.

Awwadi's head lay at a sharp angle to his bulky shoulders. The young man gazed blankly. Omar Yussef remembered the startling recognition he'd felt before Ishaq's dead, blue eyes. Faced with Awwadi's stare, he thought that it seemed no more to have been alive than the black, shiny eyeball of a fish staring back from a plate.

Omar Yussef lifted his hand to touch the dead man, but withdrew it. He was certain that Awwadi, who had either possessed the secret bank details or been confident of obtaining them soon, had been murdered because of them. *If I hadn't told him about the money, he'd be alive*, Omar Yussef thought. *That man who chased me through the casbah wasn't just trying to scare me. He'll really kill to be the first to find those millions.* He shivered and let out a quiet whimper of fear. "Close his eyes," he said.

The body was perfectly muscled and oiled, but now it would commence upon the process of decay that Omar Yussef had considered while he waited for dinner the previous night. He wondered how many more bodies he would have to gaze upon, if he continued his search for Ishaq's killer and the account details. He looked at Abdel Rahim. "May Allah have mercy upon him."

"May you yourself live long," the bathhouse manager muttered. "I was getting ready to do his massage when I heard the cry. I ran back here, but I found only Nouri's body."

"You were in the entrance hall?" Omar Yussef rose, stiff and groaning.

"No, I was mopping out the steam room after you used it. I went back to the changing room and from there I came this way."

"Was it you I heard shriek in terror?"

Abdel Rahim sucked his bottom lip under his teeth and closed his eyes.

"Could anyone have sneaked past you, after they killed Nouri?"

The masseur shook his head. He grimaced at Nouri Awwadi's back and turned away.

"Is there another way out of here?" Omar Yussef said.

The manager stared at the water dripping from the shower in the nearest stall.

Omar Yussef moved closer to him. "Abdel Rahim?"

"The Israelis were here last night to find our tunnels," Abdel Rahim said. "That's why they came."

Omar Yussef cocked his head. "Tunnels?"

"There're tunnels all over the casbah. Tunnels and passages between houses. No one knows them except those who live here."

Abdel Rahim led them to the back of the massage room and opened a door onto absolute darkness. "Down these steps, we have our heating room, the generator, the steam mechanism. There's also an entrance to a long passage. Eventually it leads to the back of a halva factory. The killer could have gone out that way."

"Did the Israelis find it?"

"I don't think so. I checked this morning and the entrance hadn't been disturbed."

Omar Yussef flipped a light switch and looked down at a spiral staircase, its worn stone steps shining in the yellow light. He put his foot on the first step to descend, but the cold draught reminded him that he was wet and wearing only a towel.

"Abu Adel," he said. "Get dressed. We must follow this passage. You'll have to do without your massage."

Khamis Zeydan looked down at Nouri Awwadi's corpse and rolled his head on his shoulders. "I prefer a stiff neck to a broken one," he said.

Chapter 18

O mar Yussef followed Abdel Rahim past three reverberating water heaters. The dense oil vapor in the basement flooded his sinuses. His head swam. He steadied himself against a grubby plastic drum of shampoo. Abdel Rahim paused before a low metal door, stroking his beard.

"This entrance is usually disguised with boxes like this one," Abdel Rahim shouted over the noise of the machines. He slapped his hand on a tea chest, lying on its side above an oil-storage tank. Another half dozen chests had been tossed behind the grimy tank.

"Maybe the Israelis found the tunnel after all," Omar Yussef yelled. He took his hand away from the shampoo drum and wiped it on his handkerchief.

"No, the boxes were in front of the door this morning when I came down to get the furnace going."

"So someone came this way today."

Abdel Rahim yanked open the heavy door. It moved no more fluidly than Omar Yussef's worn-out knees. The bathhouse manager fumbled for a flashlight in the dust behind a shuddering generator and shook the batteries inside it until the bulb was illuminated.

"It's risky for you to go in this passage, *ustaz*," Abdel Rahim said. "You aren't from Nablus and, if you happen to meet some-one, they might suspect you of being Israelis undercover."

"It'll be I who will suspect *them*," Omar Yussef said, "of murdering Nouri Awwadi."

"Perhaps you should wait for the police?"

Khamis Zeydan made his way between the raucous machines, buttoning his blue uniform shirt.

"The police force is already here," Omar Yussef said. He took the flashlight.

The ceiling of the tunnel was high enough for him to stand upright, but his instinct was to hunch in the dark, con-stricted space. A few hesitant steps in the dampness of the tunnel and the small of his back already ached with tension. Abdel Rahim shoved the metal door shut behind them and the rattling of the generators dropped to a low hum.

Omar Yussef cast the flashlight around the blackness. *You've done it again, old fellow,* he thought. *If you come across the killer, will you beat him into submission with this flashlight? Perhaps you'll distract him with a lecture about the construction of these tunnels in the time of the Ayyubid caliphate, while Khamis Zeydan sneaks up and overpowers him.*

The walls of the passage were bare stone. The floor was packed dirt, muddied by water seeping down from the baths. He bent to examine the mud.

"Are these footsteps?"

Khamis Zeydan came up beside him and leaned over his shoulder. Boot prints cut the wet dirt. "Point the flashlight at the wall," he said.

The stone was dashed with mud. Omar Yussef touched it. "It's wet," he said. "With splashes from these puddles."

"He came this way, not long ago."

Omar Yussef squinted ahead. The harder he looked, the more threatening the darkness seemed. He directed the flashlight forward. The murderer had moved quickly, again splashing mud along the wall that had yet to dry. *I know the killer came this way, but I don't know how far he went*, he thought. *He might be just in front of us, waiting.*

That thought halted him suddenly and he peered once more into the darkness. Khamis Zeydan failed to notice he had stopped and his bowed forehead struck Omar Yussef painfully in the back of his neck. Both men cursed. The air in the passage was damp and still, and Omar Yussef's breathing was heavy. He pushed on until they reached a junction of two passages. He flicked the flashlight in each direction. The tunnels stretched into blackness.

Omar Yussef glanced at Khamis Zeydan. "Abdel Rahim didn't tell us the passage split," Omar Yussef said.

"He certainly didn't. Maybe it's not the only thing he dummied up about. Want to go back and chat with him again?" Khamis Zeydan punched a fist into his palm.

"Thanks for your illustration. But the shriek I heard from him when he discovered Awwadi's body sounded genuine to me. Whatever he failed to tell us, I don't think he's the killer. Let's keep going."

Khamis Zeydan raised his nose. "He said the passage ended in a halva factory. Do you smell sesame?"

Omar Yussef detected a hint of sweetness drifting on the faintest of drafts from the right. "That way," he said.

Khamis Zeydan started to the right, but ran into the back of Omar Yussef once more. "Let's go," he said. "We'll never catch up if we have to wait for you to get your breath back."

Omar Yussef ran the beam of the torch along the wall of the passage to the left. "There're splashes of mud that way," he said. He bent to run his palm across the surface of the stone. "Still wet."

The police chief slapped his friend on the thigh. "You're quite a detective," he said. "Let's move. My shirt's sweaty from the bathhouse and it's starting to freeze me in this draft."

The left passage sloped upward, paved now with slabs of limestone slicked by green mold and stinking water. The angle of the passage and the poor plumbing suggested to Omar Yussef that they had reached Awwadi's Yasmina neighborhood, the highest part of the casbah, where the air had been rotten with the scent of broken pipes.

The tunnel grew colder. Omar Yussef tried to warm himself by thinking of the baths, but Awwadi's corpse loomed out of the steam, shining and bloodless. *Awwadi was involved in the resistance, so he would be a natural target for the Israelis*, he thought. *But it's too hard to believe that he was hit by the Israeli army in the casbah during the day. He must've been killed because of the dirt files—maybe by someone who was named in them.*

Around a corner, the passage ended in a cramped spiral of stone stairs. Omar Yussef shared a glance with Khamis Zeydan and went up. His mouth was dry. He halted and listened to the silence between Khamis Zeydan's footsteps. He came around another twist in the spiral and reached a door. A milky light crept beneath it. He turned to Khamis Zeydan, who smiled with resignation. Omar Yussef pushed against the metal door. It opened easily.

The door led into an empty storeroom with a dirt floor and a low arched roof. The air was pungent with the heavy smell of soiled straw and goat dung. Omar Yussef headed

for the steps on the far side of the room. The light seemed unnaturally golden, until he realized that he was almost outside and this was only the ordinary radiance of day. He smiled. *How quickly the glow of sunlight is forgotten by those beneath the earth*, he thought. He heard the mild stamping of feet and the goat smell grew stronger. Another few steps and he came to a dirty plank fence penning half a dozen jostling goats. He shaded his eyes from the sunshine in the courtyard of the Touqan Palace.

Running footsteps approached the palace's tall gate. Khamis Zeydan drew Omar Yussef back into the shadows of the stairway. The excited goats collided with the rough planking of their pen. A group of bearded young men entered the courtyard. Two of them carried Kalashnikovs. Holding their rifles with one hand, they fired into the air.

On the terrace above the courtyard, a heavy man ducked under a line of laundry.

"Abu Nouri, give thanks to Allah, your son is martyred," one of the young men shouted. "May Allah be merciful upon him and grant you a long life, until he invites you to sit at his side in Paradise."

Nouri Awwadi's father dropped forward and braced himself on the stone wall at the edge of the terrace. He put his hand on his low forehead. The young men cried out that Allah was most great and fired off more rounds, the reports cracking around the courtyard. The goats thrashed their heads and rolled their vacant eyes.

Khamis Zeydan tugged Omar Yussef's shirt and led him back into the storeroom. "We have to get out of here," he said.

Omar Yussef shook his head.

"Those bastards are Hamas," Khamis Zeydan said. He

rubbed his uniform insignia between his thumb and fore-finger. "I don't want to have to explain to them what one of their official enemies is doing here just after their leader's neck has been broken."

Omar Yussef handed the flashlight to Khamis Zeydan. "I understand," he said. "You go back. I'll wait here."

"With them?"

"In this storeroom. They'll go to the funeral soon. There's something I need to check here."

"What?"

"This is where Awwadi lived."

"I gathered that from what the Hamas boys said."

"I think he might have stored the dirt files here. On the other side of this wall." Omar Yussef ran his hand over the damp stone.

Khamis Zeydan stroked his mustache. He kept his eyes on the doorway. They twitched slightly with each gunshot in the courtyard.

"If you hang around, you might be able to find your file," Omar Yussef said. "And dispose of it."

His friend gave a low whistle and sat in the darkest corner of the storeroom. "I'll wait," Khamis Zeydan said.

A chorus of ululating women wailed in the courtyard as the family learned of Nouri's death.

Omar Yussef lowered himself with a snort of pain and sat against the wall. He shivered on the cold floor and hugged himself. He would hide underground until Awwadi's funeral, when the dead man would take his place under the earth. He remembered an eleventh-century Syrian poet had written that the surface of the earth was nothing but the bodies of long-dead men. *Lighten your tread*, the poet wrote,

reminding the living that their corpses, too, would become the dirt on their grandchildren's sandals.

Khamis Zeydan closed his eyes. Omar Yussef watched him. *He wouldn't have stayed with me, if I hadn't told him that the file of dirt on him might be in the next room,* he thought. *I should ask the people here if they saw anybody emerge from this passage, but they'll be in no mood to talk now. And anyway I don't want word getting around that I'm tracking Awwadi's killer.*

"I'm grateful to you for coming with me through the tunnel," he whispered. "You didn't have to."

Khamis Zeydan shrugged and swallowed hard.

He's nervous about finding his file, Omar Yussef thought. *What will he do if it's not in the room next door?*

The gunfire stopped. The wailing women moved up to the terrace and went inside. Omar Yussef lifted his head. "The men have gone to the funeral," he said.

Khamis Zeydan crept up the steps and looked out. He beckoned Omar Yussef to follow him with a wave of his hand. The courtyard was empty. The goats gazed at Omar Yussef dumbly. He put his hand behind the ears of a dark brown kid and rubbed its bony head.

"Where're the files?" Khamis Zeydan asked.

Omar Yussef moved along the wall. He shoved the gate of the horse's stable. Its bottom edge squeaked across the stone floor. He froze, fearful that he had been heard, but the women went on screeching upstairs.

The stallion was white and ghostly at the rear of the stable. He stamped and shied as the gate opened. *Sharik,* Omar Yussef thought. *Partner. A good name for a horse, until its partner is murdered.* Omar Yussef felt unaccountably guilty,

171

as though he ought to console the horse for the loss of its master. They slipped past him and down the steps at the back.

They entered another dark, damp storeroom. Omar Yussef cast the flashlight around. The room was empty. Khamis Zeydan dug his heel into the dirt floor and looked nauseous.

Omar Yussef came up the steps and stroked the dry hair of the horse's mane. He peered into the sunny courtyard. Perhaps the files had never been in the Touqan Palace after all. Awwadi may have hidden them elsewhere. But if he had kept them here, someone else had them now. Either way, Omar Yussef sensed that Awwadi wouldn't be the last person who would die for these files. No man was safe, so long as he walked above the dead bodies that were the surface of the earth. Not in the casbah.

Chapter 19

The men at the head of the funeral procession surrounded Sheikh Bader, thrusting their M-16s above their heads and chanting to Allah. Despite the perspiration and frenzy around him, the old man held his head still, glowering as though he were leading the mourners into hell to stare down Satan himself. When they left the vaulted souk, they fired their rifles into the air to honor the martyr Nouri Awwadi.

Omar Yussef clapped his hands over his ears and kept them there as the van that he had heard broadcasting Islamic songs at Awwadi's wedding jarred the street with a heavy drum beat. Another troop of gunmen followed the Volkswagen, jogging in black combat fatigues, their faces obscured by stocking caps, the green sash of Hamas around their heads. They marched in military order, lifting their knees high, clutching machine guns across their chests. A few small boys skipped along beside them.

The last of the mourners sweated past, bellowing their desire to sacrifice their souls and blood for Awwadi.

Omar Yussef intended to talk to Nouri Awwadi's father about the way his son had died. He was sure Awwadi had been on the trail of the secret bank accounts. Omar Yussef thought he might be able to use the fact that he had been with Awwadi just before he died to win the father's trust and obtain information that would be useful to Jamie King. He would have to wait until the burial was over, so he paced warily about the casbah, keeping close to the busiest streets where he thought he'd be safe from the man who had tried to kill him.

He passed the most famous *qanafi* bakery. The soporific sugariness of the dessert lingered in his nostrils as he walked on. He drank a cup of bitter coffee, and he loitered by a man selling chickens from dirty metal crates. Neither aroma conquered the cloying scent of the *qanafi*, as though he were condemned to inhale the cheese and the syrup until the funeral ended. He decided that only when he caught the smell of sweat on a worker's shirt or cigarette smoke drifting from the mouth of a passing man would he know Awwadi was under the ground.

Omar Yussef circled the cheap clothing stores in the souk and went through the lower casbah. He felt as though he were exploring the old town for the first time. When Awwadi had shown him around, he had thought that the place belonged to his guide and to the others who lived there. Now he saw that the casbah owned its inhabitants. Nouri Awwadi was muscular and powerful, but the casbah had taken him. The Touqan Palace, atrophied and decrepit, would still stand when everyone who remembered Awwadi had joined him beneath the earth.

Omar Yussef detected the bitter scent of urine in a dark corner. The sweet smell had finally left him. *The funeral must be over*, he thought, sniffing the cologne on the back of his hand.

At the Touqan Palace, he weaved through a crowd of older men who had returned to the house of mourning after the funeral, while the youngsters went to throw stones at the Israeli checkpoint. He climbed the steps to the terrace fronting the Awwadi family apartment, overlooking the uneven roofs of the casbah. A row of potted kumquat bushes quivered in the hot breeze. Omar Yussef plucked an orange fruit, inhaled its fragrance and savored the texture of its rind as he rolled it between his fingers.

A black tarpaulin shaded the mourners. A boy offered Omar Yussef a finger of thin, unsweetened coffee in a tiny blue plastic cup. He drank and wiggled the cup from side to side to signify that he didn't want a refill. He saw Nouri's father under the awning, made his way through the plastic chairs where the mourners sat, and shook the man's hand.

"May Allah have mercy upon him, the departed one," he said.

"May you live a long life," the man mumbled, letting go of Omar Yussef's hand quickly. He fiddled with a string of green worry beads like the one his son had used. Omar Yussef wondered if they had been recovered from Nouri's clothes at the baths. The man's stumpy fingers fretted the beads in his wrinkled brown hand, like an elephant's massive feet kicking a row of watermelons.

Omar Yussef lowered himself into the seat beside the bereaved man. "I'm Omar Yussef Sirhan, from Bethlehem," he said. "I was in the baths when Nouri was killed."

"Welcome."

Omar Yussef put his palm over his heart and bowed slightly. "Who would have killed your son, Abu Nouri?"

"I know exactly who is to blame." The man lifted a thick finger. Omar Yussef remembered the shaven, scented corpse in the baths. The father's gray chest-hair curled over the top of a soiled white T-shirt and he smelled of grease and sweat. His bottom lip hung heavily and his dead brown eyes reminded Omar Yussef of the dumb goats in the courtyard.

"Who did it?"

"He will pay," Awwadi's father hissed.

"Who?"

"My son had a big argument about his wedding with another young man from the casbah."

"What was the argument about?"

"This other bastard wanted to marry the same girl."

"The girl Nouri married yesterday, at the big Hamas wedding?"

Awwadi's father blinked his vapid eyes. "Nouri was killed by this man because he was jealous. We'll fight his family to get revenge."

"Who is he?"

"Halim Mareh, that son of a whore."

Omar Yussef remembered the tall young man in the blue overalls, leaning against the sacks stacked in the doorway of the Mareh family's spice store, and the harsh stare he had shared with Nouri Awwadi. "How do you know it was him?"

"I saw the murderer and his friends here in the courtyard of my own home."

The passage, Omar Yussef thought. "But Nouri wasn't killed here."

"There's a tunnel between the baths and this courtyard. They used it to escape from the baths."

"Does the tunnel go anywhere else?"

"To a halva factory. But that's a very busy place. They

would've been noticed. Here they hoped to go unseen. But I saw them come through the courtyard with their weapons. Four of them, including this jealous bastard. I thought nothing of it at first—several families live in this old palace and we all use the courtyard. Then Nouri's friends came to tell me he had been killed in the baths and I realized immediately who was guilty."

"Didn't the girl's father make the decision that she would marry Nouri?"

"Of course he did." Awwadi's father opened his clumsy hands wide. "But this jealous bastard didn't accept it. The girl's father is a follower of Hamas, and so am I. The jealous one decided he had been refused because he's a member of Fatah. That's why he killed my Nouri."

Omar Yussef tasted bile seeping over the back of his tongue. "When will the fighting begin?"

"We must give them an opportunity to make amends, to pay a blood price for Nouri's death," Awwadi's father said. "But if they don't, we'll go after their family in a couple of days. And we'll destroy them." A vein pulsed in his temple, and he slapped his thick fist into his palm. The worry beads clicked on the impact. "Even then, my existence will be over. Without Nouri, I'm finished."

Omar Yussef touched the man's knee. "I know that revenge is demanded by our tribal traditions, Abu Nouri. But as a Muslim you must also remember what happened when the third caliph, Uthman, put family ties before justice. It led to civil war, to the division of Islam into Sunni and Shia."

"What are you? A history teacher? You think I'm going to start a civil war here in the casbah?"

177

"It could be."

"In this case, there's no contradiction between family ties and justice. By the will of Allah, the guilt is on the men who killed my son. When they did that, they ceased to be Muslims. Don't speak to me about caliphs and ancient history."

"When I talked to Nouri in the baths, he told me he was about to become very rich," Omar Yussef said. "Did he mention anything to you about finding something? Something valuable?"

Awwadi's father waved his hand. "Anything Nouri had, he gave to Hamas. Ask Sheikh Bader."

"Did he give Sheikh Bader the files?"

The heavy neck lifted a suspicious face toward Omar Yussef. "Files?"

"Nouri told me he obtained some files of dirt about Fatah leaders."

"Those things? They're in the storeroom behind Nouri's horse. Sheikh Bader will send someone for them soon enough."

Not quite soon enough, Omar Yussef thought. He shook the big, limp hand and weaved back through the plastic chairs.

Omar Yussef walked through the casbah, away from the Touqan Palace. *Awwadi's father believes a Fatah man killed his son*, he thought. *Could it have been revenge for the killing of Ishaq, who worked for Kanaan, the local Fatah boss? But Awwadi was shocked when I told him of Ishaq's death. He even seemed to have liked him.*

The quiet alleys darkened in the twilight. Old Awwadi's world was at an end with his son's death. Omar Yussef wondered if anyone would feel that way, were he to die. He imagined Zuheir praying over his body at his funeral, but then he realized that he had it the wrong way around. The older Awwadi and Jibril, the priest, were fathers who had lost their sons. He gasped as he reversed the scene and saw himself weeping over Zuheir's body, shrouded for burial. His legs shook and he leaned his back against a wall for support. The stone was hot from the day's sunshine. As darkness fell, Omar Yussef felt the heat ebbing away.

Chapter 20

Jibril Ben-Tabia cradled the tarnished silver case of the Abisha Scroll like a sooty newborn, rocking on his heels as if to lull it to sleep. The old priest wore a thin smock, tight around his bony waist, and a cloth embroidered with a gold floral design twisted around his red fez. He gazed over the crowd of strangers who had come to the summit of Mount Jerizim to observe his people's Passover celebration.

Ben-Tabia appeared pleasantly bemused, like a grandfather who had expected everyone to forget his birthday, only to find himself among well-wishers whose identity he couldn't quite recall. Some of the onlookers wore dark suits, marking them out as diplomats. Photographers jostled at the front of the crowd and a handful of foreign journalists chatted together at its edge.

"Where was the body?" Khamis Zeydan lifted his foot a few inches above the chippings in the tourist parking lot and shook it.

"Your foot's bothering you?" Omar Yussef said. "It's the diabetes."

Khamis Zeydan stamped. "It just went to sleep with all this standing. The body, please?"

Omar Yussef pointed to the sloping stone where the

ancient Samaritan temple had stood. "That spot behind the priest was covered with blood," he said, "but the body was actually found on the hillside there, in the pines."

Khamis Zeydan elbowed through the crowd to get a better look at the place where Ishaq's corpse had lain. Omar Yussef struggled to catch up to him.

"The body came to rest against that tree," he whispered, pointing.

"Witnesses?"

Omar Yussef shook his head. "The caretaker confirmed that the body was left here three nights ago. There was nothing here when he closed up at night and then he found the body in the morning."

"That's not much to go on."

"Not so little. We have the body and the site of the murder, and we spoke to the victim's wife, who told us he was doing a deal with Amin Kanaan."

"So he was doing a deal and it wasn't necessarily clean." Khamis Zeydan raised his chin impatiently. "He was a Palestinian. Do you think it unusual that he should operate outside the law?"

"Sami wants out of this investigation and you don't seem to take it very seriously, either," Omar Yussef said. "Can I really be the only one interested in this poor man's death?"

"If you don't want to be the only one interested, perhaps you ought to drop it. Then you won't be alone anymore."

Omar Yussef stared at the police chief. He remembered the way Roween had touched her fingertips to the acne beside her lips and the pity he had felt for her in her lonely house of mourning. "I misspoke. I'm not alone," he said.

Khamis Zeydan rolled his tongue behind his mustache.

"We can't make too much of the location of the body," he said. "It must be pretty deserted up here most nights. You could kill someone without anyone hearing. But chances are that Ishaq was killed elsewhere and the body was dropped here later. Murderers like to move their victims. They leave fewer clues that way."

"He died up here, I'm sure of it. There was blood all over the rock." Omar Yussef turned toward the Samaritan men in their white robes flanking the priest. They were gathered at the edge of the sloping gray stone, the center of their temple.

"What rock?" Khamis Zeydan followed his gaze.

"That's the stone where Abraham bound Isaac. It's where the ancient temple was built."

"What are you talking about? That's in Jerusalem."

"This is where the Samaritans believe it was. Ishaq must have been alive when he was brought to the mountain, or he couldn't have pumped out so much blood."

Khamis Zeydan scratched his chin with the yellowed nail of his thumb.

"I think Ishaq was brought here and killed on that stone. His body was then thrown over the edge of the hillside into the darkness, and it rolled down into the trees." Omar Yussef peered into the pines.

"He knew about the Old Man's money. Did someone get the secrets of those accounts out of him and then silence him? Or is there something else?" Khamis Zeydan made a quick, summoning gesture with his fingers. "Give."

The schoolteacher exhaled deeply. "I was about to tell you when we heard Nouri Awwadi cry out at the baths," he said. "Those files of dirt on the Fatah leaders—Awwadi got them from Ishaq."

Khamis Zeydan's eyes seemed to recede into his head. "That's very interesting. Awwadi bought them from Ishaq?"

"Awwadi stole the oldest Samaritan scroll and swapped it for the dirt files."

"A straight swap? The scroll for the files? Nothing to do with Ishaq's knowledge of the Old Man's money?"

"Awwadi didn't seem to know about that. When he showed me the files, I told him about the three hundred million dollars Ishaq had hidden and I got the impression that it was news to him."

"If you were eager for the World Bank to get its hands on that money first, it wasn't so smart to tell Hamas about it."

"Don't you think someone else who was after the money might have killed Awwadi? After I told him about the secret account details, he must've started trying to find them. Someone probably killed him to stop his search."

Khamis Zeydan made a hissing sound and spat a gob of phlegm over the handrail toward the pines. "So this time *you* set him up."

"What do you mean?"

"Come on, my brother, it was a nice trick. You knew there were ruthless people who wanted to be the first to get at that money, and you also knew that they were on your scent. So you set Awwadi on the trail of the secret accounts, knowing that he'd be a greater danger than you to the bad guys, whoever they are. They had to turn their attention to him. It was a nice distraction."

Omar Yussef blinked. "You can't possibly think I'd do something so wicked?"

"You're right, I'm giving you too much credit. I was hoping you'd wised up." Khamis Zeydan spat again, wiped his mustache with the back of his hand and stared into the crowd. "Isn't that the American woman from the World Bank?"

Omar Yussef squinted toward the crowd of foreigners. At first he failed to recognize Jamie King, dressed casually and with her red hair pulled under a baseball cap. He shuffled through the throng and greeted her.

"Hey there," King said. "I wondered if you'd be here."

"I wouldn't miss it. I'm hedging my spiritual bets, in case the Samaritans are right," Omar Yussef said.

"If the Messiah comes to Jerizim tonight, do you think the Samaritans will put in a good word for you?"

"I don't like change, so I'm not interested in Paradise. I prefer to be sent straight to Hell, before all the worst punishments are taken." Omar Yussef grinned. "I want to burn for eternity in a place that's just as bad as Palestine."

"Good evening, dear lady," Khamis Zeydan said. He bowed slightly to King with his hand over his heart.

A nearby diplomat gestured for quiet. King whispered to Omar Yussef: "I was up here to look around a few days ago, but the caretaker wasn't much good at explaining the history. Is that the Samaritan temple?" She pointed to the ruined walls and domed turret, bright in the moonlight beyond the group of Samaritans.

"That's a Byzantine fortress," Omar Yussef said. "The heart of their temple is the flat stone beside where the Samaritans are standing. The temple would've been built around it, here on the peak of their holy mountain."

"Who destroyed it?"

"Religious rivals. Then the Greeks built a temple of Zeus over it."

"When the Samaritan Messiah comes, he'll rebuild it?"

"That's the idea. Although their Messiah is only a prophet, not the son of God, so I can't say how far his powers extend. He, too, may need a permit from the Israelis."

"I'll be up here again in the morning." Jamie King pointed along the ridge. "I've got a meeting with the businessman Amin Kanaan at ten. One of those big houses belongs to him."

The voice of the priest quieted the crowd. In a nasal tenor, he chanted from Exodus, the story of the first Passover. In the darkness, the Abisha seemed nothing more than an oblong blot across his white robe. The priest led the Samaritans down from the peak of Mount Jerizim. The crowd followed.

Omar Yussef detained King with a hand on her elbow. "Jamie, may I accompany you to your meeting with Kanaan?"

King hesitated. "It's World Bank business, *ustaz*. I can't just turn up with a private individual."

"Kanaan worked with Ishaq. That means he could provide important leads in tracking the money."

"My discussion with Mister Kanaan may include such topics. But there're a number of World Bank development projects that involve him, too. Anyway, I imagine he'd prefer to be interviewed about the case by the police."

Omar Yussef hid his frustration with a hand over his mouth. "I believe I would be able to extract certain information from him that you might not. It might be easier to question him in Arabic."

King looked closely at Omar Yussef and folded her arms across her chest. "I'll think about it," she said.

"I'll see you in the lobby at nine-thirty tomorrow morning." Omar Yussef smiled. Satisfied, he allowed the crowd to separate him from the American.

Along the ridge, the lights in the windows of the Samaritan village were an icy blue. Flames flared from the pits where the sacrificial sheep were to be cooked.

Omar Yussef shambled along with Khamis Zeydan at the rear of the crowd, coughing on the dust it kicked up and stumbling on the rough pavement. The police chief was silent until they reached the village, and the charcoal scent of the fire pits drifted on the air. "That's very interesting, indeed," he said.

"Those are the pits where they'll cook the sheep," Omar Yussef said. "They slaughtered them in the afternoon, fleeced them with scalding water, gutted them and salted them. Now they'll roast them and in a few hours they'll eat them to mark the feast Moussa commanded of the Israelites before they left Egypt."

Khamis Zeydan stared at him. "What?"

"They put the sheep upright on spits in those fire pits." He pointed to the small park where the white-clad Samaritans at the head of the procession were spread out.

"I'm talking about the deal Awwadi did with this dead Samaritan," Khamis Zeydan said. "Have you forgotten about that? You're usually not led by your stomach."

Embarrassed, Omar Yussef stroked his mustache. "I thought you—"

"I didn't come here to eat. I came here to investigate a crime scene."

"Only the Samaritans are allowed to eat, anyway. Their

bible says that no one outside their community may take part in the Passover feast."

"May Allah curse your father, schoolmaster. I'm not one of your foreign friends here as a tourist. Stop lecturing and let me think."

The crowd jostled Omar Yussef, as the foreigners pressed to get a view of the skewers going down into the flames, four sheep speared on each. His shoulder bumped against Khamis Zeydan and he pushed resentfully against his friend. Despite the dangers, he was more compelled to uncover the murderers of Ishaq and Awwadi than anyone else. Yet here was an ancient tradition he would probably witness only once in his life. *It's not my fault if there's room in my brain for more than just murder,* he thought.

Beside the fire pits, the door to Ishaq's house stood open. Omar Yussef turned to Khamis Zeydan, his lips pursed and angry. "You want to investigate? The dead man's wife seems to be at home. Let's talk to her again."

"There's no hurry. Really, I don't want you to miss this cultural experience." Khamis Zeydan averted his eyes. It was as close to an apology as Omar Yussef was likely to receive.

"I'm not lecturing, but I can tell you it takes four hours for the sheep to cook. We have time."

The Samaritan men tipped their heads back and sang a rough harmonized chant, monotonous and sad. Roween stood in her doorway, silhouetted by the light from her living room, listening. When the singers paused for breath, the quiet was punctuated by the spitting of fat from the carcasses in the flame pits.

Chapter 21

Inside Roween's house, Omar Yussef asked to use the bathroom. He puffed in annoyance as he undid his belt, frustrated by the effects of age on his bodily functions. He was accustomed to waking frequently at night to urinate, but lately he seemed always to be in need of a toilet. Penis in hand, he rolled his eyes and waited.

The room was clean and tiled sky blue. Every fifth tile was hand-painted with a navy blue design and lemon highlights. Omar Yussef squeezed out a few drops of urine with a grunt and a dry cough, washed his hands with soap from a neat ceramic dispenser and returned to the living room, feeling unsatisfied.

Khamis Zeydan stood close to the wall before the enlarged photo of the old president kissing Ishaq. His face twisted in disgust, as if he were recalling those wet lips puckered against his own brow, the poorly trimmed mustache brushing his skin, oily and damp. He flicked his eyes toward Ishaq's face and Omar Yussef saw him frown. *Did he feel the same strange moment of recognition I experienced when I looked into those eyes?* he wondered.

The police chief cleared his throat. "My turn," he said, unzipping his fly as he stepped toward the bathroom.

In the kitchen, Roween boiled coffee in a small tin pot. She wore the same blue cotton robe as when Omar Yussef had first seen her. The acne below her mouth and the darkness about her eyes gave her the look of a gawky teenager. *She isn't so much older than that,* he thought. He felt his chin twitching with sudden emotion and he lifted a finger to wipe a tear, disguising the motion as a casual scratch of his nose.

Omar Yussef was accustomed to consoling girls who came into his classroom upset by a gun battle in the refugee camp where he taught or by the death of a neighbor in a fight with Israeli soldiers. But he sensed in Roween conflicting emotions toward her husband, perhaps love and resentment, which made him unsure of how to comfort her. "My compliments on the beautiful tiles in your bathroom," he said. *It's not the most insightful consolation I've ever offered, but it'll have to do,* he thought. "You picked them out with a great sensitivity to art and design."

"I didn't choose them, *ustaz*. Ishaq had the eye for design in this house. He would have been much happier in a creative field like architecture or fashion. He always dressed so well." Roween took in Omar Yussef's neat French shirt with the gold clip of his Montblanc over the breast pocket, his heavy watch, and his polished shoes. "His style was a little like yours, classical and elegant—although more youthful, if you'll excuse me, *ustaz.*"

Omar Yussef waved a hand.

"He had an aptitude for finance, so he went into that field," she said. "But financial types here in Palestine so often end up drawn into dirty stuff. He was sullied by them, when he should've been picking out nice Armenian tiles for ladies to decorate their bathrooms."

189

"Them?"

Roween shrugged. She poured the coffee into small cups, took up the tray, and came toward Omar Yussef in the doorway. She smiled at him, but her thick eyebrows were low over her dark eyes. Omar Yussef sensed her devastation and felt it as his own.

"Who were Ishaq's connections in Nablus?" he asked. He forced the words out quickly, so that his voice wouldn't quaver and betray his emotion.

The woman recoiled. Perhaps his effort to exert control over himself had made him sound angry. "Drink your coffee first, please, *ustaz*. Let me welcome you to my home."

Omar Yussef heard a flush from the bathroom. "Forgive me," he said. "There are some things I need to ask you about which I wouldn't want others to hear."

"Even your colleague?"

"Not until I'm sure that these issues are relevant to the case. Personal things about Ishaq. Please, his connections? Why did Ishaq come back from France? For you?"

Roween cut short a harsh laugh. She made a show of not wanting to spill the coffee, but Omar Yussef could tell that she had heard the bitterness in her own laughter. "No, he didn't come back for me," she said. "He came back for Kanaan."

Omar Yussef took the tray from her. It shook in his hands and he put it on the kitchen table.

"Kanaan ruled Ishaq," Roween said.

"You had no children," Omar Yussef said. "Why?"

"I told you. Because Ishaq was so often away, working for the Old Man."

Omar Yussef raised an eyebrow, as he did in his classroom when a girl told him a lie—reproachful but not threatening.

Roween shook her head and her eyes became glassy. "*Ustaz*, you know what you're asking me."

"I'm trying to confirm what someone told me about Ishaq."

"I can't confirm anything, *ustaz*. What difference does it make that I thought Kanaan was my husband's lover?" Roween coughed as though her words choked her.

"But when you asked him to come back to Nablus, he didn't? He returned from Paris only when Kanaan requested that he do so?"

"Kanaan begged Ishaq to return. He was at Kanaan's mansion all the time after he came back, although he was there less in the last few weeks." Roween sniffled, pushed her dry hair away from her eyebrows, and picked up the coffee tray.

Khamis Zeydan crossed the living room to the sofa. He caught Omar Yussef's eye. His look was a warning, friendly but suspicious. Omar Yussef touched Roween's sleeve as she passed him with the tray. "My daughter, things weren't perfect in your marriage, but I'm sure that Ishaq valued a woman like you," he said. "I always say that a married man's eye may wander, but his heart does not."

"You believe that? Anyway, who said I ever had his heart?" Roween took the coffee to the low table in the living room and set it before the police chief.

Khamis Zeydan ran through the same questions with Roween that Omar Yussef had covered on his first visit. *He won't get at the truth about Roween and Ishaq*, Omar Yussef thought. *His own marriage is a mess and he refuses to address it. He could never understand what was happening in someone else's relationship.*

Omar Yussef thought that if Ishaq hadn't been killed, he might have been content to live out his fake marriage, because it provided cover for his secret sex life. Could that have been satisfactory for Roween? *Surely the needs of an intelligent woman would extend beyond a husband who decorated the bathroom in good taste*, he thought.

They were outside Roween's door, when Omar Yussef blurted over the noise of the crowd at the flame pits in the park: "Do you think Sami really wants to get married?"

Khamis Zeydan grinned. "I've told him repeatedly what a nightmare it is to have a wife and kids. Do you know some other filthy secret about marriage that will bring him to his senses?"

Omar Yussef glanced back toward Roween's house. He saw that Khamis Zeydan noticed his look. "My secrets," he said, "are of a different kind."

Chapter 22

O mar Yussef left breakfast the next morning with a fervent promise to Nadia that he would accompany her to eat *qanafi* later that day. "Even if I have to run through a volley of rifle fire to bring you a plate," he said. In the lobby of the hotel, he called Jamie King's room on the house phone and got no answer. He went over to the reception desk and found the manager picking his teeth with the green plastic cover of an official identity card.

"Have you seen the American lady this morning?" Omar Yussef asked.

The manager flinched and tried to slip the identity card into one of the pigeonholes behind him without Omar Yussef noticing. "She went out a few minutes ago, *ustaz*."

Omar Yussef glanced at his watch. It was nine-thirty. *If I move now, I can be at Kanaan's place in time to join Jamie for her ten o'clock appointment*, he thought, *whether she likes it or not*.

He hailed a taxi outside the hotel and ordered the driver to take him to the home of Amin Kanaan. The driver wiggled his hand, palm upward, to signal that he didn't understand.

"Up there," Omar Yussef said, pointing out of the window toward the mansions on the ridge.

"*That* Amin Kanaan?" The taxi driver looked Omar Yussef up and down, doubtfully.

"You can stop on the way and buy me an expensive suit, if you're anxious for me to impress him." Omar Yussef grated out a scoffing laugh. "But I won't give you a bigger tip."

"Even so, *ustaz*. There's an Israeli base up there, and Kanaan has his own guards, too. It's a long way from the town."

"You're right. He lives in a very exclusive neighborhood. So you won't have to worry about traffic."

The driver pulled off with a sullen glance at Omar Yussef in his rearview mirror.

The guards at Kanaan's elaborate iron gates sent the taxi driver to wait out of sight behind a stand of pines. One of them remembered that Omar Yussef had been to the mansion before and ushered him through.

As Omar Yussef panted along the arcade of cypresses to the house, a liveried servant came to the front door and waited for him with his hands behind his back, his blue tunic a small blot on the tan surface of Kanaan's enormous home. The sun glinted into his eyes from the windows of three big jeeps on the gravel lot beside the house. He assumed the boxy, black Mercedes G500 was Kanaan's. A dusty Cherokee with signs on each side that said TV was parked beside Jamie King's white Suburban.

"Madame isn't at home this morning, *ustaz*," the servant said, giving his mistress's title a French pronunciation.

"I'm not here to see madame this time," Omar Yussef said. He took a handkerchief from his trouser pocket and wiped the sweat from his brow. "Tell your boss to get the garden air-conditioned. I expect he can afford it."

He went into the hall. The morning sun dazzled at the far end of the foyer. A handful of silhouettes moved beyond the glass, but Omar Yussef couldn't make them out, even when he shaded his eyes.

"Shall I tell my boss you're here to sell him air-conditioning?"

"I'm with the lady from the World Bank," Omar Yussef said.

The servant grinned and opened the gilt door to the salon where Omar Yussef had met Liana. "Your colleague is in here, *ustaz.*"

Jamie King sat on the sofa in her chalk-striped suit. She looked at Omar Yussef with mild reproach. "Usually when I set a meeting with Palestinians, they either arrive late or forget altogether," she said. "This is the first time a Palestinian has kept an appointment I didn't even make with him."

"I promise this won't be the last time I surprise you." Omar Yussef smiled.

"I don't know if I like the sound of that."

"Where's the great man?"

"Mister Kanaan is outside. He has company."

Omar Yussef walked to the window, feeling the quiet air-conditioning cool him. From the shade of the brocaded curtains, he peered at the group he had seen from the foyer. A burly man with messy gray hair held a heavy video camera on his shoulder. A sticker on the side of the camera identified the foreigners as a news team from an American cable channel. A small blonde with a fluffy microphone on a short boom fiddled with the dials on a recorder strapped to her waist.

A pair of men walked toward the camera in conversation.

Both were tall. One wore the khaki vest favored by television correspondents to signal a manly taste for action. The other man did the talking, while the journalist frowned with exaggerated concentration. Omar Yussef recognized the second man, in a checked sport jacket and open-necked pink shirt, as Amin Kanaan.

The reporter stepped back so the cameraman could frame Kanaan in a close-up. Omar Yussef twisted the ornate handles of the French doors and opened them enough to hear what was said outside.

"Mister Kanaan," the journalist asked, in a resonant Midwestern American accent, "what's your response to the allegations about the death of the former president?"

Kanaan looked grave. "This is a tawdry and perilous allegation by agitators in Hamas," he said. His English was poised and distinguished. It was clear to Omar Yussef that Kanaan's full vowels and distinct *t* had been learned from an Englishman, not an American, and he imagined that Kanaan would see this as a sign of good breeding. "The president was a symbol for the Palestinian people, as well as a father and brother to all of us. Hamas has slandered the morals of the entire Palestinian people with this accusation, and they must be punished."

"Punished? How?"

"Hamas must retract the slander or face the consequences."

"Does that mean civil war?"

"We who loved the former president cannot back down. Even so, be assured we will not draw blood, unless they do so first."

The servant who had shown Omar Yussef into the salon appeared on the patio and waited a few yards behind the cameraman.

"Palestinian media report that people are upset. They think Hamas shouldn't have publicized this allegation," the reporter said. "Does this weaken Hamas politically?"

"Hamas will pay a price for its slander," Kanaan said. "I hope it will only be at the polls, because the Palestinian people love democracy."

The reporter glanced at the sound technician, who gave him a nod. "Okay, we've got it," he said, shaking hands with Kanaan.

Not exactly a grilling, Omar Yussef thought. *The sheikh made a tactical error. People are starting to resent him for making them face this possible cause of the president's demise. No one wants to think badly of a dead man, no matter what they would've believed about him when he was alive. As chief of the late president's party in Nablus, Kanaan only has to keep this story bubbling for Hamas to look worse and worse.*

Kanaan waved the news crew around the mansion toward their jeep. The servant stood on his toes and whispered into Kanaan's ear. Omar Yussef stepped out onto the red-tiled patio. Kanaan smiled at him.

Amin Kanaan appeared both coarse and cultured, like a peasant made good. He had a wide, thick nose, pitted and rough, as though it had been modeled quickly from clay between two thumbs. His skin was uniformly brown, tanned by a better class of sunshine than the intense rays scouring the people of Nablus. His gray hair seemed at once to drift on the breeze in a debonair wave and to be locked in place by lacquer. When he shook Omar Yussef's hand, Kanaan left a delicate residue of jasmine on it.

"I haven't come across that cologne before," Omar Yussef said.

Kanaan smoothed his hair back from his brow. "It's *Le Vainqueur.* Napoleon used to wear it."

"In the Empress Josephine's boudoir, perhaps. Surely not during his campaign in Palestine."

"I expect that here he would have had even greater need to disguise the foul smells all around him."

"Is that why you wear it?"

Kanaan rocked his head back and laughed. Jamie King came outside and shook the wealthy man's hand. "It's good to see you again, Jamie," Kanaan said.

He led them to a shaded gazebo at the edge of the lawn. Pink clusters of wisteria dangled from the slatted roof. The servant brought cold carob cordials in tall glasses. Mint leaves floated among the ice cubes.

"You told the foreign journalist that Hamas must be punished," Omar Yussef said, in Arabic.

"Journalists." Kanaan spoke in English and waved a disdainful hand. King smiled obsequiously. The businessman gestured to his guests to sit in the low wicker chairs arranged to face the view.

"Punished as Nouri Awwadi was?" Omar Yussef slurped the carob juice and felt immediately cooler.

Kanaan lifted his glass and watched the light come burgundy red through the cordial. "This is very good for your digestion, Jamie," he said.

"Delicious." The American took a small sip and glanced nervously at Omar Yussef.

She's worried I'm starting a fight with Kanaan, he thought. He tried to reassure her with a smile.

Kanaan switched to Arabic. "I heard Awwadi was killed by a jealous boyfriend." His lips twitched, eager to spill someone else's secret.

"The rejected suitor of his new wife? That's what his father says, but I don't believe it."

A hot breeze rustled the wisteria. "I didn't say it was his *wife's* boyfriend." Kanaan winked.

"Whose boyfriend, then?" Omar Yussef froze with the cordial halfway to his mouth. "Are you saying Awwadi was homosexual?"

"I apologize for our Arabic chatter, Jamie, we're just gossiping about mutual acquaintances here in Nablus," Kanaan said in English.

King disturbed her fixed smile long enough to take another sip of her cordial.

"Do you remember the classical Andalucian poem by Walladah about a homosexual fellow?" Kanaan said, in Arabic. "It says that 'if he saw a penis up a palm tree, he'd turn into a whole flock of birds' in his eagerness to reach it. That was Awwadi, despite his impressive wedding to a casbah girl on the back of a white horse."

Could Awwadi have been Ishaq's lover? Omar Yussef wondered. *He seemed disturbed when I told him of the Samaritan's death.*

Kanaan grinned. "Don't look so shocked. Why do you think a man in Nablus goes to the Turkish baths?"

"I imagine you have your own private bathhouse up here," Omar Yussef said. He had seen Awwadi's corpse. It wasn't something to laugh about.

Kanaan's smile faded and he looked out across the valley, where Nablus spread like so many broken white teeth. He cleared his throat and spoke to Jamie King in his punctilious English. "I'm delighted to welcome you to my home, Jamie."

"I've been in Nablus a few days and every time I look up I see these great houses," King said. "It's amazing to be able to visit one."

"Treat it as if it were your own home, please." Kanaan bowed. "Have you been to see the progress on the new school I'm funding in the casbah?"

"I have."

"I hope it gave you a good feeling about your work. If it weren't for the World Bank loan you organized for local infrastructure, even I wouldn't be able to build such a school."

"It's a wonderful project. It's unfortunate that the money may be about to come to an end." King sipped her cordial. "If the former president's secret accounts can't be traced by Friday, the bank is planning to cut off aid to the Palestinians."

Kanaan shook his head and stroked his broad chin. "By Friday? I was told about this possibility on my last trip to Washington, but I didn't know a decision was so close."

"It's only two days away."

"It would be a disaster."

Omar Yussef thought the World Bank's boycott would be less of a catastrophe for the millionaires along the ridge than for the poor inhabitants of the casbah. He cooled his palms with the condensation on his glass.

"Are you perhaps close to uncovering the whereabouts of the secret accounts, Jamie?" Kanaan spoke quietly, looking at his fingernails.

Omar Yussef watched the American. *Does she see through Kanaan's show of nonchalance?* he thought.

"I'm expecting a report any time now from one of my

investigators in Geneva," Jamie said. "I hope it will give us some new ideas."

"But here in Palestine, you have made no progress?"

Jamie shook her head. "No leads. To be frank, it seems to me that many Palestinian officials are not eager to see this money recovered."

"Why would that be?"

"They were recipients of the former president's under-the-table payments. The less that's known about all that, the better, as far as they're concerned."

Kanaan shook his head. "So people aren't being helpful?"

"Those that try to be of assistance," Omar Yussef said, in English, "find themselves dead."

Jamie looked sharply at Omar Yussef. Her cell phone rang in her briefcase. She took it out and glanced at the screen. "It's from Geneva. Maybe there's some news. Excuse me." She walked out of earshot with the phone.

Kanaan ran his finger around the rim of his glass. "Isn't it a bit boring, *ustaz*, to work for these foreigners?"

"The people I work with are fascinating," Omar Yussef said.

Kanaan puffed out his lips. "If you say so. I find Americans too serious and literal minded. In any case, I like your attitude, *ustaz*."

Omar Yussef sucked on a cube of ice. *Here comes the payoff*, he thought. *He knows Jamie won't track down the secret accounts without local help, and he thinks that means me. He wants me on his side. So that he can be the first to the money?*

"I could make good use of a man like you." Kanaan's eyes drifted to the left, as though he'd just had an idea. "Really, working on these boring development projects year after year, it must be like drinking coffee from the same dirty cup every day. I could offer you a position in my company where you would have wonderful opportunities and every day would be different."

"I always drink my coffee the same way—bitter," Omar Yussef said. "I didn't come here to be bought off. I came here to find out what you know about the death of Ishaq."

"Ishaq?" Kanaan narrowed his eyes, as though straining to focus on the distant ridge across the valley. Omar Yussef thought the rich man's jaw trembled slightly. "What does that have to do with the World Bank?"

"He was about to meet Miss King when he was killed. Did his partnership with you put him in jeopardy?"

"He was a close associate, but our business wasn't anything dangerous."

"Nonetheless, he was murdered. Then Awwadi, who was a follower of your rival for power in Nablus, Sheikh Bader, was killed—right after the sheikh slurred the man who once led your faction." The wicker easy chair creaked, as Omar Yussef leaned toward Kanaan. "It's dangerous to be either for you or against you."

"Fuck Sheikh Bader."

Omar Yussef was taken aback by Kanaan's sudden vehemence and vulgarity.

Kanaan lowered his voice. "You have me all wrong, Abu . . ."

"Abu Ramiz."

"Brother Abu Ramiz, I don't pretend that I've never been involved in questionable things. I'm a businessman, a Palestinian, and successful. You may draw your conclusions from that. But I'm no killer."

"You have higher morals than that?"

Kanaan shook his head. "I simply don't *need* to kill." He swept his hand to take in the mansion and the town below. "From this hilltop, I hear the gunshots down in Nablus, but I never know if they're killing each other or celebrating a wedding. Do you think my wealthy neighbors are all running around with guns in their pudgy little hands, settling scores?"

"As long as there's cash in those soft hands, you can find someone else to hold the gun for you. That doesn't make you blameless," Omar Yussef said. "Ishaq's killing was somehow connected to his dealings with you, even if it wasn't you who beat him to death."

Kanaan winced.

"Beaten to death, that's right." Omar Yussef brandished his glass. The ice cubes tinkled in his shaking hand. "Tortured and beaten."

The wealthy man covered his face with his thick, hairy fingers. *Was he the boy's lover, as Roween thought?* Omar Yussef wondered. *He doesn't seem to have known exactly how Ishaq died. He appears truly horrified to hear about the torture.*

"You Fatah people took a nice young man with a good head for numbers and you made him into a dirty little villain who hid your money all over the world," Omar Yussef said. "Ishaq intended to hand over the Old Man's secret account details to the World Bank. So you decided to prevent him."

"What're you saying? That I killed him?"

"Did you kill him?"

"That's insane. I loved him."

"Loved him? How?"

"I loved him, that's all." Kanaan stood and lifted both his

arms to the canopy of pink buds above him. "I don't pretend that the aims of the Fatah party are entirely pure. But neither was Ishaq. He was homosexual."

"Morals are suddenly important to you?"

"He disappointed me. Too many people knew about his preferences."

"So they suspected your sexuality, because you were close to him?"

"Don't be ridiculous. I have a wife."

"So did Ishaq."

"I have a real wife, a beautiful, accomplished woman, not a frowsy little sham wife chosen by the tribal elders."

"You loved him," Omar Yussef sneered.

"Not like that." Kanaan pulled out a fistful of wisteria petals and rolled them between his fingers. His voice was quiet. "For the sake of our society, we must be led by men of clear morals."

Omar Yussef growled out a scornful laugh. "I forgot to mention, Awwadi told me he'd obtained some files of dirt on you top party men. He got them from Ishaq. So don't talk to me about moral leadership."

Kanaan looked suspiciously at Omar Yussef. "I live amongst politicians, Abu Ramiz. I bribe them, I buy dinners and cars for them, pay for their children to go overseas for a decent education. As you see from the opulence of my home, this has proved a healthy investment." He turned to his mock-Classical palace with a resentful scowl in which Omar Yussef read the traces of all the wickedness the rich man had committed to pay for it. "But when these politicians get sick, I have to put them in quarantine, so they don't infect me."

"What was Ishaq's sickness? Why did you kill him?"

"I didn't kill Ishaq. I could never have done such a thing. I believed he had a bright future."

"Who would you not sacrifice if they got sick, as you put it? Your wife? Or is she expendable, too, in the national interest?"

"I would sacrifice everything for Liana."

Liana had inspired the devotion of Amin Kanaan and Khamis Zeydan. Yet it seemed neither man had given her quite what she wanted. Omar Yussef's impression of her had been that the course of her life had somehow been taken out of her hands, leaving her resentful. He thought Ishaq might have suffered from a similar bitterness, prevented by social constraints from finding a love that would bring happiness and bound to a partner whose fondness he couldn't return.

Jamie King snapped her cell phone shut and returned to the gazebo. She shook her head. "I don't know if this is really anything," she said. "It could be a lead from Geneva, but it may just as easily be nothing."

"What's that?" Omar Yussef said.

"I'll have the details soon. I can't say until then."

"Is there anything I can do?" Kanaan asked.

"I'd really appreciate it if you could try to break through some of the barriers I've run into at the upper levels of the government," Jamie said. "There're some people who were close to the former president and who're reputed to be corrupt. You know who I mean. See if you can get them to give me a lead, anonymously. No questions asked."

"I'll see what I can do."

"If the money does get cut off on Friday, I'll try to save

the joint projects we have underway with you, Mister Kanaan."

"Of course."

"I'd better get back to the hotel. My people in Geneva are faxing me the documents they've unearthed. I should get on top of it."

Kanaan bowed, as Jamie turned toward the house.

Omar Yussef lifted himself out of the wicker chair. Before he followed the American, he looked into Kanaan's muddy eyes. "I'm a student of history, Your Honor Amin. You might think that means I care only about the past. But the future is more important to me. I remember the future."

Kanaan opened his palm. "Pardon me?"

"I remember the future our leaders told us about when they returned from exile," Omar Yussef said. "The future as it might have been."

"It still might be, if Allah wills it."

"If Allah willed it, he would have sent the Palestinians different leaders." Omar Yussef stepped out of the gazebo and squinted into the sun over Nablus. "And Ishaq would never have met you."

Chapter 23

The manager of the Grand Hotel prodded at the inner workings of his fax machine. He slammed down the cover and rubbed his ashtray-colored face with both hands.

Omar Yussef entered the empty lobby, while Jamie King parked her Suburban. He passed the desk and pressed the elevator call button. "Peace be upon you," he said.

The manager dropped his hands to the pine desk and spoke absently: "Upon you, peace."

Omar Yussef waited for the elevator in silence. The manager breathed shallowly, his chin on his chest.

For a hotel with almost no guests, this elevator is taking a long time, Omar Yussef thought.

The manager rubbed his wide upper lip and seemed to notice Omar Yussef for the first time. "It's not working, *ustaz*," he said. "The elevator. It's under maintenance, I mean."

Omar Yussef glanced at the staircase without relish.

"There's also a message for you." The manager reached for the only envelope in the pigeonholes behind the desk.

It was a note from Maryam. She had gone to Sami's home with Nadia. "Thank you, darling," Omar Yussef whispered. "You've saved me a climb." He went outside and hailed a taxi.

Sami's place was a fourth-floor apartment on a spur of rock above the casbah. Since they had signed their marriage contract, Meisoun was permitted to visit Sami there, provided others were present. Omar Yussef assumed she had requested that Maryam come along to ensure propriety. When he entered, Meisoun greeted him warmly.

"I thought you were reluctant to visit our home, *ustaz*," she said. "I've been waiting for you to come since you arrived in Nablus."

Omar Yussef glanced over Meisoun's shoulder. Sami smiled at him through a cloud of cigarette smoke. Khamis Zeydan sat beside him on the couch, his head back, eyes closed and mouth open, dozing.

"Miss Meisoun, I was hoping you would bring some of your sisters to stay in your new apartment," Omar Yussef said. "You mentioned that they were interested in an intelligent husband. I believe I made a bad impression on Sheikh Bader, so I should like to win him over by taking another wife, as was the custom in the time of the Prophet."

Maryam came out of the kitchen. "If you're willing to pray five times a day and to fast during Ramadan, you infidel, you can have four wives, like the Prophet himself, blessings be upon him."

"My darling, the dowry for Meisoun is one camel." Omar Yussef lifted his hands to his head. "I could manage that. But how could I afford *three* new wives?"

Meisoun shook her head. "Sadly, *ustaz*, the dowry for each of my sisters is seven camels. They're larger women who will bear many children. That makes them more desirable than me, because of my small build. If it wasn't for this fact, do you think my father would allow me to marry a troublemaker from the West Bank who has a dangerous job with low pay?"

Sami grinned. "She's not much of a catch, it's true. She's all I could get."

"They say 'A fat woman is a blanket for winter.' Unfortunately, you may have high heating bills, Sami." Khamis Zeydan lifted his head and waved his hand to diffuse the smoke around the couch. "Abu Ramiz, if you want a second wife, take mine. She'll turn you to religion. One develops a belief in Paradise, when one lives in Hell. You'll be on your knees five times a day, imploring Allah to shut her mouth and leave you in peace."

"Abu Adel, you should be ashamed of yourself," Maryam laughed.

Omar Yussef coughed and wiped his stinging eyes. "Have you been smoking cigarettes, or setting fire to the sofa?"

Khamis Zeydan beckoned Omar Yussef to the couch and pointed at the television. "Someone has been setting fires, for sure."

The local station was showing the interview Amin Kanaan had given to the foreign news crew, subtitled in Arabic. When it was over, the anchor announced that he had Kanaan on the phone and the businessman proceeded to confirm the threats he had made against Hamas, in his own language this time.

"This is going to be bad," Khamis Zeydan said. "Kanaan's setting up a confrontation with Hamas. I expect he'll send out a few gunmen to put the frighteners on them."

Omar Yussef shifted anxiously.

Sami sucked on the last of his cigarette. "It'll be pretty hard to scare those Hamas guys," he said. "Particularly just now. They're angry about the killing of Awwadi. He was their main military chief in Nablus and they're ready to fight for revenge."

"Kanaan must be counting on the public to support him because of Sheikh Bader's nasty claim about the old Chief," Khamis Zeydan said. "He'll look like he's acting on behalf of the outraged public, but in reality he'll be taking advantage of the sheikh's strategic error to boost his power in Nablus with a quick fight."

"Why does there have to be any fighting at all?" Omar Yussef shook his head.

Sami and Khamis Zeydan stared at him in surprise. "Go back to your classroom, *ustaz* Abu Ramiz, before the real world pollutes you," the police chief said. "What kind of question is that? *Why?* When a Palestinian asks 'why,' he should spit first, because the answer is sure to be dirty."

"I've felt like spitting in disgust ever since I arrived in Nablus. I'm sure this impending fight is linked to the deaths of Ishaq and Awwadi," Omar Yussef said. He lowered his voice so the women in the kitchen wouldn't hear him. "Ishaq was killed after he gave those files of political dirt to Awwadi. Sheikh Bader made an announcement about the president's death that apparently came from those files. Then Awwadi was killed and the files disappeared." He gestured at the television. "This new thing with Kanaan is just another round in that dirty sequence."

"If Hamas doesn't back off when Kanaan goes up against them," Khamis Zeydan said, "we might have more than just two dead bodies on our hands."

You might have had my corpse to bury, too, if I hadn't been lucky, Omar Yussef thought. Khamis Zeydan had warned him to keep away from the mystery of Ishaq's death, so he had remained silent about the man who had tried to kill him in the casbah, because he hated to acknowledge that his friend was right. Now he wanted to recount the chase and feel protected by the police chief's presence. He wished to be told once more to leave the murder case alone—so forcefully this time that he would be compelled to remain in the apartment, safe with his family and friends, until Sami's wedding.

"I was with Kanaan this morning," he said.

Khamis Zeydan turned wide, disapproving eyes toward his friend.

"I think he's after the secret accounts, too," Omar Yussef said. "He made a show of willingness to help the World Bank woman track down the funds, but you know how easy it is to pull the wool over an American's eyes."

The police chief opened his mouth to speak, but held back when Nadia emerged from the kitchen with a small cup of coffee for her grandfather.

"May Allah bless your hands," he said, as he lifted the cup by its rim.

"Blessings," Nadia said. She put her hands on her slim hips. "I made it bitter, the way you like it. I'm starting to wonder if that's why you won't take me to eat *qanafi*— because you refuse to taste anything sweet."

"Give me a chance to rest, my darling, and then I'll take you for some *qanafi*," Omar Yussef said.

"Grandma told me the secret of why the *qanafi* here in Nablus is so good. They mix cheese made from the milk of local black goats with the sweet cheese of white Syrian goats, which is very expensive. In Bethlehem and everywhere else they use mass-produced Israeli cheese."

211

"That's very interesting. I didn't know that." Omar Yussef grinned, weakly. He felt confused. *Had Awwadi used the dirt files to blackmail Kanaan? He had said there was no file on Kanaan. Was he lying? Had Kanaan and Ishaq had some kind of lovers' argument?*

He realized that he couldn't sort out the different possibilities. He was too absorbed with fear about the dangers of the case. He chewed on the knuckle of his index finger. *Awwadi and Kanaan and Ishaq aren't my concern*, he thought. *I can't face this wickedness on my own. It isn't my job. I'm a schoolteacher and a grandfather. It's time I focused on those responsibilities.*

He took a long breath to steady himself. "Nadia, you've piqued my interest with your fascinating information about the Syrian goats. Let's go and see about that *qanafi*." He drank down his coffee. It burned his tongue, but he wanted to leave quickly and put the whole episode of the Samaritan's death behind him.

Omar Yussef took his granddaughter's hand as they stepped out into the darkening alley below Sami's apartment. Energy and anticipation seemed to pulse along Nadia's arm and into Omar Yussef's body, as though she already had consumed the sugary *qanafi*. He feared that his trepidation about the battle between Fatah and Hamas might be transmitted to her in the same way, so he let go of her hand and put his fingers in his pockets, pretending that the dusk air had chilled them.

"Are you making progress with the book you're writing, my darling?" he asked.

"I haven't written much. Mostly I've been reading Mister Chandler."

The evening breeze swept the scent of sesame through the casbah, but the doors of the halva factories were closed. Omar Yussef grew suspicious of the shuttered shops and the silence.

"Uncle Sami told me about the murder of the Samaritan fellow, may Allah have mercy upon him," Nadia said.

Her pale skin was ghostly in the twilight. Omar Yussef thought of his mother, who had looked so much like this girl. He wondered if Nadia's youthful enthusiasms would end in the same depression that had gripped his mother after the family had fled their village during the first war with Israel. He took his hand from his pocket and held her fingers, sensing how fragile she was, fearing that he couldn't protect her from the awful world into which she had been born.

"Uncle Sami says you haven't told him everything you know about the murder of the Samaritan. He says good detectives always keep something for themselves, even from the people who're helping them." Nadia grinned mischievously. "You can tell me, though."

"But you'll write all my secrets in your book."

Nadia ran her fingers along her tight lips and shook her head.

Omar Yussef rested his hand on her shoulder. "The poor Samaritan's murder is linked to information about dirty things done by important people—information that could be used to blackmail them." He glanced down an alley and recognized it as the entrance to the baths where Awwadi had been killed. He picked up his pace.

Nadia nodded gravely. "To put the bite on them."

"Bite them?"

"'Put the bite on them.' It's what Mister Chandler writes when he means someone blackmailed someone else."

213

"Let's put the bite on some *qanafi*. The most famous place to eat it is around this next corner."

The broad alley where Aksa Sweets sold its celebrated dessert was empty. On the coppery green shutters of the store, an old poster commemorating the death of a gunman in a fight with Israeli soldiers flapped in the breeze.

"Grandpa, why is everything closed?"

Omar Yussef remembered what Khamis Zeydan had said about spitting before asking *why*. He swallowed hard, but he had no spit. "I've been told that the very best *qanafi* is actually not made in the casbah these days," he said. "There're some good restaurants just south of the old town. Let's go there for our dessert, my darling."

Nadia's footsteps became quiet and cautious. "Grandpa, maybe we should turn back. I know you said you'd walk through bullets to get me some *qanafi* today, but I hope you didn't really mean it. It seems like something bad is about to happen."

"The author of *The Curse of the Casbah* can't be turned back so easily, can she? Aren't you hungry any more?" Omar Yussef said.

"I don't want to eat *qanafi* because I'm hungry. Thanks to Grandma, I'm never short of food. I want to try the *qanafi* because they make it better in Nablus than back home in Bethlehem. But we don't have to get it right now."

"We'll be all right," he said. He let go of Nadia's hand, so she wouldn't feel the sweat in his palm.

Omar and Nadia emerged from the casbah into a wide square that was usually noisy with belligerent yellow taxis. It was empty now, except for three dozen figures in camouflage fatigues with Kalashnikovs slung across their chests.

The men clustered around a few jeeps at the base of a twenty-foot statue of a coffeepot, a symbol of the town's hospitality. Omar Yussef realized that the stores had closed because these gunmen were assembling to enter the casbah.

The men smoked intensely and shifted from foot to foot, like athletes before a race. *This is what Khamis Zeydan predicted*, Omar Yussef thought. *And I've walked into the middle of it with my favorite grandchild.*

A tall man in camouflage pants and a black leather jacket climbed onto the back of one of the jeeps. He lifted his arms to signal silence. "Brothers, you heard the slanders against our chief and our symbol, the Old Man," he called out. "Now it's time to cut out the deceitful tongues and punish the liars. Allah is most great."

The gunmen started for the casbah. Omar Yussef stared at the tall man on the jeep—he knew him from somewhere.

Nadia tugged on his sleeve. "I'm not hungry," she said. Her face looked whiter than ever and Omar Yussef cursed himself for not turning back earlier.

He put his arm across her shoulder to hurry from the square, just as the man on the jeep noticed him. When the gunman's hard gaze turned toward him, Omar Yussef recognized Halim Mareh, whose hostile glare he had seen directed at Nouri Awwadi outside the spice store in the casbah. Mareh bared his teeth and jumped from his jeep, jogging toward Omar Yussef.

Mareh would know these streets well. Omar Yussef couldn't outpace him, but he had to lose him somehow. As he passed Aksa Sweets, the martyrdom poster seemed to flap more urgently in the wind. Omar Yussef's breath was quick. He squeezed Nadia's bony shoulder.

"Don't worry, my darling," he said. "I've been walking these alleys for days. I know my way around. I'll get you home without any trouble."

Nadia's eyes flickered up and down the alley. The gunmen's heavy boots echoed through the casbah.

They'll head for the Touqan Palace at the center of the casbah, Omar Yussef thought, *to trap the Hamas people who are probably gathered there with Awwadi's father for his battle against Mareh's family.* "Let's go this way, Nadia," he said. He'd circle around to the north and come to Sami's apartment from that direction.

He pulled his granddaughter along the main commercial alley, past the old tombs where he had hidden from the man who had tried to kill him and through the square where Nouri Awwadi had ridden his white horse to marriage. He cut uphill and plunged along a covered way so dark that he couldn't see Nadia, though he held her hand. His pulse drummed in his ears when he heard the first shots. He had been correct: the gunmen were south of him, approaching the Touqan Palace.

He glimpsed a slice of light to his right, alive with a cloud of midges. He stepped toward the glow and stumbled over a bottle. It rolled away noisily on the flagstones. He staggered, off balance, and bent double in the darkness. He reached for the wall to right himself and felt the cool stone against his hands. Both hands. *Nadia*, he thought. *I let go of her when I slipped.*

He called her name, but his voice fell dead and echoless in the dark alley, and there was no answer.

Heavy boots came closer, running in a group. Someone shouted something that Omar Yussef couldn't make out, a harsh call that could have been a command to a subordinate or a warning for an enemy to surrender.

Omar Yussef retreated into the darkness. When he had dodged to the right, it had been a wrong turn, taking him toward the gunmen and the Touqan Palace. Nadia must have kept going straight ahead, after he let go of her hand. His mouth filled with midges. He tried to spit them out, but his tongue was dry. He groped through the darkness, panting and coughing.

Nadia called to him. She seemed a long way off. He responded with a whisper, in case the gunmen should hear him, and tried to pick up his pace. He came up a short flight of stairs and into a small courtyard. It was empty.

"No, not Nadia," he said. "Not Nadia." He put his hand on his forehead.

He heard a light footstep and turned. Nadia peered out from a deep stone doorway. She recognized Omar Yussef as he stepped out of the dark stairwell and ran toward him. He was surprised that her thin arms could hold him so tightly.

"This isn't a book, Grandpa," she mumbled into his shoulder. "It's real."

"Don't worry. It's good research for *The Curse of the Casbah*, my darling," he said, stroking her long black hair.

She shook her head and nuzzled against his sweating neck. Then he felt her shoulders grow tense. He followed her eyes and saw Halim Mareh framed by a low arch, his Kalashnikov across his chest.

The gunman's lazy, blank eyes chilled Omar Yussef. He stepped toward Mareh, gently pushing Nadia toward the edge of the courtyard.

"I didn't read any of those files," he said.

Mareh tipped his head to the left and was quiet.

"The files in Awwadi's storeroom. When I went to find them, they were gone."

Mareh shrugged.

"I mean, if someone wants to silence me so that I don't reveal the contents of those files, it's unnecessary. I know nothing."

The gunman licked his lips. "I can't argue with that."

"Let me take my granddaughter home and I'll be happy to come to see you later. We can talk about this."

"We must thank Allah, because that really puts my mind at rest," said Mareh, mocking and scornful. He raised his weapon. "But you'll understand that I need to put you to rest, too."

Omar Yussef's neck muscles quivered with fear, but he took another step toward the assault rifle. "How is this civil war between Fatah and Hamas going to benefit you or your people in the casbah?"

"Awwadi's family is about to attack mine. I'm striking first."

"You're doing Kanaan's bidding, that's all. This isn't really about a family feud. You're a slave to that rich bastard."

Mareh said nothing, but something hardened in his deep brown eyes and betrayed his boss to Omar Yussef.

"I'm right, aren't I?"

Mareh cursed.

"Watch your tongue in front of the child," Omar Yussef said.

"Nasty words won't be the worst thing she learns today." Mareh leaned close and grinned.

Omar Yussef smelled cardamom on the man's breath. "Kanaan sent you to beat up Sami Jaffari, too."

"I was the one who slapped you." Mareh smiled broadly. "Little Grandpa."

Omar Yussef quivered with rage. He heard Nadia's feet shuffle, nervously. His knees jerked back and forth and his jaw trembled. He raised his hand and slapped Mareh's face.

It was a feeble blow, but the gunman stared at him, astonished and affronted. Mareh's lips tightened. He braced his rifle against his hip and shoved the barrel into the schoolteacher's belly.

Omar Yussef shut his eyes. He heard a shot. Nadia screamed. Then he looked.

Mareh squirmed on the ground with a bullet wound in his neck. The gunman pressed his hands to his throat, but blood spewed through his fingers.

Khamis Zeydan came breathlessly to Omar Yussef's side. Nadia rushed to hold her grandfather tight once more.

"You shot him?" Omar Yussef asked.

The police chief grunted and pointed over his shoulder.

"I'm not so good with my left hand, Abu Ramiz." Sami holstered his gun. "That's why the bastard's still struggling."

Omar Yussef's legs were weak. "Sami, Nadia mustn't . . ."

The young policeman beckoned to them. As Omar Yussef rounded the corner, Khamis Zeydan stood above Mareh. Nadia shuddered when she heard the shot.

Khamis Zeydan followed them into the alley.

"You just finished him off?" Omar Yussef whispered, his eyes wide.

"Because slapping him in the face like a girl won't stop him trying to kill you again." Khamis Zeydan grabbed Omar Yussef's elbow. "Come on, he saw Sami shoot him.

He saw me, too. If he'd lived, he'd have been after all of us. I prefer to share my secrets only with the dead."

"What were you doing here?"

"Sami and I got hungry for some *qanafi*, so we thought we'd join you."

Omar Yussef recoiled when Khamis Zeydan turned his eyes on him. The habitual blithe confidence of the police chief's gaze, his ability to be at once as hard as nails and yet to take nothing seriously, was gone. In its place a naked wildness oscillated. He hauled Omar Yussef along the passage.

Nadia was pale and she whimpered with every gunshot that echoed through the casbah.

Sami was right about Ishaq's murder, Omar Yussef thought. *The amount of money involved is so great, it was bound to interest powerful people who would pay someone like Mareh to take my life without hesitation. I ignored Sami and I exposed my sweet Nadia to the killing of a man. And still I'm not safe, just because Mareh's out of the way. They'll send someone else.*

I have to get to them first.

At the bottom of Sami's stairwell, Omar Yussef leaned on the metal banister, exhausted and wheezing. Nadia mounted the first flight of steps. "Come on, Grandpa, hurry." He waved her on, but she stayed where she was, until he followed her.

In Sami's apartment, Maryam hugged Nadia and gave Omar Yussef a look of reproach and concern. He puffed out his cheeks, thrust open the bathroom door and let himself down onto his aching knees. He gripped the cold rim and vomited.

Chapter 24

Though the assault weapons in the casbah splintered the quiet, the women fell asleep in the bedroom, where they had gone to comfort Nadia. Omar Yussef drowsed on the black leather couch. The chase through the old town with his granddaughter disturbed his dreams. He plunged back into the panic he had felt when he had let go of Nadia's hand. Shivering with desperation, he awoke, gasping, detecting cardamom on the air and fearing that Mareh wasn't dead after all.

Khamis Zeydan watched him from an armchair, tapping his pinkie on the leather.

Omar Yussef's breath was quick. A shot sounded close to the apartment block and he let out a frightened grunt.

"Sami ought to have bought an apartment that was less noisy," Khamis Zeydan said. "After his marriage, he'll find the nightlife of the casbah too exciting for a steady family man."

In the kitchen, Sami boiled a pot of coffee. *At least that's the source of the cardamom*, Omar Yussef thought. *I must have smelled it in my sleep.* He shuddered at the thought of the gunman's breath, hot and sweet on his face.

"I couldn't afford Amin Kanaan's neighborhood," Sami said. "Not on a policeman's salary."

"Serves you right for being an honest policeman," Khamis Zeydan said. "You should accept some bribes."

"As a police officer, I have a good role model." Sami smiled at Khamis Zeydan. The police chief waved a dismissive hand at him.

Omar Yussef's sons had arrived while he slept.

Ramiz sat on the edge of the sofa, biting his knuckle and sucking on the mouthpiece of a *nargila*, his eyes nervous. The water rumbled in the glass bulb at the bottom of the *nargila*.

Zuheir held himself taut and upright on a dining chair, his elbows close to his sides, his hands folded on his lap, watching his brother.

Another volley of gunfire rattled through the casbah.

Ramiz exhaled a blue cloud of *nargila* smoke. He offered his brother the brightly striped pipe.

"What're you smoking?" Zuheir sniffed. He grimaced at the fruity odor of the smoke. "That's Bahraini apple tobacco. I'm not touching that cheap crap. Why don't you get something good?"

Ramiz shrugged. "I was in Amman last month and I found *nargila* tobacco scented with something called 'Frappuccino.' Whatever that is."

"Foreign nonsense, that's what. The oldest tradition is to flavor the tobacco with roses, and that's how it should continue. Isn't that right, Dad?"

Omar Yussef stared at his sons. "I dreamed that I lost Nadia."

Ramiz sucked on the *nargila*. Water rumbled in the pipe.

A low crack resonated out of the casbah. "Grenade," Khamis Zeydan muttered.

"I don't know why you can't just hang around the hotel and chat with the other wedding guests, Dad," Ramiz said, irritably. "Why must you always take these risks?"

"Your father is on the trail of some big money," Khamis Zeydan sneered. "Somehow he seems not to have grasped that there are sure to be some nasty types trying to get to it before him." He looked hard at Omar Yussef. "Your friend Amin Kanaan wanted to get you out of the way, before you could help the World Bank woman find the money."

"Kanaan might not be the only one tracking the bank accounts," Omar Yussef said. "I could be getting in the way of other powerful people who want those riches for themselves."

"Sami, the schoolteacher has finally come around to our way of thinking," Khamis Zeydan called toward the kitchen. "At last, he agrees that this is too big and dangerous for him."

"I just mean that there could be a lot of people who might have sent Mareh to kill me."

"But Kanaan was the only one who created a mini-civil war in the casbah with Mareh as his commander on the ground."

"These Fatah people disgust me," Zuheir exclaimed. Ramiz gestured for his brother to lower his voice and swept his eyes toward the door of the bedroom where the women slept. Zuheir gave an exasperated growl.

"What's your problem with Fatah, anyway? Hamas started this," Ramiz said, "by saying the president died of that disease."

"Who cares if they say he was the bastard offspring of the Israeli prime minister and a lame donkey?" Zuheir slapped his thigh angrily. "They can say what they want. It's just words. Why does it always have to end in gunfire and death?"

Sami spoke from the kitchen door. "Would you say that, if it was one of the famous Hamas martyrs who had been slandered?"

"You think I'm Hamas? Just because I have a beard and I pray five times a day? I sometimes wonder if we Palestinians are real people with our own individual identities or just caricatures."

Khamis Zeydan poured a slug of Johnnie Walker. Zuheir tutted, but the police chief ignored the young man's disapproval of the alcohol.

Omar Yussef shuffled into the bathroom to urinate. He felt feverish as he strained against his recalcitrant bladder. When he came back into the living room, he was conscious of the heavy smoke of the cigarettes and the water pipe. He needed air. He wrenched at the window, but it wouldn't budge.

Sami leaned over his shoulder, clicked a catch and slid the window open easily. He handed a cup to Omar Yussef. "Here's some coffee for you, Abu Ramiz."

"May Allah bless your hands." Omar Yussef put his head out of the window and inhaled deeply. The night was cool and moonless, and the domed rooftops of the casbah were black and indistinct. As he breathed the clean air, he felt the nightmares recede.

He pulled his head back into the room. "Kanaan says he didn't kill Ishaq," he said.

He turned to face Khamis Zeydan. The police chief's eyes were fixed on Omar Yussef.

"I believe him," Omar Yussef said. "He seemed truly shocked when I told him Ishaq had been tortured. He said he loved Ishaq, but he denied that he was Ishaq's lover."

"Ishaq's lover?" Khamis Zeydan hawked up some phlegm and worked his jaw. "Where did you get that idea?"

"Nouri Awwadi said Ishaq was homosexual, and Ishaq's wife suspected that Kanaan was her rival for her husband's love."

"Why didn't you tell me that before I questioned her?" Khamis Zeydan grunted and slapped his thigh just above the knee. "Bastard leg."

Sami folded a cheap tartan blanket around Khamis Zeydan's legs and feet. "Before you lecture me, yes, I know it's the diabetes," the police chief said to Omar Yussef. He put his hand on Sami's head, as the young man tucked the blanket into the armchair. "You're going to have to delay the wedding if this gunfight continues for a few days, Sami. The guests won't be able to move about safely."

Sami shoved his good hand into his pocket.

"My permit expires one day after the scheduled date of the wedding," Omar Yussef said. "The same for Maryam and Nadia, Zuheir and Ramiz, too. If the wedding is delayed, we'll have to return to Bethlehem and miss the big party. The Israelis will never give us an extension."

"Why don't you get your pal Kanaan to intervene?" Khamis Zeydan spat into a tissue.

A disjointed volley of gunfire sounded, close and loud. Omar Yussef moved away from the window and sat on the end of the couch. "When the fighting dies down, perhaps we should go and confront Kanaan, tell him he's exacted enough revenge on Hamas, and ask him to stop."

Khamis Zeydan stared. "Are you serious, schoolteacher? Screw your sister, you're insane."

"So you'll come with me?"

"If it's the only way to stop this fighting and to make sure Sami's wedding goes ahead, of course I'll come with you."

Omar Yussef smiled with one corner of his mouth. "Ramiz, give me your cell phone, please."

His son handed him a silver Nokia. A photo of Ramiz with his wife and children lit up the screen when Omar Yussef touched the keypad. He took Jamie King's business card from his pocket and clumsily plugged her mobile number into the phone. "How do I make it dial?"

Ramiz sighed. "Press the button with the little green telephone on it, Dad."

Omar Yussef brought the phone level with his ear. "There's something wrong with it. Nothing's happening."

Just as Ramiz reached for the phone, a voice came from the handset.

"Jamie?" Omar Yussef said. He held the phone a few inches from his head and looked sideways at it.

"Speaking." Jamie King's voice sounded clearly.

"This is Omar Yussef Sirhan. The grandfather of Nadia, your partner in crime."

"Since you came to Kanaan's place with me, I guess you're now my coconspirator, too. How're you, *ustaz?*"

"Fine, thanks be to Allah."

Khamis Zeydan and Ramiz, who knew Omar Yussef's suspicions about the health hazards of cellular phones and his ineptitude with technology, sniggered at the mistrust with which he eyed the phone in his hand.

"Get off the line quickly, before it gives you radiation sickness," Ramiz said.

Omar Yussef scowled and turned to the window. "I'm sorry to call you so late at night."

Jamie King laughed. "Don't worry about it. It's not easy

to sleep in this town, anyhow," she said. Another shot reverberated in the dark outside.

"You're quite right." Omar Yussef lowered his voice. "I wondered if your fax from Geneva contained anything useful."

"It took a long time for me to receive the whole thing," King said. "The fax at the hotel isn't very reliable."

"I've noticed."

"My investigators in Switzerland managed to turn up a couple of small accounts. Nothing like as big as we're looking for."

"That's disappointing."

"My staff happened to be the first to inform the people at one of the banks that Ishaq was dead. It turns out he left instructions with this particular bank that, in the event of his death, they're to transfer a half million bucks to a Nablus account in the name of Suleiman al-Teef."

"Who's he?"

"No idea. The manager of the bank where the account is held refuses to tell me anything about it without permission from his boss in Amman. That won't come through until at least next week, which is too late to stop the funding boycott. In any case, that's only half a million bucks. It leaves us still more than two hundred and ninety-nine million short of our target."

Omar Yussef nodded at the phone, until King spoke into the silence to ask if he was still on the line. "Yes, I'm here. So the World Bank really is going to cut funding?"

"Friday afternoon the board turns off the cash."

"What time is it now?" He looked at his wrist watch. Before

he could read the time, he noticed that it was scratched. *That must have happened when I stumbled in the casbah, before Mareh tried to kill me*, he thought. He clicked his tongue and rubbed his thumb across the face. *Such a beautiful watch.*

"It's three a.m. It's already Thursday," King said.

"We have less than two days."

"That's not much time, *ustaz.*"

Omar Yussef held his watch to his ear. It was still ticking. "I'll do my best, don't worry."

"Hey, keep trying."

He was about to hand the phone to his son, when he remembered what he had wanted to ask the American. "Jamie, when we first met, you said that Ishaq told you he could lay his hands on the bank documents within an hour."

"That's right. I spoke to him by phone to arrange a meeting. We talked only briefly before he was killed."

"The documents must be in Nablus, if they were so close at hand. Did he say anything else about where they were?"

"Nothing substantive." King was quiet for a moment. "I'm trying to remember his exact words. He said something like, 'I put them out in the open, where anyone could see them. But no one except God would ever know they're there.'"

Out in the open. Omar Yussef remembered Roween telling him that Ishaq had said he was involved in something so dangerous that he wanted to bury it behind the temple. *Does that mean the altar on top of Jerizim? That's where offerings were left, where the Samaritan God would see them, and that's where their temple was.* "Didn't you think that was strange? You didn't ask him to explain what he meant?"

"Everyone in the Middle East is always making references to God, *ustaz.* In my limited experience, it usually means

228

nothing. I thought he'd tell me exactly where the documents were soon enough."

"Thank you, Jamie." In his tiredness, Omar Yussef forgot to speak English. "May you have a morning of goodness."

"And may you be of the family of goodness," King responded in Arabic. "That much of your language I've managed to learn, *ustaz*."

Omar Yussef smiled and gave the phone to Ramiz. "I've finished."

"You didn't hang up. You see, you have to press this red button."

"Sami, is there a Fatah guy in Nablus named Suleiman al-Teef?" Omar Yussef asked.

Sami tapped his good hand thoughtfully against the cast on his right forearm. "It doesn't sound familiar, Abu Ramiz."

Omar Yussef leaned against the window frame. He listened to the bursts of sporadic gunfire and waited for the sun to show across the valley. When it came, the gunmen would sleep and await the cover of the next night to rejoin their battle. He had not much longer than that—thirty-six hours—to find three hundred million dollars. It seemed too short a time. In Nablus, there were centuries of wickedness to uncover beneath every ancient stone.

Chapter 25

Khamis Zeydan hobbled to his jeep and tossed his keys in the air. Omar Yussef juggled them, snatched them to his chest, and frowned at his friend.

"You expect me to drive?" he said.

"My foot's all numb," Khamis Zeydan said. "I can't work the clutch."

"It's not an automatic? I can't drive this car."

"It's not a car. It's a jeep."

"I'm a bad driver, even with automatic transmission and good roads. You think I'm going to drive up that mountain on a tiny, twisting road in an enormous damned jeep—and change gears at the same time?"

Khamis Zeydan slapped his hand on the turquoise hood of the police jeep. "Later today I'll see if I can trade this in for a nice comfortable Audi sedan at the police depot— something with only one previous lady owner, if that suits you. In the meantime this will have to do," he said. "And I'm sorry it doesn't have a cup holder and a CD player and air-conditioning. I'm also sorry that the ashtray is full. But most of all I'm sorry that I have to stand here listening to you complain. Just drive."

Omar Yussef lifted himself toward the driver's seat with

a grunt. His shoulders felt weak and he dropped his trailing foot back to the pavement. "Why do they make these vehicles so far off the ground?"

"So pedestrians will be able to duck underneath the chassis when *you* run them down." Khamis Zeydan leaned over from the passenger seat, grabbed Omar Yussef's shoulder, and hauled him inside.

The jeep hopped along the road. Omar Yussef clenched his teeth, trying to avoid the pedestrians wandering out of the casbah. A taxi came up behind him and sounded its horn impatiently. "Shut up, you son of a whore," Omar Yussef muttered.

Khamis Zeydan laughed quietly and lit a cigarette. "Mind the tomato cart," he murmured, with the Rothmans between his lips.

A drop of perspiration stung the corner of Omar Yussef's eye. "Mind the what?" he said, blinking to clear the sweat. He heard a sound like the sudden crushing of a cardboard box and then a shout.

He rolled the jeep to a halt. At the passenger side window, a bony man with a keffiyeh wrapped like a turban around his head yelled that they had overturned his cart. Khamis Zeydan took a brief look at the tomatoes spread like poppies across the dirt at the roadside and grinned at the vendor. "Show me your market license," he said, "or get out of my sight."

The man pulled off his keffiyeh and flung it toward his tomatoes with a curse.

"We should help him pick them up," Omar Yussef said.

"Let's go. And no more stops for vegetables," Khamis Zeydan said.

"A tomato is a fruit." Omar Yussef stabbed at the gear-shift.

"What?"

"It's not a vegetable. It's the fruit of the tomato plant."

Khamis Zeydan stared. "Just leave the grocery shopping to your wife, schoolteacher."

"I'm looking forward to the empty road above the town." Omar Yussef sighed. "I can't keep track of all these things coming at me in so many directions."

The engine roared as they climbed the hill. Khamis Zeydan advised Omar Yussef to keep the jeep in second gear. When the apartment buildings at the edge of Nablus thinned out, they turned onto the twisting, narrow road to the peak of Mount Jerizim.

Khamis Zeydan threw a cigarette out of the window. He dropped his eyes to Omar Yussef's right foot. "We'll never get there at this rate. You can give it more gas, you know. The engine's noisy, but it isn't going to blow up."

At the entrance to the Kanaan mansion, Omar Yussef tried to pull over, but the engine stalled and he let the jeep come to a halt in the middle of the road. He pushed open his door and dropped to the ground.

Khamis Zeydan leaned over and yanked the hand brake with his good hand, just as the jeep started to roll backward. "Were you planning on walking down to the town, after you wrecked my jeep?"

Omar Yussef tossed the keys into his friend's lap and pushed his door shut.

The servant at the mansion's main entrance greeted Omar Yussef with a twitch of his mustache. "Sorry. Still no air-conditioning in the garden, *ustaz*," he said.

"We're here to see His Honor Kanaan."

"The boss isn't here, but you can see Madame."

Omar Yussef felt a pulse of frustration. He wanted to confront Kanaan about the man he had sent to kill him and the war he had started in the casbah. He didn't need anything from Liana, but it would be impolite to leave now and Khamis Zeydan would want to see her again, anyway.

The servant led them across the polished hallway, held open the door to the salon, and glanced at Khamis Zeydan's limp. The policeman noticed and elbowed him in the ribs as he passed. The servant snatched Khamis Zeydan's arm and shoved him into the room. "Mind your step," he said. "Don't fall on the rugs. You'll make them dirty, and they're very expensive."

"But you're cheap," Khamis Zeydan said.

The servant smiled, straightened the gold brocaded hem of his blue tunic and closed the door behind him, leaving them alone.

"What's eating you?" Omar Yussef said.

"Did you see the way that bastard looked at my foot?"

He's about to see the woman he loved when he was young and vigorous, and he's going to be limping on a diabetic foot, Omar Yussef thought. *He ought to be happy I'm around to make him look virile by comparison.*

"I can't stand the disrespect," Khamis Zeydan said. "It's bad enough that I have to put up with insubordinate young policemen in my division. They saw a little action as gunmen during the intifada, so now they all think they're heroes and they won't take orders from me."

"It's the same problem with all our young people," Omar Yussef said. "The older generation failed to liberate Palestine, so in their eyes we deserve no respect. You should hear how the girls speak to my staff at the school."

"They should be thrashed."

"Is that what you do with your policemen?"

"It's what I'd like to do to that servant, the arrogant bastard. I'll hang him up by his girly little pencil mustache."

The servant opened the door and leaned back against its raised giltwork, looking down his nose at Khamis Zeydan.

Liana moved quickly into the room and greeted them. She wore a sleeveless red silk dress that pouched a little over the slackness in her gut. Her eyes were painted more heavily than they had been when Omar Yussef had seen her before, and her face was stiff and joyless.

A second servant carried a tray of coffee to a low table.

Liana invited her guests to sit. "I'm afraid you've just missed my husband. He's already gone down to Nablus this morning on business," she said.

"A deadly kind of business," Khamis Zeydan said.

Liana looked closely at him. "Dear Abu Adel, don't misunderstand what I said about my husband when last we met. He may not be pure, but whatever he does, it's never against the interests of the Palestinian people."

Khamis Zeydan drank his coffee with a noisy slurp, a surreptitious raspberry blown at Liana's husband.

Omar Yussef sat on the edge of his armchair. "Dear lady, your husband has embarked upon some kind of small war with Hamas in the town."

"As I said, he never acts against the interests of the Palestinian people." She lifted her chin.

She looks strong and defiant, when she holds herself that way, Omar Yussef thought. *I have to admit it's attractive.* "This fighting can't possibly benefit the people."

"He's fighting for a good reason, not for the fun of it." Liana continued her scrutiny of Khamis Zeydan. "He's not that kind of man."

Khamis Zeydan growled once more and set his cup on the table, rattling it in the saucer.

"What's his reason, then, for taking on Hamas?" Omar Yussef asked.

"He had to get something back from them, something important," she said, "and now Hamas is fighting back."

Suddenly Liana's more interesting than I expected, Omar Yussef thought. "Something important? What exactly?"

Liana ran her tongue across her painted lips. "Documents that were stolen from him."

The dirt files. "Did Suleiman al-Teef steal them?"

"Who?"

"What did these documents contain?"

"Information on top Fatah men," Liana said. "He had to get them back. If they remained in the hands of Hamas, they'd use them to cause a real civil war. You heard how they slandered the Old Man."

"How did Hamas get the documents?"

"They were stolen from my husband."

"By whom?"

Liana shrugged.

"How did your husband come to possess these documents?" Omar Yussef said. "They originally belonged to the Old Man. Who gave them to Amin?"

Liana looked hard at Omar Yussef. "I didn't say that they had belonged to the president. What makes you think that?"

Khamis Zeydan rolled his upper lip like a camel protesting the whip.

I messed this up, Omar Yussef thought. "I must have confused these papers with something else. Forgive me," he said. "I've come across two dead bodies in four days. It's very disorienting for an old schoolmaster."

Liana raised one of her painted eyebrows. "The documents were gathered by my husband, not by the Old Man. They contain dirt on top party people. They were meant as an insurance policy, in case Amin were ever threatened."

"Or blackmailed?"

Liana's eyes were half closed, but alert. "Blackmailed about what?"

Khamis Zeydan sucked in his breath. "My friend Abu Ramiz has heard some unsavory rumors about your husband's sexual appetite, Liana," he said.

The woman's eyes widened and she raised her voice for the first time. Omar Yussef detected a vicious edge that was at odds with the silk and gilt all around her. "You have quite the wrong idea about my husband," she said. The skin on her throat shook and she turned to Khamis Zeydan. "Whatever grudge you may bear against Amin from the old days in Beirut, Abu Adel, I expect you to stand up for the reputation of a man who has struggled and sacrificed for his people."

The police chief glanced at a porcelain statue of a leaping nymph on the side table by his armchair. He pushed a button by the nymph's foot and a lamp set in her outstretched hand lit up. "Yes, he's a great struggler for our people."

Liana's face grew stiff. She leaned over and clicked the button to shut off the light in the nymph's grasp. Her hand lay on the table by the lamp. Against her fingers, tanned and freckled, the gold in her wedding ring seemed unnaturally bright. Khamis Zeydan gripped the arm of his chair, until his knuckles were white. Omar Yussef sensed the tension and knew that the former lovers would have touched, had he not been present.

"Perhaps *you* could tell me about Amin's relationship with Ishaq?" he said. "So I don't have to listen to what others might say about it."

Liana drew a long breath and stared at her hand on the table. She lifted it and touched her forehead. "Amin had a big argument with Ishaq before his death."

"He died four days ago. When did they argue?"

"A few weeks back."

"Did it have something to do with these files about the Fatah leaders?"

Liana shook her head.

"Did Amin speak to you about it?" Omar Yussef asked.

"He didn't have to. I was there."

Omar Yussef wet his lips. "What happened?"

"Ishaq burst in here, very angry." Liana covered her eyes. "He made accusations, against both me and Amin. They weren't true. I told him so, but he refused to believe me. He ran out of here and I never saw him again."

"Was it the last Amin saw of him?"

"Amin talked to him afterward by phone. I don't know what they said. I couldn't stand to think of the boy's rage. He was so close to us."

"What was the accusation?"

Liana shook her head, her hand over her face.

Khamis Zeydan reached for her arm and stroked it. His blue eyes were glassy. "That's enough now, Abu Ramiz." He stood and touched Liana's head, his fingers reaching into the blow-dried hair, pressing lightly on its lacquered bulk. When he took away his hand, her hair rose slowly to its original height.

Omar Yussef followed Khamis Zeydan out. The servant crossed the hall, his face blank and insolent, to open the front door. As he stepped into the sunshine, Omar Yussef heard a sound like the baying of a jackal. It came from the room where they had left Liana.

Chapter 26

O mar Yussef turned the key in the ignition, revved hard and gripped the wheel as the jeep bounced and stalled. Khamis Zeydan knocked the lever out of gear with his prosthetic left hand. "You've uncovered a few dead bodies this week," he said. "Are you trying to make a corpse out of my jeep, too?"

"I told you I'm a bad driver." Omar Yussef turned the starter and pressed the gas pedal to the floor. The engine bellowed like a *taboun* oven when its flames catch a new log.

"You have to put it in gear, my brother."

The guards at Kanaan's gate coughed on the thick exhaust fumes. Omar Yussef blushed and fumbled with the gearshift, until the vehicle shook into motion. Once he had rattled into second gear, he stopped holding his breath.

"I can't concentrate on driving. I keep thinking about what Liana just told us," he said. "Kanaan and Ishaq had an argument."

"I heard."

"Don't you see what that could mean?"

"Could?" Khamis Zeydan snorted.

Omar Yussef turned the jeep across the road and backed into a three-point turn.

Khamis Zeydan looked doubtfully over his shoulder at the steep drop down to Nablus. "A hill start? This isn't a driving test."

Omar Yussef ran the engine noisily and lowered the hand brake, so that the jeep roared up the hill. One of the guards at Kanaan's gate put his fingers in his ears.

"I'm turning around because we're not going back to Nablus yet," Omar Yussef said.

"What's the plan?"

"We're going to the Samaritan village. I want to see the priest."

"What for? You want to check whether his Messiah came, after all?"

"Amin Kanaan had the dirt files, according to Liana. Then Hamas had them, because Ishaq handed them over. Liana said they were stolen from her husband. Did Ishaq steal them from Amin?"

"Awwadi stole the ancient Samaritan scroll and gave it to Ishaq in return for the files. And Ishaq gave the scroll to the priest." Khamis Zeydan stared through the dusty windshield of the jeep.

"I don't see why Kanaan would agree to that. They were important files and he got nothing out of the deal. Unless he *wanted* the Samaritans to get the scroll back."

"It seems like that'd only be important to the six hundred Samaritans, not to Kanaan."

Omar Yussef scratched his chin.

The Samaritan village showed white beyond the windbreak of pines on the ridge.

"Ishaq wanted the scroll back, for the Samaritans. It's their holiest relic," Omar Yussef said. "Maybe he was supposed to give something to Kanaan in return for the dirt files."

Khamis Zeydan leered. "A little fireside companionship on lonely nights?"

Omar Yussef gave a slow, hesitant shake of his head. "It must have something to do with the secret account details."

The police chief's leer became a scowl. "Three hundred million dollars."

"Does that sum of money make your diabetes feel more or less troublesome?" Omar Yussef laughed.

"It makes me want to throw up. That was our money." Khamis Zeydan pointed toward the houses of Nablus in the valley. "Their money."

"What would you do for it?"

Khamis Zeydan grimaced. "You want to know if I'd kill for it, schoolteacher? Killing's not always so difficult, when the cause is just."

"Are there things more shameful than killing?" Omar Yussef asked. What did his friend's file contain that would still shame this acknowledged killer? *Something worse than murder*, he thought.

Khamis Zeydan watched the Samaritan village grow closer. "Are you intending to drive all the way in second gear?" he said, turning a hostile frown on Omar Yussef. "Or are you just trying to annoy me?"

Omar Yussef shifted awkwardly into third gear and the jeep picked up pace. He tensed his shoulders, struggling to hold the next curve, then he braked and let the jeep creep slowly along the ridge.

"The account numbers and passwords—that's what

Kanaan must have received from Ishaq," Omar Yussef said. "Hamas got the dirt files. Ishaq got the scroll. Kanaan got the money, or at least the details of how to lay his hands on it."

"Very neat. Everybody's happy."

"So why is Ishaq dead?" Omar Yussef thumped his fist against the steering wheel. "Kanaan was *supposed* to get the money. But he didn't. The woman from the World Bank said she hadn't traced any transactions indicating that such a sum of money had been moved. Ishaq must have held out on him, so Kanaan killed Ishaq."

"He murdered his boyfriend?" Khamis Zeydan shook his head. "I'm prepared to believe almost anything about that bastard, but would he kill a kid he loved?"

"For three hundred million dollars? That's real money, even to one of the richest men in Palestine."

Khamis Zeydan raised his eyebrows.

"Ishaq said something to his wife about burying the financial details behind the temple, and he told the American from the World Bank that he had put the documents where anyone could find them," Omar Yussef said. "Maybe they're hidden on Mount Jerizim. Up there. Where Ishaq's body was discovered." He pointed toward the gray, square stones of the Byzantine fortress over-looking the Eternal Hill, the rock at the center of the ancient Samaritan temple.

As the jeep entered the village, a teenager scratched his mis-shapen ears and stared at Omar Yussef, his mouth wide and dumb, a basketball jammed between his elbow and his ribs.

"We've got one day to figure this out," Omar Yussef said. "Or the World Bank is going to make this mess a problem for every Palestinian."

They came to the small park beside Roween's house. Charcoal blackened the rows of concrete flame pits, still smoking from the Passover feast, and the dry grass had been shredded by the feet of celebrating Samaritans.

Omar Yussef let the engine stall and stepped onto the curb in the silent village. When he swallowed, the movement of his Adam's apple seemed loud in his throat.

A resonant thump cut the quiet. The boy with the strange ears shambled down the road. Every few paces he bounced his basketball, clutched it with both hands, and pulled it to the side of his head. Omar Yussef listened: the ball made a shadowy metallic chime after the deeper impact. The boy bellowed, frustrated that he couldn't grab the ball quickly enough to hear that high note close to his ear. *He senses that it would be beautiful*, Omar Yussef thought.

He lifted a hand and called to the boy: "If you please."

The boy held his basketball in front of his thighs. He slumped his shoulders and stared at Omar Yussef, his head twitching and his jaw hanging low.

"Where is the house of Jibril the priest, my boy?" Omar Yussef stepped closer.

The boy jerked his eyeballs up into his head and made a choking sound.

"Abu Ramiz, remind me not to marry my grandsons to my granddaughters," Khamis Zeydan said, pointing a finger at the boy.

The teenager's head jerked to the side. Omar Yussef felt a burst of pity for the kid, playing alone on this quiet mountaintop. It made him angry with Khamis Zeydan. "If what you say about your family relations is true, no one will care to ask your opinion on the matter of marriage," he said. He put his hand on the boy's shoulder, bent close to his face and spoke gently. "Clever boy, the house of Jibril the priest?"

The boy bounced his ball and shuffled toward a white house with pink window frames on the corner of the street. Omar Yussef followed him, smelling urine and stale sweat. At the lacquered cherrywood door, the boy put his ball under one arm and shoved down on the handle. He went inside, leaving the door ajar.

Omar Yussef waited in the shadeless street. He mopped the back of his neck with his handkerchief and glanced at Khamis Zeydan. "I apologize for my temper, Abu Adel," he said. "If I weren't a schoolteacher, perhaps I wouldn't care. But I've been around so many children in my time, I hate to see them mocked. I know how much they suffer."

"I've lived in a world of men," Khamis Zeydan said. "We didn't have our children with us when we were on operations in Europe or during the war in Lebanon. I never learned the first thing about kids. Maybe that's why mine hate me."

"Wasn't it a world of women, too? Liana was there, after all."

"No, I never understood women. Least of all Liana."

The boy loped out of the house onto the pavement, head down. He bounced his ball and grabbed for it, then he ran between Omar Yussef and Khamis Zeydan and disappeared into the trees beyond the park. Omar Yussef looked up at Roween's house. A curtain on the second floor fluttered, as though it had just been dropped by someone watching from the window. He kept his eye on it, until the curtain was still.

A sturdy woman in a long red embroidered gown appeared at the door of the priest's house. The skin of her fat, wrinkled face was the color of wet sand. She lifted her arm for them to enter.

The sun filtered through light-weight pink curtains in the reception room. Along the wall, black-and-white photographs of white-bearded men wearing the tarboosh of the priesthood stared down. The earliest portraits were distinguished by the priests' lack of spectacles, but all the men looked otherwise alike—high foreheads, long noses, innocent eyes.

Omar Yussef heard Jibril approach, his legs swinging against the loose skirts of his robe.

The priest took Omar Yussef's hand in both of his own. "Greetings, *pasha*."

"Double greetings."

"You are with your family and as if in your own home," Jibril said. The top of the light cotton robe he wore next to his skin was ripped from the neck to the breastbone—a sign of mourning for his son. He smiled restrainedly and extended the same greeting to Khamis Zeydan.

"Are you also a policeman?" he asked.

Khamis Zeydan's eyes swung toward Omar Yussef, who cleared his throat, uneasily. "I'm the police chief in Bethlehem," Khamis Zeydan said.

"Welcome." The priest swept his hand above the couch, as though spreading a silk upon it. He sat in an armchair that commanded the room. "Welcome to our village."

"I'm sorry for the loss of your son," Khamis Zeydan said. "May Allah be merciful upon him. If that's what you say in condolence. You Samaritans, I mean. Pardon me."

"It's an acceptable wish. May you be granted a long life."

The priest fingered his robe. "It has been an exhausting week. We must mourn my son Ishaq for seven days, as is our tradition. But we also had to celebrate our Passover festival."

"We saw the rites," Omar Yussef said. "It was very interesting."

The priest pulled his beard. "I admit, this was a difficult festival for our people, because of the murder," he said, softly. "But I'm pleased you found it of interest."

The thickset woman entered with two tiny coffee cups, breathing loudly through her wide nostrils like a heavy sleeper. Omar Yussef and Khamis Zeydan each drank a bitter slug. The woman looked at the priest, who closed his eyes briefly and shook his head. She shut the door behind her.

"Do you have developments to tell me about?" Jibril asked.

Omar Yussef frowned.

"About the investigation into the death of Ishaq?" the priest went on. "Did you not come here to tell me you have found the killer?"

"I'm sorry to say that we're far from that stage, Your Honor," Omar Yussef said. "We have some further questions which we believe are important to the progress of the investigation."

Jibril nodded slowly.

Omar Yussef sat forward. "The scroll that was returned on the same night as Ishaq's death—"

"The Abisha Scroll."

"Yes. Tell me exactly how it was returned to you?"

"I found it on the steps of the synagogue."

"Was there any message attached?"

"Nothing."

246

"Isn't it odd that such a valuable object should be placed there, where anyone could have picked it up?"

"But no one else could have found it. You've seen that the doors are set back some distance from the street. No one goes up the steps, unless it's one of us on our way to the synagogue, and they'd almost always be accompanied by me, because I'm the only one with a key."

"Even so, it seems a strange way to return the scroll."

The priest poked his tongue into his cheek and rolled it around.

"Was there any damage to the Abisha?" Omar Yussef asked.

"Thanks to Allah, no. I examined it thoroughly."

"Where is the scroll now?"

"After the Passover celebration here on Jerizim, I returned it to the safe in our synagogue."

"When we were together in the synagogue, I believe you told me that most of your people's important historical documents are kept here in your house."

"One of the leading priests traditionally safeguards these documents in his home."

"May we see them?"

The priest gripped the side of his armchair, pushing himself to his feet. Omar Yussef and Khamis Zeydan followed him into a spartan study, darkened by rolling blinds lowered halfway to block the bright morning sun. Against the nearest wall was a desk, its surface covered in brown leather nicked with light scratches. Across the room, a tall wooden cabinet displayed a series of tubular casings behind glass doors.

Omar Yussef put his face close to the glass. His breath misted it. "These are amazing," he said.

"We keep twenty-six copies of the Books of Moses here," Jibril said. "This one is the oldest, from the fifteenth century."

Omar Yussef followed the priest's gesture. The Torah was encased in a tube of goatskin about eighteen inches in length. The handles at the top were of tarnished silver and the front of the case was decorated with a silver panel molded to its curve. Omar Yussef looked more closely and tapped the glass. "This silver is embossed with the same image of the ancient temple as the Abisha Scroll," he said.

"The scrolls themselves are from different historical periods, but it's possible that the cases were made and decorated around the same time," the priest said.

"Has there ever been an attempt to steal these scrolls?"

Jibril shook his head. "The Abisha is much more valuable. That's why we keep it in the safe at the synagogue, rather than here in my home."

Omar Yussef tapped his finger against the glass once more. "Before he died, Ishaq said something to his wife that I think might be important."

The priest regarded Omar Yussef expectantly.

"He told her he was involved in something very dangerous. So dangerous that he wanted to bury it behind the temple and forget about it." Omar Yussef looked at the monumental towers of the temple on the weathered panel encasing the scroll. "Those were his precise words, according to his wife."

Jibril puffed out his cheeks. "What does that mean?" he said, slowly.

"I hoped you might have an idea." Omar Yussef watched the priest run a hand through his short beard and shake his head. "Roween said you argued with Ishaq over something immediately before his death. What was the argument about?"

"It's not appropriate for me to say bad things about my son after his death."

"Why does the argument reflect badly on Ishaq?"

"To curse his father is a shameful thing."

"He cursed you? Why?"

The priest moved toward the window. He yanked on the chord, pulling the blind open. Omar Yussef blinked in the strong light.

"I told him to divorce Roween," Jibril said.

"Were they unhappy?"

"I wanted a grandson."

"Ishaq was your only son. But you told me you have two daughters. Are they childless?"

The priest shook his head. "You Arabs have a saying: 'The son of a son is dear. The son of a daughter is a stranger.' The male line is most important. You understand that."

"I understand that this is what convention dictates, Your Honor, but I can't agree with you," he said.

"Easy for you to say," Khamis Zeydan said. "You only have sons."

Omar Yussef looked with irritation at his friend. He turned back to the priest. "You argued with Ishaq. Did he refuse to end his marriage?"

"He refused." Jibril leaned his face on the windowpane, squinting into the sunlight.

"Because he loved Roween?" Omar Yussef stepped toward Jibril in the corner. "Or because he knew a change of wife wouldn't make him any more likely to father a child?"

The priest straightened quickly to his full six feet and raised his chin. He glared at Omar Yussef.

"You know what I mean, don't you?" Omar Yussef said.

Jibril slackened his fingers and let the blind rattle down. In the sudden darkness, the priest's voice was raw and dry. "Roween is a very plain girl. If Ishaq had a more beautiful wife, he might not have become a *Louti*, a sodomite," he said.

"How harshly did you criticize him?" Omar Yussef moved close to the priest. He smelled raw onion on the man's breath. "Did you tell him you hated what he was? Did he blame you for his unhappiness? For making him live on this lonely hilltop with a wife to whom he could never be a real husband?"

"I'm a priest of our people." Jibril's voice was quiet. "I'm a symbol. My family must be above reproach."

"So you made him return from Paris. Don't you think he might have been happy there? In the liberal West, he might have found love."

"What kind of love? A filthy, sinful love."

"You made him pay a fine to rejoin the community. You made him come back to this remote, conservative place, where he would be isolated. Where he would fall under the spell of the only other cosmopolitan character around."

"What're you talking about? Whom?"

"Amin Kanaan."

"What does this have to do with Kanaan? Ishaq did some work for him, that's all."

Khamis Zeydan snorted. "Hard work for you or I, maybe. But quite to Ishaq's taste, it seems."

The priest shook his head, his misty eyes rolling.

"If it were Roween's fault that they had no children,

everyone would expect Ishaq to divorce her. But he refused to end the marriage. No divorce and no kids: people in the village would have realized Roween wasn't the cause of the childlessness." Omar Yussef raised his voice. "Did Ishaq tell you about his secret life? Did you kill him because of that? Because of the scandal there would be if people found out that the priest's son was gay, that he was having an affair with a powerful businessman?"

Jibril's slender shoulders shook. "It wasn't that way," he said. "I loved him." His words became a moan and his legs gave way. He slipped down the wall onto his haunches and crouched with his hand on his forehead. His other hand gathered the skirts of his robe and twisted them.

Chapter 27

The lonely teenager bounced his basketball somewhere behind Roween's house. Omar Yussef leaned on the police jeep. Khamis Zeydan limped to his side. "You seem to be leaving some tearful scenes behind you today."

"These have been painful conversations," Omar Yussef said. "My head's killing me." He stretched across the front of the jeep and dropped his forehead to the hood. The metal was hot in the early afternoon sunshine. *By the time the sun rises this high tomorrow, I must have my hands on those account details, or I won't be the only Palestinian with a headache*, he thought.

He looked up at the sun. "Even people driven to suicidal despair are clear-minded enough to climb to the fourth story before they end it all," he said. "I feel like I'm throwing myself again and again from a ground-floor window. I get hurt, but I can't make it count."

"I've always warned you that a detective needs to be hard," Khamis Zeydan said. "You have to be able to manipulate people, to make them like you, hate you, fear you. But you should be dispassionate. Don't feel what they feel."

"How can I fail to feel the anguish of Liana and this

priest?" Omar Yussef inclined his head toward the house with the pink window frames. "That'd be inhuman."

"Murder is inhuman." The police chief picked a strand of tobacco off his lip. "You need to feel the inhumanity, so that you can walk beside the murderer and read his mind."

Omar Yussef shook his head. "You're forgetting that passion and love might figure in it. I prefer to enter the head of the killer by feeling those emotions, rather than hate and violence."

The boy with the basketball loped around a corner. When he saw Omar Yussef, he halted with the ball at his ear and his feet wide apart in the middle of the road.

Omar Yussef approached him and beckoned. The boy didn't move. Omar Yussef sweated as he shuffled along the empty street. From the corner of his eye, he caught another movement in the curtain behind Roween's window.

"Clever boy," he said, "where is the house of the man who looks after the visitor center on top of the mountain?"

The boy stared and rolled his eyes.

"A fat man." Omar Yussef held his hands far in front of his belly, puffed out his cheeks and waddled from side to side. The boy sucked in his chin and wagged his head. *He's laughing*, Omar Yussef thought. "A fat man who wears a cap with the name of his cigarettes on it."

The boy moved along the street, the ball tucked beneath his arm. Khamis Zeydan limped up beside Omar Yussef. "If you're intending to shoot some baskets with this kid, I warn you my leg's in no state for me to jump," he said.

"I imagine you'd offset your handicap by playing dirty," Omar Yussef said.

The boy came to an alley between two squat apartment blocks and pointed into the darkness.

"Thank you, clever boy," Omar Yussef said.

The boy headed toward the park, tossing the ball awkwardly in the air and jerking forward at the waist to catch it, his arms sagging each time as though it were a tremendous weight.

Omar Yussef moved into the dark alley. The breeze cooled him now that he was out of the sun. Behind one of the apartment blocks, a lurid green awning flapped lightly over a yard filled with junk. Against the bare cinderblock wall of a shed, the frame of an old Japanese motorbike leaned, stripped of its parts like desert carrion, the springs cutting through its dusty seat. A blackened oil drum, punctured to ventilate a fire during colder months, stood beside an upended ceramic sink and a mattress rotten with mold. In a worn leather armchair, the caretaker who had found Ishaq's body snoozed with his cap over his eyes. His dirty white undershirt had slipped up over his belly and the sweat shone on his hairy stomach.

Khamis Zeydan flicked his cigarette. The butt landed on the undershirt and smoldered. The caretaker came upright with a gasp, swatting the cigarette away. When he saw the policeman's uniform, he gripped the arms of his chair and dropped his jaw.

"Evening of joy," Omar Yussef said.

"Evening of light, *ustaz*," the man mumbled.

"I brought a senior colleague with me." He gestured to Khamis Zeydan. "He's a brigadier."

The caretaker swallowed hard and bowed to the policeman.

"Welcome, *pasha*," he said. Khamis Zeydan stared at him without expression.

Omar Yussef stepped forward quickly and looked down at the caretaker. The man's eyes opened wide with surprise. "You lock that place every night?" He lifted a finger toward the summit of Mount Jerizim, visible over the tin roof of the shed.

"That's right," the caretaker said.

"You lock the gate by the parking lot?"

"That's the only entrance, *ustaz*."

"Who has the key?"

"Only me."

"Ishaq's body wasn't there when you locked up in the evening, but you found it in the morning."

The caretaker nodded dumbly. Khamis Zeydan took a small step toward him and the fat man pressed himself deep into the cracked leather of his armchair.

"So how did the body get there?"

"I don't know, *ustaz*."

"Whoever took the body to the mountain must have had the key."

"No, that's not possible."

"Unless they had your help."

The caretaker removed his baseball cap and wiped his bald head with his forearm. He looked at the front of the cap. Sweat soaked the band. He ran a hairy finger across the logo of the cheap Israeli cigarettes. "There's a path in the pines beyond the village. It goes through a hole in the fence behind the fortress."

"What's the point of locking the gates, if there's a hole in the fence?"

"No one knows about the hole in the fence, except us. Anyway there's nothing up there to steal."

"Who's *us?*"

The caretaker bit his bottom lip. "The people from the village."

"The Samaritans?"

The caretaker kept his eyes on Khamis Zeydan. The police chief shuffled closer and stroked the leather glove on his prosthetic hand.

Omar Yussef moved closer, too. "Ishaq was taken up to the peak of the mountain after he died, or he was killed there. But he certainly didn't go through the gate, because it was locked. He must have entered through the hole in the fence—a hole known only to the Samaritans."

"So the body must have been taken there by a Samaritan." Khamis Zeydan smiled. "That narrows things down."

"A Samaritan would never defile our holy place that way."

Omar Yussef thought for a moment. "Unless he was doing it for the good of the Samaritan people," he said.

"How could a murder be good for us?" The caretaker raised his arms. The dark hair in the pits glistened with sweat.

Omar Yussef watched the man closely. "Who's up there now?"

"No one." The caretaker opened his palms. "I have to take a break sometime, don't I?"

"We may be back to talk to you again."

The fat man bobbed his head. "Welcome, *ustaz.* Welcome, *pasha.*" They left him examining the cigarette burn on his undershirt.

When they reached the street, the police chief's upper lip curled. He lifted a thumb and gestured back down the alley. "My dear father used to say, 'When the wolf comes, the guard dog disappears for a shit.'" He turned to Omar Yussef. "Convenient that he wasn't around when the murder occurred, eh?"

Omar Yussef scratched his cheek thoughtfully. He led Khamis Zeydan toward the jeep. "Ishaq told his wife he wanted to bury the dangerous thing he was dealing with behind the temple. That must have been the account details. I think he meant that he hid them up there on Mount Jerizim."

"Behind the temple? What does that mean?"

"The temple of the Samaritans once stood at the summit of this mountain. We have to look there."

"You wanted to climb up high enough that falling would be fatal. Maybe you found the right spot. The only place higher than that temple is heaven."

The distant sound of rifle fire disturbed the silence of the village. "The entertainment started early today," Khamis Zeydan said.

Omar Yussef blinked into the vivid blue sky. The gunfire was ugly and incongruous on the quiet mountaintop.

A deeper sound punctuated the cracking of the rifles. Omar Yussef brought his eyes down to the street. The boy with the misshapen ears caught his basketball as it rebounded from the side wall of Roween's house. He stopped and watched Omar Yussef, then threw once more at the wall. He grabbed the ball and made his way through the flame pits, halting to stare at Omar Yussef before moving on again.

Omar Yussef looked at Khamis Zeydan, lifted his chin

toward the boy, and headed after him. The police chief sighed and followed.

Thin smoke rose from the coals at the bottom of the pits where the Samaritans had made their sacrifice. The air was thick with the aroma of lamb fat. Fed by the grease, it might take days for the fires to burn themselves out.

The boy led them to a stand of trees at the edge of the park. The smell of the sacrifice mingled with the sauna scent of pines in the sun. Their footsteps crunched the carpet of fallen needles.

A figure in a blue gown watched them from a small glade. In the clearing, Roween caressed the boy's cheek and tidied his hair. Sweat glowed along the fringe of darker brown skin edging her lips and in the fine auburn hairs that spread onto her cheeks. She pulled back into a shadowed corner and sat on a rock.

"He's my brother," she said to Omar Yussef, with her hand on the boy's arm. "Ishaq was very close to him." She whispered in the kid's ear and he loped through the trees toward the village.

Omar Yussef watched him go and wondered at the bond between the homosexual, his retarded brother-in-law, and his stumpy, ill-favored wife. The misfits had shared some sort of tenderness in a community bound by rough convention.

Khamis Zeydan positioned himself on a rock with his back to the clearing, guarding the approach.

Roween turned a faint smile of conspiracy to Omar Yussef. *This woman has her secrets*, he thought. *Ishaq may not have been the husband she bargained for, but they were joined in some kind of love and they shared things no one else knew.*

"Is this the way to the gap in the fence? To get onto the mountaintop when the gate is locked?" he asked.

"The path starts here. But you can take the road to the very upper edge of the village and join it there, to shorten your walk." Roween looked quickly back toward the Samaritan houses and rubbed the sweat from her lip. "You were at the home of Jibril the priest."

Omar Yussef remembered the movement of her curtain as he had entered the priest's house. "We talked about Ishaq," he said, "and the return of the Abisha Scroll."

"What did you learn?" Roween rolled her tongue in her cheek.

"I discovered that Samaritan priests are no more likely than Muslim sheikhs to confront the hardest truths. Am I about to discover that Samaritan women will only hold back their full knowledge for so long, once they see that they're talking to a genuine friend?"

Roween smirked with one side of her mouth. "*Ustaz*, Ishaq was in between Kanaan and Hamas. They both wanted something that only he could get for them."

"Ishaq obtained scandal files on top Fatah men from Kanaan and gave them to Hamas."

Roween nodded.

"Hamas gave Ishaq the Abisha Scroll, which they had stolen, and he passed it on to the priest," Omar Yussef continued. "Ishaq had the details of the old president's secret accounts and he was supposed to give them to Kanaan, in return for the files."

"But he didn't."

Omar Yussef heard the pine needles crackling as Khamis Zeydan rose. *Roween has caught his interest*, he thought.

259

"Ishaq was killed because he held onto the account details." Omar Yussef took out his handkerchief and wiped his face. The cloth came away gray from the smoke by the flame pits. "He must have known it was dangerous to keep those documents."

"The priest told him not to give them to Kanaan."

"Jibril? His father?"

"He wanted the scroll *and* the old president's money," Roween said.

Khamis Zeydan stepped to the middle of the clearing. "The priest got the scroll. Awwadi got the scandal files. But Kanaan didn't get the account documents. It's as we thought: Kanaan's the disappointed party. There's your killer."

Omar Yussef scratched his chin. "Did Kanaan kill Ishaq, Roween?"

"Never. I'm sure of it. Kanaan loved Ishaq very dearly. He always helped Ishaq and promoted him. I can't imagine him turning against someone so close to him."

Khamis Zeydan rubbed his fingers against his thumb, his hand in a loose fist. "Three hundred million dollars would turn love into hate, don't you think?"

"Kanaan isn't short of money, but he didn't have anyone else like Ishaq," Roween said.

"How did Ishaq's father have such power over him?" Omar Yussef asked. "Couldn't Ishaq have simply said that it would be too risky to hold onto the account documents?"

Roween grimaced. "When Ishaq came back from Paris, he was forced to be very contrite before the village elders, so that they'd reverse their decision to expel him from our people. It was humiliating, because they referred to his—his proclivity in a disdainful way. I think Jibril may have threatened to make him appear before the elders once more."

"What about you?"

"Me?"

"Would Jibril have made you go before the elders?" Omar Yussef averted his eyes. "To testify that Ishaq was unable to perform the duties of a husband."

Roween dropped her chin to her chest. *She hadn't considered that,* Omar Yussef thought. *Did Ishaq risk everything to protect his wife?* Roween stared at Omar Yussef with her eyes wide and aghast. "I would've lied for him," she said.

"In the event of his death, Ishaq ordered that half a million dollars be sent to a man named Suleiman al-Teef at a bank in Nablus. Is that one of his friends in the Fatah Party?"

Roween looked away. "He can't be anyone important. Half a million isn't much compared to three hundred million, is it?"

An appalled dreaminess had descended upon her. "I'd lie for him," she repeated, and she stood and went through the trees toward the village.

Omar Yussef watched Roween emerge into the sunshine and pick her way between the smoking pits. She held the skirt of her gown above her thick, pale ankles, as she moved over the uneven ground. She came to the yard behind her home and disappeared through a green metal door.

Omar Yussef crossed the clearing and leaned against a tree. He dabbed the back of his neck with his soiled handkerchief. "I'm hot," he said. "I think we ought to go somewhere with air-conditioning."

"What are you talking about?" Khamis Zeydan pointed

up the slope through the trees. "Aren't we going to search the mountaintop for the financial documents?"

"That could take hours. We don't have time for it now, not after what Roween told us. We need to take care of something more urgent. Then we can come back here." Omar Yussef raised his handkerchief to his sweating forehead. "I think Liana was lying when she said Kanaan was down in Nablus. We didn't pass him on the road up from town. I think he's in his mansion and this time he'll see us, because we know why he didn't get the account documents from Ishaq. We need to press him on this."

"Don't make *him* cry, too. Your weepy scenes have already exhausted my compassion today." Khamis Zeydan screwed up his face and limped through the trees.

The gunfire intensified in the valley below. It was late afternoon. The nightlife of Nablus was gearing up.

Chapter 28

At the door to Amin Kanaan's mansion, Khamis Zeydan muttered a curse and expectorated. Omar Yussef frowned at the oyster globule, gleaming in the sun. A servant hurried onto the gaudy fan of marble steps, startled and outraged, as though the phlegm had landed on his cheek. *It may have been better to leave Abu Adel in the jeep,* Omar Yussef thought. *My friend might be saving some spit for Kanaan. Even so, I need the security of the gun on his hip to enter the home of the man who tried to have me killed.*

"Tell your boss we know exactly how Ishaq let him down," Omar Yussef said.

The servant sniffed and showed them across the hall, its polished floor warmed to a pale coral with the first glow of sundown through the tall windows. In the salon where they had sat with Liana, they waited for her husband.

Khamis Zeydan paced across an antique Tabriz rug and opened the glass doors. The distant shooting sounded louder. "Screw your mother," he said, kicking the wall lightly.

Omar Yussef twisted in his gilt armchair. "Are you going to behave yourself? Because if you can't keep a lid on your anger, you'd better wait outside."

"I wouldn't give him the pleasure."

"What pleasure?"

"Of seeing me cowering in his garden."

"You'd prefer him to see you lose your cool?"

"I won't lose my cool."

Omar Yussef stared at the police chief. Khamis Zeydan waved his hand impatiently and lit a Rothmans.

The servant entered and held the door open for Amin Kanaan. He came smoothly over the Persian carpets in a pair of claret suede moccasins, wearing a sky blue Italian shirt with the top three buttons open and the collar high at the sides of his neck. He extended a soft handshake to Omar Yussef.

"Before we begin to talk, I warn you that I already know you aren't really an employee of the World Bank, *ustaz*." Kanaan wagged a scolding finger at Omar Yussef.

"I didn't say I was. You neglected to ask the right question."

Kanaan smiled. He circled the rococo sofa to greet Khamis Zeydan, spreading his shoulders and pushing out his broad chest. "My dear Abu Adel, welcome to my home," he said. "You're in your own home and as if you were with your own family."

Khamis Zeydan's eyes dropped to the intricate palmettes on the rug. "Your family is with you," he whispered, as though the formulaic words were jagged in his throat.

Kanaan clutched the police chief's shoulders and gave him three kisses. He moved to the sofa and reclined. "Please sit down, Brother Abu Adel," he said.

"I'll stand." Khamis Zeydan played with the handle on the open glass door and held his head just outside, as though to escape the aroma of wealth on his old rival's body.

"You always did do things your own way," Kanaan said.

"I disagree. I took orders. I did what the Old Man told me to do."

"Come on, he didn't issue orders. He gave hints. You had to interpret them, just as I did. It's what made him so treacherous. It's how he kept all of us in his power. You never knew when he was going to pull the rug from under you and deny everything. He did it to you in Damascus once, don't you remember?" Kanaan turned to Omar Yussef. "Our friend Abu Adel was sold out to the Syrians, who put a bullet in his back."

"He told me all about that," Omar Yussef said.

Kanaan glanced at Khamis Zeydan. "Did he?" he said, slowly. "Did he indeed?"

"We're not here to reminisce," Omar Yussef said. "I have some questions."

"I thought you told my servant that you had some information. But, anyway, wait for the coffee, *ustaz* Abu Ramiz," Kanaan said. The servant returned with a silver tray and three small cups, each painted with a golden cartouche.

Omar Yussef took his coffee. "May Allah bless your hands," he said to the servant.

"Blessings," the servant said.

Omar Yussef turned formally to Kanaan. "May there always be coffee in your home," he said.

Kanaan watched Khamis Zeydan receive his cup, balancing the saucer between thumb and forefinger. "There certainly will be, *ustaz*," Kanaan said. He kept his eye on Khamis Zeydan, smiling at the police chief's reluctant acceptance of his hospitality. "You can be sure of that."

By the window, a pedestal of jade-colored marble rose to the height of Khamis Zeydan's chest. It was designed to hold a bust, but it was empty. He laid his coffee cup on it.

"Your double health, Abu Adel," Kanaan said, lifting his own cup. "Welcome."

Khamis Zeydan shifted from foot to foot.

Kanaan licked his lips with pleasure at the policeman's discomfiture. "Abu Adel—"

"Fuck your mother," Khamis Zeydan yelled. "I won't touch your coffee. I won't pretend I don't wish you were dead."

"And I thought you came here to accuse me of killing Ishaq," Kanaan said. "Instead I discover that perhaps you've come here to kill me."

"Don't be ridiculous, Your Honor Amin," Omar Yussef said. He raised a finger at Khamis Zeydan. "Be careful, Abu Adel."

"Ridiculous? I wouldn't be the first one to die because your friend decided to settle a score," Kanaan said. "This fellow was the party's top assassin for two decades. He hates me because I know him for who he really is."

"What do you mean?" Omar Yussef said.

Khamis Zeydan gripped the head of the marble pedestal and stared fiercely at the tiny coffee cup in its center.

"Since he returned from exile to live in Bethlehem, I've kept an eye on Abu Adel. I had to. I never knew when he might try something against me, given our history." Kanaan sneered. "He portrays himself as an honorable policeman. But men like him gave Palestinians a bad reputation, with their terrorist attacks all over Europe and their airplane hijackings and their war in Lebanon."

Khamis Zeydan backhanded his coffee cup off the pedestal. It smashed onto the floor. "If it was down to me, there'd have been peace decades ago," he shouted. "But people like you made too much money out of the chaos, the lack of rules, the opportunities for corruption. You kept me fighting and others dying, so you could exploit our people and get rich."

"But we both got what we wanted out of it in the end. I got rich, and you got excitement, the chance to be a tough guy." Kanaan raised his eyebrows mockingly. "We both got what we wanted."

Khamis Zeydan lurched toward Kanaan and grabbed the sofa. Kanaan jerked back, expecting a blow.

"No, we didn't," Khamis Zeydan said. His breath came loud through his nose. He leaned close to Kanaan, his lips spread, showing his teeth, like a dog preparing to pounce. "I didn't get what *I* wanted."

Kanaan composed himself. "I suppose you didn't," he grinned.

Liana, Omar Yussef thought. *My friend didn't get her, and now it seems to him she was all he ever wanted.* "Abu Adel, perhaps it would be best if you waited in the garden," he said.

Khamis Zeydan rolled his pale eyes. He slammed the French doors behind him and hobbled across the lawn to the gazebo.

Omar Yussef drained his cup and laid it on the Armenian tiles of the coffee table. He wiped the dregs from his mustache. "Abu Adel is a dear friend and I don't think it's fair of you to continue this animosity from so long ago," he said.

Kanaan put his hand to his heart. "Isn't it your friend who harbors the grudge?"

Omar Yussef leaned his elbows on his knees. "You sent Mareh to kill me, but you're lucky that I'm more forgiving than Abu Adel. I'm not after you. I have a different aim. I want to know the truth about you and Ishaq."

Kanaan shrugged.

"Aren't you going to protest that you already told me the truth?" Omar Yussef said. "That you're offended I should suspect you of covering something up?"

"I have nothing to hide," Kanaan said. "You're welcome to ask me whatever you want."

"You gave Ishaq files of dirt on all the top Fatah people," Omar Yussef said. "In return he was supposed to give you the information on the Old Man's secret bank accounts. But he backed out."

"That's not a question."

"Why did he back out?"

"I don't know."

"Did you ask the priest Jibril why the deal wasn't completed?"

Kanaan blinked and spoke slowly. "*Should* I ask him?"

"What did you want the money for?" Omar Yussef said.

"I don't understand your question. Does one need a reason to want money?"

"What I mean is, don't you already have plenty of it?"

"The money wasn't for me. I wanted it to go into the official Palestinian treasury, where the international donors intended for it to be in the first place."

"Do you think I'm naive enough to believe that?"

"After your last visit, I thought it best to learn more about you, *ustaz.*" Kanaan aimed his index finger at Omar Yussef. "First I discovered that you weren't with the World Bank. Then I heard that you have something of a troublesome background."

"What do you mean?" Omar Yussef felt a jolt of adrenaline.

What does this man know about me? He experienced a surge of guilt for things he knew he had done wrong and anger at false accusations that had been made against him over the years.

"You were fired from your job at a nice school. Why was that? Was it your alcoholism? Or did something happen with one of the pupils? For some men, a school is full of sexual temptation."

"How dare you."

"You had some trouble with the Jordanian authorities when you were a student radical, too, didn't you? Murder, wasn't it? You're probably going to tell me that the charges were dropped. But in an Arab country, with our corrupt justice systems, that doesn't exactly clear your name. I also gather you had some dubious connections in Damascus, when you were a student there."

"You're just rehashing old nonsense."

"Then why are your cheeks burning?" Kanaan stroked his gray sideburns. "Really, as you point out, I don't need this money for my personal use. I've made many millions in construction and banking. But the Palestinians are poor."

"Because of men like you."

Kanaan waved his hand as though wafting away a bad smell. "I wanted to collect all the money hidden around the world by the old president and use it to build hospitals and schools for our people. If you insist on seeing me as entirely selfish, then look at it this way: if I could help cleanse Palestine of corruption and build good infrastructure, international investors would put money into the economy and my holdings here would appreciate in value."

Omar Yussef dropped his gaze to his knuckles. *Have I been blinded to this man's better intentions by the animosity Khamis Zeydan feels for him? Perhaps he's telling me the truth now.*

"If I tried to put you out of the way, it was because I didn't know your objectives," Kanaan said. "You can't blame me for assuming that if you'd found the money you would have kept it for yourself, or for some faction allied to your friend Abu Adel. I already paid off everyone else who might have considered going after the money, because I wanted to make sure that I'd be the one to trace it. Then I planned to deposit it in the Palestinian treasury."

"If someone refused to be paid off, then you employed Mareh and his own special methods?"

"I used extreme measures, because the fate of our nation rests on the recovery of this money."

"How about Suleiman al-Teef? Did you buy him?"

"I don't know who that is."

"If this is true, why didn't you coordinate your search with Jamie King. The World Bank could've helped you."

"Foreigners like her just get in the way."

Omar Yussef flexed his fingers. "Ishaq took the dirt files. Then he failed to hand over the account documents?"

"Correct."

"So you killed him?"

Kanaan's eyelid fluttered and something beneath his suave calm quivered. "I could never have done such a thing. I loved him."

"You can't kill someone you love? Love's usually the most popular reason for murder."

Kanaan glanced out of the window toward the gazebo

where Khamis Zeydan sat, hunched and sullen. "Don't you think that if I was that kind of man I'd have killed other people who were close to me? Ishaq wasn't the first person I loved who betrayed me."

His wife, with the dashing young field officer who's now sulking in his garden, Omar Yussef thought. "Liana?"

"In Beirut, I had an understanding with her. We were promised to each other, though not formally engaged. Then I discovered that she had loved another man, too."

Kanaan took Liana as his wife even after that betrayal, Omar Yussef thought. *His attraction to her wasn't only a matter of sex. He loves her as if she were his own flesh.* Omar Yussef raised his head. *His own flesh.* "Ishaq was your son."

Kanaan's chin dipped like a man on the verge of sleep. "He was my son," he said. He pyramided his fingertips at the end of his clumsy, wide nose and closed his eyes. "Liana and I had relations before our marriage. You should have seen her, *ustaz.* She was brave and intelligent, the most beautiful woman in Beirut. Were you ever there?"

"Not since I was a student."

Kanaan smiled dreamily. "The spirit of Beirut back then swept me and Liana into each other's hearts. She rejected the conservative morality of our culture and even convinced me that I could join this rejection. She had spent time in Europe and seen how young couples lived there."

"You don't look like a hippie to me."

"We were radicals, not hippies. In those days, revolution was something creative and idealistic. Artists and theater people used to visit our headquarters. I met the great English actress Vanessa Redgrave more than once."

Omar Yussef rolled his eyes, but Kanaan appeared not to notice.

"No one knew who would be alive the next day. You could be killed by the Syrians, the Israelis, the Christian militias, the Shiite gangs, by one of the other Palestinian factions, or even by the Old Man himself." Kanaan gazed into the sun, glinting off the tall windows of his salon. "If you found someone who would love you, you loved her back with all the life you had, all the life that might be snuffed out the next day, the next hour."

Omar Yussef sneered. "Liana became pregnant."

"Shortly after we became engaged, I sent her to Nablus to have our baby," Kanaan said. "I had to get her out of Beirut, where all the other PLO people were, to avoid a scandal. She couldn't go to her family in Ramallah, because everyone knew her there. Nablus is my home. When she gave birth here, I paid the Samaritan priest to adopt the boy. I chose to hide my son with people so much on the fringe of the town that no one who knew me would ever discover the truth, but he would still be close enough that we could watch him grow up."

"Why didn't you go to live in Europe with him?"

"That's what Liana wanted. But I realized that it was only she who could live outside our people's morality and traditions. Only she could leave Palestinian society. I was too weak." The sickly yellow around Kanaan's irises glowed with desolation in the fading light. "After our marriage, it was too late to get the boy back without admitting what had happened. It would have been a dreadful slur on my wife's reputation, to have acknowledged that we had physical relations before our wedding."

Omar Yussef understood the dilemma. Many women had been killed for staining the honor of their families with even the suspicion of sex outside marriage, let alone an illegitimate birth. *Liana's family might have been a little more modern about it than that, but they could easily have disowned her,* he thought. *Certainly Kanaan's business career would have been destroyed by the scandal.*

"But I funded Ishaq's schooling and I promoted him in the party," Kanaan said. "How else do you think an obscure Samaritan kid became the financial adviser to our president? I propelled Ishaq as I would have my legitimate son."

Kanaan stared at the shining marble floor. For a moment, Omar Yussef wondered if he was still breathing, then the man covered his face with both hands and groaned. Omar Yussef knew that now, when Kanaan was weak, he had to push him. "Ishaq died as his biblical namesake Isaac was intended to die," he said.

"What do you mean?"

"Isaac was bound, ready for sacrifice, on the peak of the mountain where the temple would later be built. His father, the Prophet Ibrahim, or Abraham, as the Jews call him, was to carry out the killing."

"You think I'm Ibrahim? Ibrahim didn't kill Isaac in the end, and anyway that's just an old story." A wave of Kanaan's cologne floated across the coffee table to Omar Yussef. "Ishaq threatened to blackmail me if I made a fuss about him failing to give me the account documents."

"He put the bite on you?"

"What're you talking about?"

Omar Yussef thought of Nadia and her American detective story and he hid his smile behind his hand. "He threatened to reveal who his real parents were?"

273

Kanaan ran his fingers through his hair. "It would have destroyed my wife."

"And you?"

"By now I've made too much money for any dirt to stick. Too many bastards need me on their side. They stifle their moral outrage easily enough. But my wife is more vulnerable than I am. She couldn't have taken the scandal."

"How did you respond to Ishaq's blackmail?"

"I gave in. I agreed that he could keep the secret bank documents. I told him it would be dangerous for him to hold on to that information, that deadly people would discover the truth and force him to hand over the account details. I had paid people to leave the secret funds to me, but if I didn't get hold of the accounts quickly enough, those same people would consider the field open once more." Kanaan spread his hands wide and let them slap down onto his tastefully cut linen pants. "And of course they—whoever they are—found him and killed him."

"Who has the secret account details now?"

"I don't know. Whoever killed Ishaq, I suppose."

"And the files of dirt on the Fatah people?"

Kanaan smiled bitterly. "I reclaimed them."

"You saw no reason to be bound by your agreement with Ishaq once he was dead."

"I didn't receive what I was supposed to get out of the deal. I sent my people to Awwadi's place and took the files back."

"Why did you have Awwadi killed, too?"

"I only wanted the files. Mareh had some private reason for murdering Awwadi, so he killed him."

The quarrel over Awwadi's bride, Omar Yussef thought. He rubbed his chin. "Why didn't Ishaq stay in Paris?"

"He came back because he thought he was a Samaritan. He was lonely and he wanted to be with them. Even though he didn't have to hide his sexual proclivity in Europe, he didn't feel at home. A few weeks ago he discovered the truth about his birth and came here in a rage. He didn't look like himself at all." Kanaan winced. "There always used to be something in his eyes at times of action that suggested he enjoyed danger. But not then. His eyes were exploding. It terrified me."

Omar Yussef frowned and stroked his chin. "I know what you mean," he said. "How did Ishaq find out?"

"I assume the priest gave us away, because no one else knew. I told Ishaq I had kept his birth a secret for Liana's sake, but that only made him furious with her, too. The person we loved most in the world turned against us."

"That leaves you with only one person to love."

Kanaan flushed beneath his even tan. "I'll give you anything to keep this quiet."

"You're still worried about scandal? The boy is dead."

"I have to think about my wife. Ishaq's death has made her—" he looked for the right word "—fragile. I'll give you anything in my power."

Omar Yussef stood and stepped toward the French doors. *Why does everyone want to conspire with me?* he wondered. *Do I seem dishonest? Or am I their confessor, like the priests to whom Roman Catholics go for remission of their small, venial sins. A priest can't forgive mortal sins, though.* He tapped his knuckle softly on the glass. *Can I?*

Khamis Zeydan paced across the lawn with his back to the house. A hoopoe dipped its long, thin beak into the grass and came up with a worm. It skipped a few paces and

275

dropped the worm, picked it up again, extended its wings to show its black and white stripes, and flew into the branches of a sycamore.

Omar Yussef put his hand over his mouth and stroked his chin. He smiled at the stricken face of Amin Kanaan. "There *is* something I can think of that you can get for me," he said.

Chapter 29

O mar Yussef cut the engine and waited for something in the silence to ambush him. When Khamis Zeydan wheezed, he realized that they had both been holding their breath, anticipating the momentous discovery they hoped to make up the hill and fearful that they would find someone else, someone murderous, searching there too. Stepping out onto the dried pine needles around the jeep, he skirted the woods until he found the path to the Byzantine fort winding around a patch of rocks. Khamis Zeydan's pistol glinted in the moonlight.

"Put that gun away," Omar Yussef said. "We might walk into someone perfectly innocent and you'll have shot them before we get a chance to see who they are."

"I'll aim to wound," Khamis Zeydan whispered. "If there's anyone up there now, after the gates have been locked, I doubt that they're innocent."

"We'll probably be searching for hours for the place where Ishaq buried those secret documents. If you shoot at some shadow, the whole village will come and catch us. We won't be able to do this by day without being noticed, and tomorrow the World Bank cuts off its aid. We have to do this tonight. Don't blow it."

Khamis Zeydan puffed out his cheeks. He kept his gun hand raised, the barrel pointing at the branches above, and paced carefully ahead of Omar Yussef, as though he expected the ground beneath each advancing step to blow up.

They passed through the break in the fence and the pines started to thin. Stones, long tumbled from the old walls of the fortress, spread irregularly over the hillside like a shoreline wavering in the shifting moonlight.

"Can you make it up here with your foot in that condition?" Omar Yussef asked. "It looks like a rough climb over these fallen blocks."

"You'd prefer me to wait at the bottom for your corpse to come rolling down?" Khamis Zeydan shook his foot and slapped his thigh to get the blood moving.

"Since you put it that way, my brother," said Omar Yussef, "stick close."

He stepped onto one of the stones and saw that his leg shook with fear. His apprehension made him feel foolish. He was a schoolteacher, not a man of action like the policeman who walked behind him, pistol at the ready. Yet here he was, ascending a pile of ancient stones in the night, unsure of what awaited him at the end of his climb.

His ankle turned and his shoe slipped off. He winced, bending to pull it back on, and leaned against a stone to right himself. It was rough with lichen and the weathering of ages. "Now we both have a bad foot," he said.

"At least I had some fun boozing and eating badly to get mine into the condition it's in," Khamis Zeydan said.

"Aren't we having fun now?"

Khamis Zeydan bent low, the pistol still raised. "I'm

loving every minute." He smiled grimly. "I'm starting to hope there's actually someone up there."

"There isn't." Omar Yussef flexed his ankle. "The documents Ishaq hid are up there, somewhere near the flat stone where the ancient temple stood. That's all."

"It never pays to be surprised. Get yourself ready for a welcoming committee."

They climbed side by side over the stones. Omar Yussef bowed to use both hands where the slope was most acute. Khamis Zeydan kept his gun in his hand and balanced with his prosthetic limb. They moved quietly, though Omar Yussef thought their labored breathing might as well have been a shout in the hush around them. His pulse thundered in his neck like a Ramadan firecracker.

The spray of rocks on the hillside brought them to a rise at the foot of the fortress's walls. Beyond a soft dip in the ridge, the stone that had been at the center of the ancient Samaritan temple angled down the slope from the peak of the mountain, a silvery charcoal. At its center, a darker spot marked it. Omar Yussef squinted. The spot on the rock seemed to roll to one side. *Is that a shadow cast by the clouds passing across the moon?* he wondered. Something stretched out of the darkness at the center of the flat stone. It jerked upward, then it bent. It was an arm.

"Someone's there," Omar Yussef said.

They hurried over the grass toward the temple stone.

Omar Yussef stepped onto the holy rock and felt electricity rise through his feet and into his legs. The charge quickened his breath, squeezing his heart between two pounding fists of adrenaline.

The body moved again. An arm flapped, then collapsed with a crack of knuckles against the rock. The forearm, which fell out of a blue gown, was lightly covered in black hair. Omar Yussef went onto his knees and held the outstretched limb, rubbing its cold fingers between his hands.

"Roween, can you hear me?" he said.

The Samaritan woman opened one eye, as far as the contusion surrounding it would allow. A bloodied slash flayed her skin from the bone of her cheek and concealed the other eye. She sucked air desperately over smashed teeth. Her gown rode above her knees, showing her stocky legs, bruised and scratched. She exhaled and Omar Yussef thought it was the death rattle.

Khamis Zeydan turned a full circle. "There's no one around, as far as I can see," he said, holstering his pistol.

"Who did this to you, Roween?" Omar Yussef asked, squeezing her fingers.

Roween choked and dribbled blood from the corner of her mouth. "Abisha," she spluttered.

"The scroll? Did a man named Abisha do this?"

"Abisha." She gagged again and the force of her coughing almost brought her upright. She grabbed at a pain in her belly and rolled onto her side.

Omar Yussef felt moisture chill his face. He wiped the back of his hand across his cheek and it came away dark. Roween had coughed a spray of blood over him.

"Where are the account details?" Khamis Zeydan knelt beside the battered woman. His voice was harsh and clear. "Where are they?"

They're in the Abisha Scroll, Omar Yussef thought. *She*

knows we came here to find the secret bank documents. She's telling us Ishaq hid them inside the scroll's box. That's what he meant by 'behind the temple.' It has nothing to do with the location of the ancient temple. He meant the silver image of the temple decorating the Abisha's box. He lifted a hand to restrain Khamis Zeydan. "Let her rest," he whispered. "She's nearly gone."

Khamis Zeydan shook his head and leaned closer to Roween's face. "Where?" he said.

"Synagogue." Roween's voice was barely more than a breath. Her glassy eye fought to focus on Omar Yussef's face. He came closer, took his handkerchief from his pocket and wiped the blood from her cheek and mouth. "He knew," she said. "Kanaan."

"What? Kanaan knew what? That Ishaq was his son?" Omar Yussef whispered gently.

"He knew about Kanaan," she said.

"Ishaq knew he was the son of Kanaan?"

"Ask her about that other guy." Khamis Zeydan nudged Omar Yussef. "What's his name?"

"Roween, do you know who Suleiman al-Teef is?" Omar Yussef asked.

The woman's lip twitched, as though she wished to smile. "My brother," she murmured.

Omar Yussef thought of the handicapped boy bouncing his basketball alone and of the kind brother-in-law he had lost. Now he was to be robbed of the sister who had loved him.

Roween's eye closed. Her body convulsed and she grasped Omar Yussef's hand until he felt the bones in his fingers might shatter.

He looked helplessly at Khamis Zeydan and grabbed his friend's collar and pushed him close to the dying woman's face. "Can't we do something? You're always bragging about assassinations and battles," he wailed. "Haven't you ever tried to save someone's life? Can't you stop her bleeding?"

The police chief removed Omar Yussef's hand from his shirt and held it softly in his own. He stayed close to Roween's face, waiting for one final word.

The word didn't come. Khamis Zeydan closed his lips, as if to avoid inhaling Roween's dying breath. Omar Yussef traced his fingertips tenderly over the woman's scabby acne. A cloud shaded the moon and the bruises and cuts on her face became no more than shadows. She looked like a girl merely asleep.

He sobbed and laid Roween's hand at her side. The stone was still warm from the sunshine of the day, as he touched her fingers to it. He brought his handkerchief to his face, finding a segment not damp with Roween's blood, and rubbed at the tears of desperate tenderness in his eyes.

Down in Nablus, a machine gun rattled.

The schoolteacher gritted his teeth and screwed his burning eyes shut.

"Maybe the documents aren't hidden up here at all. Maybe they're at the synagogue," Khamis Zeydan said.

"I think that's what she wanted to tell us, yes," Omar Yussef sniffled. "Temple. Isn't that what the Jews call their synagogues? It could be the Samaritans use the same word for it. That might be what Ishaq meant. It's also where they keep the Abisha Scroll, remember. I think the documents could be hidden in the scroll, at the synagogue."

"She must have told someone else what Ishaq said, and they beat her to death because they thought she knew more."

"Maybe she's dead because she wouldn't tell them anything." Omar Yussef thought of the love there had been between Roween and Ishaq. It wasn't the usual attachment between a husband and wife. Omar Yussef wondered if Roween had actually been repulsed by the prospect of a husband's rough, scrambling attentions and had been happier with her sensitive partner, even if he wasn't what her family would've wanted for her.

"My brother," Khamis Zeydan said, with a gentle caress of Omar Yussef's shoulder.

Omar Yussef looked out from the mountaintop. The valley was unlit, as though Nablus was in hiding. But the guns ensured that it wasn't quiet.

He came to his feet. "Let's go," he said.

"To the synagogue? Down to Nablus?" Khamis Zeydan looked into the dark valley, listening to the gunfire.

"We can't wait until light. Whoever killed Roween may have the same information as us. They're probably on their way to the synagogue now. If we don't get there first, hundreds of millions of dollars that were supposed to improve the lives of our people will fall into the hands of the bastards who killed this woman."

Omar Yussef closed his eyes. In the wind along the ridge, he could still hear Roween's final breath.

Chapter 30

They knew they had missed the narrow road into Nablus, when the jeep hit deep tank tracks, throwing dust into the cab. "This must be the trail the Israelis use for their night raids," Khamis Zeydan said. "Turn off the headlights."

The jeep pitched on its squawking suspension over the scarred dirt road. Omar Yussef took the steep sections leaning back into his seat, his elbows locked and his foot shaking with strain on the brake. "I hope your diabetes isn't still acting up tomorrow," he said, "because I've done all the driving I can stand."

"If you get us through Nablus without running into an Israeli tank or a jeep full of Hamas gunmen, you won't have to drive any more, because I'll carry you around on my back all day out of gratitude," Khamis Zeydan said.

They came to the first silent white apartment blocks at the upper reaches of the town and soon were on a paved section of road. The driving was easier and Omar Yussef relaxed, until the shooting in the valley reminded him that he was heading into danger and operating on a tight deadline. He imagined the members of the World Bank board would be heading to dinner parties in Georgetown at that moment. When they reached their office in the morning, they'd cut his people's financial lifeline. He thought of Sami and Zuheir and Ramiz, of Nadia, of the better Palestine he wanted them to live in someday. *I won't fail them,* he thought.

Outside the Samaritan synagogue, Omar Yussef switched off the engine and listened. A car alarm wailed and a machine gun stammered in the casbah. Under the discordant sounds, he detected a breathless silence, like the energetic anticipation of a child behind a sofa in a game of hide and seek. The night was waiting for him. He narrowed his eyes. *I'm ready.*

Khamis Zeydan hobbled up the first flight of steps to the synagogue. Omar Yussef went beside him. He felt alert, youthful, determined.

The doorway of the synagogue was dark. Khamis Zeydan pulled his gun to shoot out the lock. Omar Yussef grabbed his wrist. The police chief hesitated, then holstered the pistol. Omar Yussef eased down on the door handle, felt the lock slip and drew the door back carefully. *Was it left unlocked by accident,* Omar Yussef wondered, *or is there someone inside?* Khamis Zeydan peered into the darkness within, frowning. He nodded and the two men entered.

The main hall was quiet and murky. The door to the staircase at the back of the room emitted a flickering light. Hurried footsteps ascended the stairs and a man came into the hall, his long robe and tarboosh silhouetted by the pale blue of the stairwell.

Omar Yussef snapped on the lights.

In the door to the stairway, Jibril Ben-Tabia blinked as

the fluorescent tubes shuddered to life. He clutched something to his chest, rolled in the folds of his robe, like a mother protecting her child. The shock of discovery registered for a moment, then the priest's old, lined face hardened into outrage.

"How dare you enter this building?" he shouted, raising a leathery finger toward Khamis Zeydan. "The security forces aren't allowed in here without a warrant."

"I'm not wearing a uniform, your honor," Omar Yussef said. "Do I need a warrant, too?"

"What do you want?"

"I see that you have the Abisha Scroll."

"You've come for our most priceless treasure?" The priest retreated toward the stairs. "You've come to steal it once again?"

Omar Yussef sneered. "We're not thieves and you didn't come here to protect the scroll."

"Don't you hear the gunfire? You Palestinians are having a civil war. Anything could happen in Nablus tonight. I came to take our precious relic back to the village on Mount Jerizim, where those swine won't be able to rob us of it."

"You came to search inside the scroll for three hundred million dollars," Omar Yussef said.

"What're you talking about?"

"Roween told you that Ishaq said he'd hidden those documents 'behind the temple,' didn't she. Perhaps at first you thought, as I did, that they were hidden on Mount Jerizim." Omar Yussef put his hands on his hips and leaned toward the priest. "You took Roween to the temple up there, because you thought she could show you the exact spot where Ishaq hid them."

"This is just empty talk."

"But she knew no more. You beat her and now she's dead, yet you learned nothing."

"She's dead?"

"Then, you remembered the silver decoration on the scroll's calfskin box, the image of the temple on the cover. You concluded that Ishaq hid the account details somewhere in the box or inside the scroll, when Nouri Awwadi returned the Abisha Scroll to him. You left Roween to die and came here to get the scroll."

The priest glanced at the Abisha, cradled in his arm. He ran his fingers over the raised depiction of the temple; his eyes closed and his face became enraptured, like a man exploring his lover's features in the dark. "I don't believe you," he said. "Roween isn't dead. You're trying to trick me."

Khamis Zeydan took a step toward the priest. "I don't care if you've killed all six hundred Samaritans, old man. I came for that scroll."

Jibril hugged the Abisha. "And *I* don't care if the entire world has to die, no one shall possess this scroll but my people."

"You admit it, then. You killed Roween." Omar Yussef stared angrily at the oblong box in the priest's arms. "After she told you what Ishaq had said, you continued to beat her, until you realized that was all she knew. But by then she was beyond saving."

Jibril smiled. "*Pasha*, it was you who told me what Ishaq said to Roween about the temple. I tried to force Roween to tell me even that much, but she kept her mouth shut."

"I told you?" Omar Yussef faltered. *When I was in the priest's house, did I tell him then?*

Jibril licked his upper lip. "If we're pointing fingers, then you killed her."

Khamis Zeydan stepped past his friend. "I've heard enough of your crap," he said to the priest. "Give me the scroll."

Jibril hurried to the head of the stairs. "I'll lock this door before you can get to me," he said, "and I'll destroy the secret documents rather than give them to you. You government people allowed us Samaritans to be forced out of our ancient neighborhood. I won't let your unclean fingers touch the Abisha Scroll or have the money."

Omar Yussef laid his hand on Khamis Zeydan's forearm. "Wait, Abu Adel, let's talk to him," he said.

Khamis Zeydan let Omar Yussef pass. The priest made to retreat once more, but Omar Yussef lifted his hands. "Your Honor, I'm younger than you, but I'm in no great shape," he said. "If I tried to catch you, you'd be down the stairs before I'd even have my hand on the doorknob."

Jibril touched his fingers to his beard. "You policemen don't understand what has happened to our people."

"I'm not a policeman. I'm a history teacher."

The priest was confused for a moment, then his expression became pleading. "So you know our history in this town, *ustaz*," he said. "Nablus was entirely ours in the days of the Byzantines. Then the Muslims came. We lived beside them for centuries in the casbah, until we found ourselves caught between them and the Israelis. First we moved out of the casbah to this neighborhood, then we had to leave Nablus completely, for our new village on the top of Mount Jerizim."

"To be close to your holy place."

"That's what we tell people, but mainly it was to get away

from the dangers of Nablus." Jibril jabbed a finger toward Khamis Zeydan, as though the police chief were the embodiment of the violence his people had fled. "The money in the Old Man's secret accounts will be recompense for the historic injustice we Samaritans have suffered. Your leaders already stole it from you. Who'll notice if it ends up in our hands, instead?"

"The World Bank is on the trail of that money," Omar Yussef said. "They'll notice. You can't just make the money disappear."

"They haven't traced it yet. Ishaq hid it well."

"You talk about injustice. What about the injustice Ishaq suffered? He was your son."

"He liked to be screwed by men. He deserved what he got."

Omar Yussef took a step back, startled by the priest's sudden venom. "I saw how you wept for him earlier today," he said. "I know you didn't hate him."

"I raised him well." The priest bared his teeth maliciously. "Look how he turned out."

Omar Yussef's cheek twitched below his left eye. "You killed him, didn't you?" he said. "You killed Roween, but first you killed your own son."

"He was adopted."

Omar Yussef thought of Miral and Dahoud, whom he had adopted after their parents were killed. *I feel more love for them after one year than this priest is capable of displaying for Ishaq after two decades*, he thought. "Adoption is no different from blood parentage," he said.

"My blood son wouldn't have been a dirty little homo." The priest brandished the Abisha Scroll. "There's enough money in these secret bank accounts to make my people secure for decades. But there's also some for you. What do you say?"

Omar Yussef raised his finger at the priest. His hand shook with rage. "Roween's last words were, 'He knew about Kanaan.' When she said that, I thought 'he' was Ishaq—that Ishaq knew Kanaan was his father. I thought she was trying to tell me he had refused to hand over the secret accounts to Kanaan because he was angry with him for concealing his true paternity. But 'he' was you. You knew, of course, that Kanaan was Ishaq's father, because Kanaan came to you with his illegitimate child and paid you to adopt him."

"You said you were a history teacher," the priest said, "but now you're a detective, after all?"

"You tried to blackmail Ishaq into giving the bank details to you, instead of to Kanaan. You threatened to make public that he was the illegitimate son of the Kanaans."

Jibril lifted the scroll and looked invitingly at Omar Yussef. "A million dollars. For each of you," he said. "Two million."

"Ishaq didn't do quite what you wanted. He gave you the scroll, but not the money," Omar Yussef said. "It served as a bargaining chip to keep you quiet about his scandalous birth and protect his real parents. He hid the account documents. You tortured him to make him say where he'd hidden them, but you pushed his body too far and he died."

"Why would I have been in a hurry to get the money? If Ishaq had it, he'd have given it to me in the end."

"You were running out of time. Ishaq intended to meet a woman from the World Bank who's investigating the Old Man's secret finances. Ishaq was going to hand over the account details to her, so the money could be made part of the official Palestinian budget and be used to build hospitals and schools. You had to get the documents before that happened."

"It's true that I loved him." The priest choked, his eyes cast to the floor, all his malice spent. "But wasn't my people's future more important than Ishaq's life?"

Khamis Zeydan stepped to Omar Yussef's side, his gun in his hand. The priest looked up, his eyes widened, startled and scared. He turned toward the stairs, but the policeman raised his gun. Omar Yussef ducked, as the pistol went off by his ear.

His hearing returned with a hiss like escaping gas. The priest lay on the ground by the door. Khamis Zeydan walked quickly to him and rolled him onto his back with his boot. He picked up the Abisha Scroll and held it toward Omar Yussef.

"Let's see if you're right about the money," he said.

Omar Yussef stared at Jibril's face. The priest's tarboosh rolled across the floor. His head was bald and small without the hat. Omar Yussef pointed weakly at the dead man. "Why?"

"He was getting away with the scroll," Khamis Zeydan said. "He was going to destroy the account documents." He shoved the calfskin case into the schoolteacher's arms and scowled at him.

Omar Yussef felt his pulse beating in his palms, where the box rested, charged with so much knowledge and history. He looked up at Khamis Zeydan, his eyes wide with awe.

The police chief sighed impatiently and snatched the box away.

"Be careful with it," Omar Yussef said. He followed Khamis Zeydan to the synagogue's rear bench.

Khamis Zeydan wrenched the finials from the end of the case. He spread the Abisha Scroll along the seat.

Omar Yussef shrieked and grabbed at his friend's arm. "You'll damage it."

Khamis Zeydan shook him off. "Do you want to find these account details or not?"

"Not if we destroy this ancient artifact in the process."

Khamis Zeydan yanked the end of the scroll. It unspooled along the bench and onto the floor. "By Allah, it's long," he muttered.

"If you'd ever bothered to read the Bible, you'd know that already."

"This is the entire Bible?"

"The first five books only."

"Thank you, Father Abu Ramiz. So you're a Bible reader now? When I first met you, you were a leftist who hated religion."

"Not as much as I hated ignorance. Please, put it back before you damage it beyond repair."

Khamis Zeydan rolled the scroll loosely, held it upright and shook it. The sheepskin crackled in his fingers. "Nothing in here," he said. He dropped the scroll to the bench and sat with his back to Omar Yussef, staring at the body of the priest.

Omar Yussef gathered up the scroll. He twisted the handles until it was wound tight and slipped it back into its box. He ran his hand over the calfskin cover. "They made these boxes with the skin side on the exterior," he said. "But the hair of the calf's hide is still on the inside. Look."

Khamis Zeydan grunted.

Omar Yussef fingered the edges of the silver plate on the front of the box with the raised image of the temple. *Could this be what Ishaq meant by 'behind the temple'? Not in the scroll, but behind this piece of silver?* He slipped a fingernail beneath the rim of the plate. A shred of black gum came up. *This hasn't been opened in a while,* he thought. He worked at the edge of the silver panel until he could push a finger behind it. He pressed down on the calfskin and slipped his hand inside. He came out with nothing but a rancid film of four-hundred-year-old calf's grease on his palm.

"Well, that's it," Khamis Zeydan said. "Ishaq's secret died with him."

Omar Yussef dropped the Abisha Scroll to the bench and came swiftly to his feet.

Khamis Zeydan glared at him.

"That's what Ishaq told Roween," Omar Yussef said. He stared toward the front of the synagogue.

Khamis Zeydan followed his gaze. "O peace, what's up with you now?"

"Ishaq told her that the thing he was working on was a secret between him and the old president and Allah. The president's dead, and Ishaq said that when he died, too, it would be 'a secret known only to Allah.'" Omar Yussef stumbled into the aisle and hurried to the front of the synagogue.

"So you've somehow figured out Allah's secret?"

"Exactly." Omar Yussef nodded. "Allah's secret."

"Really, the god of the Samaritans decided to share it with you?"

"No, but the priest did." Omar Yussef climbed onto the dais. "When I came here with Sami, the priest told me the

Samaritans never destroy old religious documents, even after they become unusable. They put them inside this trunk."

He lifted the long lid of the pine bench. The sharp scent of aging parchment rose from the yellowed rolls inside. He turned to Khamis Zeydan.

"The priest said they call them 'Allah's secrets.'" Omar Yussef kneeled, dug his hands into the pile of parchment and pulled out an armful.

"The secret Ishaq shared with his god?"

Omar Yussef nodded. "In here."

Khamis Zeydan reached into the trunk and tossed out a heavy scroll. He coughed at the dust rising from the recesses of the cabinet.

Scrolls and books in frayed bindings piled on the floor around them and the air grew dusty and sour. Khamis Zeydan coughed so hard he retched.

Omar Yussef slid his fingers to the bottom of the long trunk. He felt the seam of the old dry wood. The parchments at the bottom were brittle as baklava pastry.

Then he touched it. Plastic. He pulled against the weight of the documents on top and brought out a manila folder encased in a freezer bag. The folder was thick with spreadsheets and columns of numbers, all headed with the eagle of the Palestinian Authority and the address of the president's office in Ramallah.

Khamis Zeydan whistled quietly.

"Banks in Switzerland, companies registered in the Caribbean," Omar Yussef said, leafing through the file. "This is it."

"By Allah," Khamis Zeydan whispered.

Omar Yussef returned the folder to the freezer bag and

held it to his chest with both hands. He noticed that the pulse of excitement he experienced when he set foot on the temple stone and when he touched the Abisha Scroll was absent. The file felt heavy with death.

Khamis Zeydan pulled out his cell phone. "I'm calling Sami," he said. "I want him to take care of this. I don't want any other officer asking me questions about that dead Samaritan over there, and I certainly don't want anyone else to know that you have three hundred million dollars in your shaky little paws."

Omar Yussef knelt by Jibril. The dead man's skin was as bloodless and dry as the parchments piled on the floor around the ark. He must have had help when he took Ishaq and Roween to their deaths on the hilltop. He would have been too frail to overpower either of his victims alone. But Omar Yussef would never find out who had aided the old priest, now that Jibril lay dead.

Khamis Zeydan muttered to Sami on the phone. When he hung up, Omar Yussef turned to him. "Did you really shoot the priest to prevent him destroying the account documents?" he asked. "Or was it to protect the reputation of your old lover? With Jibril dead, no one knows about Liana's illegitimate son, except her husband."

Khamis Zeydan lit a Rothmans and shot the match over the synagogue benches with his thumb. He stared toward the ark. "That's another of Allah's secrets," he said.

Chapter 31

Night receded to a mauve fringe on the ridge of Jerizim. Omar Yussef watched it slink away and breathed the unsullied cool of dawn. He kept his eyes on the mountain until the blue sky overcame its final taint, and still he stared. He twisted his mouth into a sour smile. He didn't trust the darkness to be gone. If he turned down the hill toward the casbah, he was sure he'd see its somber essence lurking there. The sun might simmer Nablus in the heat at the valley's bottom, but it would never burn off the shadows. In the alleys of the old town, it was always an ominous midnight.

Sami came down the steps outside the synagogue. Omar Yussef rolled the account documents and stuffed them awkwardly into the hip pocket of his pants.

"Concealing evidence?" Sami smiled.

"Are you going to search me?"

"I wasn't anxious to investigate all along. I'm not about to begin now."

Khamis Zeydan slouched out of the synagogue and leaned over the railing by the steps.

"The priest interrupted another attempted theft of the

Abisha Scroll," Sami said. "The thieves killed him, but they panicked and left the scroll behind. That's the official version. What do you think?"

Omar Yussef touched his mustache. "Sami, what's wrong with the truth?" he said. "Abu Adel was doing his job as a police officer by stopping a criminal. I'm sure we could explain the priest's death honestly."

Sami's eyes darkened above his bony cheeks. "The truth is in your pocket, Abu Ramiz. The truth is that the former president salted away hundreds of millions of dollars in secret bank accounts, while ordinary Palestinians lived in crappy refugee camps and studied in crowded schools. What's wrong with the truth? A great deal is wrong."

Omar Yussef saw the hardness in the young man's eyes. Khamis Zeydan expectorated into the basement yard of the synagogue. *Is this the moment when Sami becomes like his mentor,* Omar Yussef wondered, *dirtied and compromised?*

"It's the truth, nonetheless," he said. "Don't give up on that, Sami. At least this money will no longer line the pockets of corrupt leaders. I don't expect you to become idealistic about the Palestinian people, but tell me I've restored a little of your faith."

Sami shoved the protruding roll of documents firmly into Omar Yussef's pocket. "Watch out or you might lose them," he said. The hardness left his face. "Really, Abu Ramiz, is it the job of a detective to make sure everyone knows just how bad things are?"

Omar Yussef lifted a finger, as he did when he lectured in his classroom. "Detectives are like the cloth that polishes a tarnished piece of silverware. The silver is displayed

proudly, shining and admired. The cloth is tossed into a cupboard, filthy and unseen, imprinted with a record of the dirt everyone else believes to have been erased forever."

Sami smiled. "You promised me you'd be cheerful by the time my wedding came around, Abu Ramiz."

"You're going ahead with the party?"

Sami raised his good arm, then tapped a knuckle against his cast. "My bride will walk on my left in the procession, and there's no other reason to delay, anymore. Listen, what do you hear?"

"Nothing."

"Precisely. The gunfire has stopped," Sami said. "The battle in the casbah came to an end around the time when you and Abu Adel were in the synagogue with the priest. While we've been photographing the position of the corpse and dusting for prints, Amin Kanaan's men have taken complete control of Nablus."

"So the fighting is over?"

"Hamas conceded for now. They were at a disadvantage after Awwadi was killed. He was their military leader in the casbah. The people were angry, too, about the way the sheikh slurred the Old Man. Hamas had to back down. My wedding will take place this afternoon."

"A thousand congratulations."

Sami went up the steps. He slapped Khamis Zeydan gently in the lower back and gave a nod to a pair of paramedics. They entered the synagogue with a folded, orange stretcher and emerged a few minutes later with the corpse of Jibril the priest.

The priest's hand dangled from the stretcher, bumping the steps as they descended. Omar Yussef halted the paramedics.

He lifted Jibril's arm and laid the hand on the blanket covering the dead man. He rested his palm on the leathery skin and felt the thin bones.

One of the medics adjusted his grip on the handles, jolting the body on the stretcher, and for a second Omar Yussef thought the old priest had come to life. It left his pulse quick and anxious, even as the paramedics descended the last steps to the street.

At the curb, Jamie King watched the stretcher pass. She took the steps to Omar Yussef three at a time, her brown work boots loud on the stone, and clasped his hand in both of hers. She was dressed for the chill of early morning in a purple fleece and black jeans, but her palms were clammy with excitement.

"I'm amazed, *ustaz*," she said. "When did this happen?"

"In the middle of the night," Omar Yussef said. "I would've called you immediately, but the police asked me to wait until the man's nearest relatives could be notified, up there." He gestured toward the Samaritan village on Jerizim.

"That was the priest I just saw on the stretcher? What happened to him?"

"He couldn't keep a secret." Omar Yussef glanced up the synagogue steps.

Khamis Zeydan stared into the sparse gardens of a neighboring apartment building. Sami came out of the synagogue. He lit a cigarette and handed the smoke to Khamis Zeydan. The older man took it without lifting his head. Sami rested his hand on Khamis Zeydan's back.

"Jamie, can you give me a ride to the hotel? I need to get some rest. I have a wedding to go to later," Omar Yussef said.

He pulled himself into the high cab of Jamie King's Chevrolet. King shut her door, turned to Omar Yussef, and raised one eyebrow. Omar Yussef took the manila folder from his hip pocket and unrolled it. He handed it to her.

The American opened the freezer bag. She flipped quickly through the papers, sucking her freckled lip behind her lower teeth.

"How much is there?" Omar Yussef asked.

"It looks like almost everything." King didn't raise her eyes from the documents. She fanned the papers in the file with her thumb. "Hundreds of millions of dollars."

"You have time to prevent the boycott?"

"I'll write my report to the board in D.C. as soon as I get back to the hotel. I'm sure this'll convince them to scrap the boycott. Just in time."

The American slipped the documents into the map pocket on the driver's door. She wiped her sweaty hands on her jeans and grinned, excited and embarrassed. As she started the engine, she turned to Omar Yussef. "You could have been very rich," she said.

"I'm a Palestinian," Omar Yussef said. "I'm giving you this money to spend on my behalf, Jamie. After years of official theft, the money is mine at last, because it's finally in the right hands."

"It'll be transferred to the Palestinian Ministry of Finance," King said. "They've instituted proper accounting procedures to track the money now."

"Keep your eye on them, Jamie." Omar Yussef grated out a guttural laugh. "Not everyone in Palestine is as pure as I am."

Chapter 32

N adia preened before a mirror in the foyer, stroking the lacy pink shirt her grandmother had bought for her at the *souk*. Maryam took her hand and led her toward the women's hall for the wedding celebrations. "Remember, I want you to tell me everything that happens at the men's party, Grandpa," Nadia called.

Omar Yussef raised his arm to wave and felt a jab in the ribs from the wad of documents stashed in the inside pocket of his jacket. He moved politely through the bland stream of women in their loose gowns of brown or navy blue or beige, cream scarves pinning their hair out of sight. He heard a series of sharp clicks and noticed Liana approaching in high-heeled shoes and a yellow suit.

"Greetings, *ustaz*," she said.

"Double greetings, my lady."

Heavy black kohl ringed Liana's eyes. It seemed to Omar Yussef that her eyeballs themselves had been painted in and that the woman before him would have receded into complete invisibility had her sadness not been adorned with gold jewelry and Parisian couture.

"It's a shame you're unable to mourn as you should for

the loss of your husband's associate Ishaq. But you can at least take comfort that his murderer is now dead."

Liana appeared to be short of breath for a moment. "Who was it?" she gasped.

"Jibril the priest. He was shot by our friend Abu Adel."

The woman's eyes flamed briefly, a lick of passion and pride amid her frozen features.

Omar Yussef looked hard at Liana. "I wonder for whom Abu Adel fired that shot?" he said.

Her features became cautious and stony again.

"Did he shoot a criminal in the act of committing an offense? Did he kill him to protect your secret?"

"My secret?"

"Or did he do it for the boy?" Omar Yussef thought of the pale blue eyes staring out of Ishaq's corpse and the queer feeling of recognition he had experienced in that moment. He remembered the pain with which Liana's wealthy husband recounted her infidelity. He recalled that, when he had told her of Ishaq's murder, she had wanted to be alone with Khamis Zeydan.

Liana inclined her head toward the corner of the room and Omar Yussef followed her.

She stood with her back to a tall potted plant and scanned the room. She spoke without moving her lips. "What is it you want, *ustaz?*"

"Want?"

"For your silence."

Though she took him for a blackmailer, Omar Yussef sighed with pity for Liana. "Dear lady," he said, "your husband has already bought my silence."

The kohl ran in a tear from Liana's eye, but she caught

it quickly with a tissue. She twitched her face taut and cleaned up the black streak. She looked expectantly at Omar Yussef. He blinked, signaling that the track of her tear had been erased, and she put the tissue in her handbag.

"What was the boy like?" he asked.

"He was handsome, brave and impulsive, with a great capacity for tenderness. But he also had an explosive temper. Like his father."

Omar Yussef recognized the traits. "Did you tell him? When I left you together in your salon on the evening that I told you Ishaq was dead?"

"I thought I would, but I just couldn't." Liana covered her eyes. "I wanted to be with him in my moment of loss, but after the boy's murder it was too late to tell him."

"I'll never speak of it to him."

Two musicians wearing white shirts and baggy white cotton pants pranced into the building. The first of them played a trilling, breathy melody on a *shabbabah* flute. The second held a circular *darbouka* and beat a rhythm with his fingertips.

Sami and Meisoun came in from the sunshine behind the musicians. Sami's black jacket was draped over his shoulders and his broken arm slung across his blue dress shirt. His dark skin shone with sweat and he smiled broadly. Meisoun's white lace dress was tight around her slim torso. Under her veil, her head rocked from side to side with the rhythm. The women in the hall ululated, and the men who arrived with Sami clapped their hands and swayed to the eight-four time of the *zaffah* wedding march.

Khamis Zeydan danced behind Sami, snapping his fingers above his head. *His foot must be feeling better,* Omar

Yussef thought. The police chief turned his smile toward Omar Yussef. He noticed Liana, who dropped her eyes to the potted plant, rubbing one of its leaves between her fingers. Khamis Zeydan followed Sami into the men's hall, as the women led Meisoun next door. He glanced over his shoulder, but Omar Yussef avoided his eye.

"I couldn't wait for him," Liana said. "When I saw Abu Adel in the hospital after he was wounded, the doctors told me he would die. I wanted to tell him I was pregnant, but he was too drugged up to recognize me and, in any case, he was already married. All my silly fantasies about escaping to Europe or America disappeared. You understand the disgrace I faced? My family would have disowned me. Amin had been courting me and I convinced him the child was his. I accepted his offer of marriage."

"Did you try to think of a way to raise the child as your own?"

"Even if we married in a hurry, he would have been born too soon afterward. My father was a prominent diplomat and there was Amin's career to think about—and my honor. Despite all my supposed radicalism, I realized that I was ashamed to go against our traditions. I couldn't allow people to think I had such intimate relations with my fiancé."

"You had no other choice, dear lady." Omar Yussef glanced toward the men's hall. "Do you still love him?"

The foyer was almost empty. The final guests were entering the halls to celebrate with the bride or the groom.

"It's different now," Liana said.

Her love for Khamis Zeydan was passionate in Beirut, Omar Yussef thought, *but its memory has been made melancholy by years of lies.*

"I hate Amin like a donkey hates the man who rides it, no matter how well fed and watered its master keeps it," Liana said. "But I'm afraid to leave my husband."

"Why?"

Liana split a leaf from the stem of the potted plant. "He knows too many of my secrets," she said.

She caught another streak of kohl and smiled so that her tears would end. Omar Yussef looked into her brown eyes, and he remembered the sky blue irises in the dead face of her son. *Why are all our eyes colored with one of these two sad hues?* he wondered.

As she went into the women's hall, Liana pulled her shoulders back and lifted her chin. The canary yellow suit merged with the somber robes of the other women. Omar Yussef crossed to the men's hall.

The dance moved around Sami. Ramiz and Zuheir laid their arms across Sami's shoulders and the three men stepped side to side, shaking their hips and rolling their necks. At the fringe of the crowd, Sheikh Bader stood, sullen and still. Across the hall, Amin Kanaan wiggled his head to the music, though it would have been beneath his dignity to dance with the mob. The sides of his mouth lifted in a smooth grin, accepting the greetings of those who approached him.

The music came to an end and Sami climbed onto a dais. He smiled at the faces in the crowd, holding each man's eyes a moment. He sat in a comfortable armchair, as Khamis Zeydan ascended the platform and reached down for a radio microphone. The police chief tapped the head to be certain it worked and waved his hand for the men's attention.

"Peace be with you," he said. "May you experience abundance from Allah, O Sami."

Some in the crowd returned the wish loudly. "With the protection of Allah," said the man next to Omar Yussef.

"Sami Jaffari has a wonderful family," Khamis Zeydan said, "and Hassan is an admirable father."

Sami's father raised his hand near the front of the crowd to acknowledge the cheers.

"But I've always felt Sami to be like a son to me, because I'm the father of Lieutenant Sami the policeman," Khamis Zeydan said.

The laughter was warm. Khamis Zeydan waited for quiet. "Sometimes I worry about the risks Sami takes."

Sami grinned and raised his broken arm.

"But I know that he faces these dangers because he wants to enforce the law and protect our community. I'm proud of the way he carries out his duty."

Omar Yussef thought of the boy Khamis Zeydan had sired in Beirut. *A son is linked to his father as the Turkish buildings of the casbah are bound to the Roman remains far underground,* he thought. *Even when they're unaware of each other's existence, the blood beneath the skin is shared.* Though he had never known his true father, Ishaq had moved in the same treacherous circles as Khamis Zeydan. After Ishaq's death, the police chief had unwittingly avenged his boy with the bullet that killed the priest in the synagogue. *A war separated this father and son. A murder reunited them.*

"Sami, when you went to Our Honored Sheikh Bader to begin the process of marriage, he required you to say a prayer," Khamis Zeydan went on. "Sometimes we pray without thinking about what we say, but let's remember the words of that prayer. It required you to request a chaste wife who would 'from her womb bestow a pure son who will be my sweet reminiscence in my life and after my death.' Sami, may your son one day bring to you the same sweetness that you have brought to me, for whom you are like a son."

Sami rose so that Khamis Zeydan could kiss his cheeks. The police chief came down from the dais and moved across the dance floor, taking the slaps of congratulation and the handshakes.

Amin Kanaan nudged one of his acolytes, pointed at the departing police chief, said a few words and smirked. *For someone who just missed out on three hundred million dollars and lost the boy he believed to be his son, he's pretty cheerful*, Omar Yussef thought.

Sheikh Bader watched the wealthy businessman with a glower so savage that it seemed to clear a space around him in the crowded hall. It was then that Omar Yussef knew Kanaan had double-crossed the sheikh. *Kanaan lured him into a fight so that he could take control of Nablus*, he thought. *He planted a fake autopsy in the dirt files, which Ishaq intended to give to Hamas. He knew the sheikh would publicize the autopsy's finding that the Old Man died of that shameful disease, giving him a pretext to confront Hamas.*

"You're not dancing, Dad?" Zuheir slapped his hand onto Omar Yussef's shoulder, smiling.

"When I was a student, I danced with ladies at a café in Damascus. It's no longer the fashion," Omar Yussef said, gesturing toward the crowd of men on the dance floor, "but I developed a taste for it and I simply don't like to dance any other way."

"You'd better keep that quiet, or Sheikh Bader will issue a *fatwa* against you."

"We all have our secrets."

Zuheir stopped smiling. "I've been keeping a secret myself."

"What is it, my son?"

"I'm getting married, too."

Omar Yussef blinked.

"I met a Lebanese woman on a research trip to Beirut. We're hoping to marry. That's why I'm leaving Britain to live in Lebanon."

"I thought you were—"

"A crazy religious extremist who hates the West? Well, I'm not crazy and, no matter how we differ on certain things, I'll always be proud to be your son."

Omar Yussef felt his eyes grow wet and he reached for Zuheir's hand. "A thousand congratulations, my dear boy." He kissed his son five times, moving from cheek to cheek.

"What happened with the woman from the World Bank?" Zuheir asked. "Were you able to help her find the money?"

Omar Yussef nodded. "The bank will continue its aid."

Zuheir shook his head with admiration. "Thank you, Dad."

Omar Yussef tried to make his habitual staccato laugh of self-deprecation, but it caught in his throat. He touched his son's arm and he turned toward the door.

He crossed the foyer of the wedding hall and went into the bathroom, where he found Khamis Zeydan splashing water on his face. The police chief looked at his friend with reddened eyes and a sheepish smile. "I got choked up," he said.

Omar Yussef pulled a wad of papers from the inside pocket of his jacket, unfolded them and held them out to Khamis Zeydan.

The police chief dried his face with a paper towel. "What's this?"

"Haven't you been wondering about the dirt files that went missing from Nouri Awwadi's basement?"

Khamis Zeydan's blue eyes opened wide. "By Allah." He grabbed the papers. "Where did you get these?"

"I made a deal with Amin Kanaan." The file had been waiting for Omar Yussef when he returned to the hotel, just as Kanaan had promised.

Khamis Zeydan looked up from the documents. "Were you searching for dirt on me?"

"I don't expect you'd have clean hands, even if you spent the rest of the day scrubbing at that basin," Omar Yussef said, "but you're my dear friend, above all else, so you're in the clear. I didn't even read the file."

Khamis Zeydan shuffled the papers, glancing briefly at each one. "There's not much here," he said.

"Are you disappointed? Perhaps you're not as bad as you make out."

"Perhaps I'm not."

Omar Yussef smiled. "Put those papers in your pocket. Go and enjoy the wedding."

Khamis Zeydan kissed Omar Yussef's cheeks. "You're a true friend, my brother," he said. He ran a fingertip beneath his eye. "It's a day for crying tears of happiness."

Omar Yussef put his hand on his friend's shoulder. "Tears? A tough guy like you?"

"No one has more reason to weep than a hard man." Khamis Zeydan left the bathroom.

From his other pocket, Omar Yussef took a thick sheaf of papers. He went into a toilet stall and locked the door. He ripped the rest of Khamis Zeydan's file into tiny shreds, dropping them into the bowl and flushing until everything was gone.

When he left the bathroom, Omar Yussef saw his granddaughter at the entrance to the men's hall. Nadia stood on her toes, searching for someone among the dancing men. He called to her and she came toward him with a smile. She held two small paper plates, each with a square of shredded wheat soaked in lurid orange syrup. She gave one plate to Omar Yussef and handed him a plastic fork.

"I decided not to wait any longer for you to take me to the casbah for *qanafi*, Grandpa," she said. "Thankfully Meisoun ordered some for the wedding buffet. Eat it with me, and may you have double health in your deepest heart."

Nadia's laughter was musical and light. Omar Yussef cut a small slice of the warm *qanafi* with the edge of his fork and, closing his eyes, he put it in his mouth. It was sweet.